MY FRIENDS

*By the same author in PAN Books*

MY FRIEND MADAME ZORA
MY FRIEND COUSIN EMMIE

# MY FRIENDS THE MRS MILLERS

JANE DUNCAN

UNABRIDGED

PAN BOOKS LTD: LONDON

First published 1965 by Macmillan & Co. Ltd.
This edition published 1968 by Pan Books Ltd.,
33 Tothill Street, London, S.W.1.
330 02008 0

*Printed in Great Britain by*
*Cox & Wyman Ltd., London, Reading and Fakenham*

I should like to dedicate this book to all my West Indian friends with whom I have long lost touch and who have probably forgotten me. There were too many to name them all, but the names below are a representative cross-section.

Marion Skinner          Albert Philipson
Noel Skinner            Wilfred Brown
Ivanhoe Morrison        Lester Ledgister
Lloyd Plummer           Nurse Dalrymple

'Every valley shall be exalted and every mountain and hill made low, the crooked straight and the rough places plain.'

A prophecy of Isaiah as paraphrased by Handel in the oratorio *Messiah*

# PART ONE

## *The Valley*

# 1

I THINK it must be a commonplace with most of us that we are from day to day so taken up with the trivia of life that we give little thought to life itself. This is certainly my own experience and I would liken my life to the traversing of a tract of flattish unexplored country where I have come through a wood here, crossed a moor there, hacked my way through a thorny little thicket somewhere else and dawdled, sometimes, in a green sunlit meadow. As I have travelled, I have seldom thought of where the path I am following was leading, for the wood, moor, thicket and meadow have occupied my mind from day to day. Only once or twice have I seemed to emerge on an eminence from which I could see the path leading away into the future but these eminences, although not very high, have been little peaks close to the clouds and it is into the clouds that the path to the future disappears. I cannot see any further ahead than when I am in the wood, moor, thicket or meadow but, for a moment, I am conscious that this unexplored country that contains all of these is greater than them all. Momentarily, I become overawed with its greatness, its grandeur, its mystery and, at the same time, I am filled with gratitude that all this wide territory is open for me to discover.

I think it is possible that the reason why I see life in this way as a tract of unexplored country viewed from an eminence is that I was born and lived until I was ten years old at a small croft called Reachfar which lay upon the summit of a hill in Ross-shire. It was not a very high hill – only some six hundred feet above sea-level – but for the first ten years of my life it was the highest hill on whose summit I had ever stood, and our own summits are higher than the Everests of other men, just as our own depths are lower than other men's Great Pacific Deeps. From that hill, I could see for twenty miles and more in every direction and to me, as a child, all that distance that I could see represented country which, one day, I would explore and, in later life, when I have seemed to reach some turning-point in my small experience and have become conscious for a moment of the future lying ahead, it is as if I find myself standing on an eminence, like the hill of Reachfar, but Reachfar in a November mist, when all the distance is obscured and the road round the granary gable and down the hill disappears into a white swirling mystery. I know that the road is there but that is all.

I can look back on some of these little eminences of mine such as when, at twenty-one, I was ready to leave Reachfar for the south of England to begin to earn my living; or when, in 1939, I looked in the glass and saw myself for the first time in the uniform of the Women's Air Force; or in 1947 when I came back from my honeymoon journey and looked about the few rooms which were my new home; or in 1948 when I landed from the aeroplane that had brought me to St Jago in the West Indies for the first time. These are small eminences, for mine is a small life, but they are my Everests.

In mid-July of 1952, I had a consciousness of having once more emerged on an eminence, and the moment of realization took place, oddly enough, at the airport of St Jago once again. My husband and I had just been seeing off home to England a friend called Miss Morrison. We watched the airliner roar down the runway, detach itself from the earth spurning gravity away, tip over in a wide sweep above the bush-covered hills and head out to become a silver mote over the wide sea and, suddenly, the unexplored territory that was life was as limitless and mysterious as the hazy space into which the silver mote disappeared.

'Well, good luck to her and a happy landing,' my husband said as we turned away.

'I shall always regard her as a pivot point,' I said, detaching my gaze from the dazzling distance and blinking my eyelids.

'Not that she had anything to do with it, really, but she marks the point in time.'

'What point?'

'You and I having decided that our future doesn't lie in this island.'

'Cousin Emmie had no bearing on that.'

She was a cousin of our friends the Dulacs but we always referred to the old lady between ourselves as 'Cousin Emmie'.

'She had a sort of bearing on *me*,' I said. 'She brought to the surface what I truly feel about this island and our way of life here.'

We had come to the door of the airport restaurant. 'Let's have something cool to drink,' my husband said and we went into the pleasant, cool, air-conditioned place and sat down. 'Yes?'

'Nothing really. I've said it all before – what I think about us white people in this black country. Since we came here I have been like a child picking flowers in what I thought was a meadow but really, all the time, I have known that it was a quaking morass but I was ignoring that. That's no way to live. It's an ignoring of one of life's basic dimensions, the dimension of place. It is a falsification of life to skate about on the surface of this island in the way I have done. And now we are going back to Britain for good in two years or less. It's a bit late to start exploring the real St Jago but these years I have wasted will always be a small private shame lying at the back of my mind.' I was looking towards the door of the restaurant as I spoke and I now added: 'There is a woman over there who has just come in and she is looking very hard at the back of your head.'

'Who is she?'

'I have no idea, idiot, but I think she knows *you*.'

'What is she like?'

'Elderly, dignified, thin with white hair. Very good-looking. Very well-dressed too.'

'Naturally she will be all that if she is a friend of mine. I'll have a look in a minute.'

But before he could turn round, the woman had left the table she had thought of taking and came over to ours.

9

'Mr Alexander, isn't it?' she said. 'How do you do?'

My husband got up. 'Mrs Miller! How are you? I don't think you have met my wife. Janet, this is Mrs Miller of Hope. Remember I told you about meeting her on the Mount Melody road one night?'

'Of course! How d'you do, Mrs Miller? Won't you sit down and have something cool to drink?'

'Thank you.' She sat down and began to take off her white gloves. 'I am so happy to meet you at last, Mrs Alexander. I have had a guilty conscience ever since that night your husband towed my wretched car to the garage and then took me home. So *far* out of his way – you must have been worried.'

'I am afraid I never worry about Twice,' I said.

'Twice?' She looked from one of us to the other.

'The names I was given are Alexander Alexander, Mrs Miller,' my husband explained, 'and they have earned me the nickname of Twice. Janet is responsible.'

'I see. Twice,' she repeated. 'There is something very apt about it anyway.'

'And you'd really better call him by it,' I said, 'for he hardly answers to anything else.'

'I shall indeed. Thank you. And have you also been seeing friends away?'

We agreed that we had been and Twice added: 'And it sent Janet into the twilight – she hates parting with people.'

'Some people,' I corrected him and Mrs Miller laughed.

'Yes, indeed. Some! I have just been seeing my son and daughter off to New York with two friends they had down. One of the friends was charming but I found it extraordinarily easy and pleasant to part with the other. Dear me, it *is* hot! How people contrive to live in the town and on this coastal plain I cannot imagine. It is fairly hot at Paradise too, I should imagine?'

'Nothing like this,' I told her.

'But Mrs Miller would find Paradise hot, Flash,' Twice said to me, and then at a glance from Mrs Miller he explained: 'Flash is my retaliation for the Twice, Mrs Miller. When my wife was younger, she had a temper with a remarkably low flash-point.'

10

'One more reference to my advancing age and the flash-point won't be all that high even now,' I said.

'But going back to what I was saying,' Twice continued, 'Mrs Miller would find Paradise pretty hot. How high are you at Hope, Mrs Miller?'

'The house is at two thousand feet. A lot of the land is much higher, of course.'

'It must be quite lovely,' I said. 'I have heard and read a great deal about Hope House. It is one of the island's historic places, isn't it?'

'As a site, yes. The Spanish governors of the island had a palace there but that's all gone, of course. The present house is only about the same age as the Great House of Paradise. Hope, Paradise and Horizon Great House were all planned by the same architect between 1770 and 1780. Our date-stone has 1774 on it.'

'Paradise is 1775,' I said.

'Yes. I think Horizon is the earliest.'

'Is yours one of the island regicide families, Mrs Miller?' Twice asked.

'Oh dear me, no! We are not a bit grand or romantic in that way. No. Hope was left to me by an uncle. It was bought by a naval ancestor of ours in 1808 with the prize-money he acquired in the course of the Napoleonic Wars and he retired out here and turned himself into a planter.'

'I think that is just as grand and romantic as being a regicide!' I said. 'And a sight more decent, actually. The romance part of the regicide families is just a trick of time, it seems to me. There was nothing very romantic about old Cromwell and his crew.'

'Old-Wart-on-his-Nose, as Sir Ian calls him,' Twice said.

'How is Sir Ian? And Madame Dulac?' Mrs Miller asked.

I listened to Twice talk to her about Madame Dulac and her son Sir Ian on whose estate of Paradise we lived and listened with great interest for, some months ago, when I had told Madame that Twice had found a Mrs Miller on the road after dark with her car broken down and had taken her home, Madame, after a few inquiries, had said: 'Oh, yes, Millicent Miller. And what was she doing on the Mount Melody road

11

after dark in any case? A very strange young person, Millicent Miller.'

From this and from the fact that in the course of my several years at Paradise where all the white people in the island were entertained at one time or another and yet I had never met Mrs Miller of Hope, I gathered that between her and Madame Dulac there existed one of those rifts that split the white society of the island into a series of cliffs and chasms just as the mountain torrents split its physical landscape into a crazy chaos of near-perpendicular mountains and seemingly bottom-less gullies.

I looked across the table at Mrs Miller. 'A young person,' Madame had called her, and, indeed, by comparison with Madame, who was in her eighties, Mrs Miller was young, for she could be no more than sixty and a very young-looking elegant sixty at that. She was not elegant in the fashion-par-lance sense of being 'well-groomed'; she wore no make-up and her clothes were not strikingly fashionable but she had what my grandmother would have called 'style'. Her hair was silver-white, her skin was clear and fine and she had striking blue eyes under brows that were still dark and was tall and slim of build with good legs and narrow feet that were clad in very good white buckskin court shoes. I am always attracted to decorative people, especially those that are decorative in an elegant as opposed to a pretty way, and I listened with pleasure as she talked to Twice as if he were an old friend.

'And do you enjoy life at Paradise, Mrs Alexander?' she asked me after a little.

'Very much.'

'Janet has a bit of a gift for enjoying life nearly anywhere,' Twice told her. 'As a matter of fact it is pretty dull at Paradise a lot of the time. I am away a great deal.'

'How do you amuse yourself?' she asked.

'In lots of ways. I have a garden, I sew a bit – embroidery and odds and ends of cotton frocks in an amateurish way – I read a lot, I write a lot of letters and then there is Madame and all her charity work. I am her sort of private secretary for a lot of that. I find lots to do but I suppose it sounds very idle

12

to you when you are accustomed to running a big property like Hope?'

'Hope is very small by comparison with Paradise but, yes, running it keeps me very busy. But then, I like it. I am terribly interested in my cattle.'

'What breed do you have?'

'Bits of everything but my good lot is my Island Black herd.'

'I think the Island Blacks are beautiful,' I said, 'but then I would think so. I was brought up to believe that the only real cattle were Aberdeen Angus and there is enough of the Angus in the Island Blacks to make a strong appeal to me.'

'So you are of farming stock? So am I. My father was a canon of the Church, actually, but I threw back to his forebears and spent most of my young life with a farmer uncle in Wiltshire. Where is your home?'

'In Ross, in the north of Scotland. It is only a croft really – a very small holding, called Reachfar, but it is in very good farming country and we have some very famous herds on some of the bigger farms round about.'

'Reachfar? What a beautiful name!'

'It is a remarkably beautiful place,' Twice told her. 'It's on top of a hill and you can see for miles in every direction over firth and hills and sea.'

'I don't know Scotland,' she said. 'In fact, I hardly know England now. I married when I was twenty and came out here. I go over every other year of course and the children were educated partly in England and partly in the States but I am really more of a St Jagoan now.' She smiled at me. 'But you aren't. You are still what the Negroes call an over-the-water person.'

'I think she always will be,' Twice said. 'She has just never become used to the island – she still feels the heat, the mosquitoes bite her as much as on her first day here and the suddenness of the weather and so on still astonishes her.'

'Are you homesick?' Mrs Miller asked me.

'Oh, lord, no! No, it isn't like that. But Reachfar seems to have taken a great hold on me when I was a child and I never quite get away from it. I use it as a yardstick for other places,

13

as it were, a standard for measuring them. And if their weather is different from Reachfar weather, that weather astonishes me, as Twice said. It's all rather silly.'

'Not at all. We all have – and need – a yardstick of some kind. Reachfar sounds fascinating. Tell me more about it.'

If Mrs Miller had set out deliberately to make me like her, she could not have chosen a surer way to go about it but I do not think that this was her motive. She was a country-woman, very intelligent and interested in the farming both of animals and crops, and her interest in Reachfar had nothing personal towards me or Twice in it.

'You know,' she said to Twice at last, 'I feel that I have kept you two here this morning for much longer than you intended to stay, but this has been very pleasant. And I have a suggestion that I would like to make. I know it is pointless to ask you both to visit me at Hope because you are always too busy, Twice, but next time you are springing off on one of your visits to the other islands, couldn't your Janet come to me? It would be a change for her from the heat of Paradise and I can offer her more interesting crops than sugar cane to look at. Sugar is *so* dull, I think!'

'So do I!' I said. 'Paradise is just one vast sea of green sugar cane and if it sends up some of those lovely silver plumes like big pampas grass, they send people in to chop them down because they don't like the cane to flower like that. And sugar isn't just dull – it *stinks*! I don't think there is a worse smell in the world than what hangs around the sugar factory and rum distillery!'

Mrs Miller laughed. 'It is odd,' she said, 'that so many things that make a lot of money should be so offensive to the nose but if you come to Hope, I can promise you nicer smells. We crop a lot of limes and pimento and both are very good-smelling things.'

'I'd love to come to Hope.'

'Then that is splendid. I have no telephone but if you will write to me when Twice is going away next time, I'll drive over to Paradise to fetch you. Twice told me, I think, that you yourself don't drive.'

We said goodbye to her in the car-park and watched her

drive out and turn east along the coast road before we ourselves drove out, turning west, towards the hot, crowded township of St Jago Bay to do a little shopping before going back to Paradise. Later, as we drove homewards in the heat up the twisting road which was no more than a shelf cut into the face of the cliff above the river gorge, I thought of the cool, elegant Mrs Miller, another typical châtelaine of another of the magnificent great houses on the island.

'I should think Hope will be very beautiful,' Twice said, as if catching my thought in the air. 'It was pitch dark the night I took her home but it is magnificent inside – in far better taste than the Paradise Great House.'

'That wouldn't be difficult.'

'That's true. But Hope is in near-perfect taste. Would you like to go there while I am away? You don't have to if you don't want to.'

'Oh, yes, I'd like to go. I liked Mrs Miller enormously, darling, but I feel that it is just some more of this grand, segregated, artificial life of the white people that I would like to get away from.'

'That's true. But it is going to be difficult to get away from it now. We are connected in the minds of the whole island with Paradise, you see.'

'That is what strikes me as sort of unfair. You and I came to this island with open minds and in a completely fortuitous way got caught up in an island-white stronghold. However, there it is. I sound discontented, darling. I'm not, really. But our time in this island is limited now and I feel I've been led into wasting my time here. As I was saying at the airport, I am glad our time is limited. I don't want to spend the rest of my life here but before we go I'd like to know a little more of the real people of the island. But it's not important and, as you say, it will be difficult at this stage. But it doesn't matter. After all, to know Janet Alexander or be known by Janet Alexander is not going to affect the St Jagoans one way or another.'

'I don't believe that and neither do you. The ultimate solution of the colour problem lies in Janet Alexander knowing and liking John Crow and in more and more Janet Alexanders knowing and liking more and more John Crows. But it's

15

difficult. It's difficult in a million ways – the accidental way that it has been made difficult for us through our connexion with the Dulacs is only one of the ways.'

'It is difficult and ridiculous,' I said. 'I have been here off and on – mostly on – since late 1948 and I have never met any Negroes except my servants and a few of the estate people. There is a class barrier there. You seldom get to know people who are out of your own class even in Britain – it takes a cataclysm like a war to make people like Monica and me get to know one another in Britain even in this year of grace. But surely if I met some of the Negroes with something like my own slight education we could reach some common ground?'

'Madame and Sir Ian would say not.'

'Are you convinced they are right, Twice?'

'No, I'm not.'

'Of course, it's so much *easier* to stick to the Mrs Millers,' I said, 'and that is how I shall probably end up. After all, I can't walk up to some coloured woman in the streets of the Bay and say: "Do let's be friends!" You can't do that with anybody.'

'Not with any real hope of success,' Twice agreed, smiling.

2

WHEN we arrived home, the overseas mail was lying in the hall and I picked out two letters with the postmark 'Achcraggan Ross', one of which was from my friend Monica and the other from my friends George and Tom. George is really my uncle and Tom our general helper at Reachfar but they do not figure in these terms or under these titles in my mind. I opened the letter from George and Tom first. It was very short, for to write a letter was always a tremendous effort for them and they are growing no younger and Twice and I have the great distinction of being the only people they write to at all. It was written on one of these airmail forms that can be bought from the post office for sixpence, and half of it was written by Tom and half by George and Tom's half said that George would likely give me all the news in his bit so that he, Tom, must not take up too much room but was just writing this bittie to say that he was very well and sending his best love. George's part of the letter told us that there was very little news, that Tom had probably given us it all and that he, George, hoped we were well, he was very well himself and so was Tom and they were both sending their best love. Then there was a postscript: 'We suppose we will soon be hearing from you about Mrs Miller' and that was all.

'Well, come on, what are they saying?' Twice asked.

'They are simply exasperating!' I exploded. 'And besides, they give me a touch of the creeps. You'd think they had Second Sight. They say they will soon be hearing from us about Mrs Miller.'

Twice stared at me. 'What's that?'

'You heard! Have you ever heard of a Mrs Miller?'

Twice regarded me solemnly. 'Now, Flash, down at the airport this morning —'

'Oh, shut up! I mean a Mrs Miller that *George and Tom* would know!'

'I don't know what you're talking about. May I see the letter?'

I handed him the blue form and he read what was written on it which, goodness knows, did not take long. 'Who is Mrs Miller?' he asked then, looking at me with bright interest.

'I was asking *you!*'

'Why ask me? You're the one they are talking to about this Mrs Miller!'

We glared at one another, breathing heavily, and then when we had Mrs Miller-ed ourselves into a near quarrel: 'Let's just carry on as if nothing had happened,' Twice suggested. 'This Mrs Miller of George's and Tom's will come out in the wash sometime. Is that a screed from Monica?'

Monica is a friend I made during the 1939–45 war and she is now married to Sir Torquil Daviot, the laird of Poyntdale which lies just to the north of Reachfar. Monica writes a very good letter although she took to it rather late in life – not, indeed, until after Twice and I came out to the West Indies. In her younger days, she corresponded mostly by telegram. But good as her letters are, she does not write them very often, reserving them mostly as birthday or Christmas treats. As Twice's birthday is in April and mine is in March and Christmas is not in July, I looked hard at the outside of her letter before I opened it. There is something about the whole personality of Monica that leads to the unexpected. Twice says that this is a facet of her personality that shines out only in the light shed by myself but, be that as it may and although I love her dearly, I opened her letter with suspicions of the sinister.

However, there was nothing sinister about it this time for I will say in Monica's favour that if she is going to be sinister she does not beat about the bush. The letter told us all about everything that was going on at Reachfar and in Achcraggan which is our local village; how George and Tom had got a new housekeeper who seemed to be a little simple-minded but very nice; how my Aunt Kate was thrilled to bits, as we had probably heard, with New York and her new home in Brooklyn and about how happy she was now that she was married to her admirer of thirty-five years' standing. It told us about the new stud bull at Poyntdale; it told us about George and Tom having taught her six-months-old son Anthony to spit when being fed, and then it said: '– but what I am really writing about is a Mrs Miller who once lived around here and who is going out to St Jago with her son. Your father knows more about her history than I do and he will be writing to you. He is very doubtful whether you will remember her at all but George and Tom are sure that you will because her mother-in-law was in Miss Tulloch's shop the day you let your ferret loose among all the women and wanted to have you and Davie the Plasterer arrested by Constable Campbell for disturbing the peace. They said that if I told you this, you would remember. And the Mrs Miller who is coming to St Jago was married to this Mrs Miller who was in Miss Tulloch's shop's son Tommy. "Chust tell her that and she will mind on her fine," Tom said.'

'Crikey!' Twice said. 'The Mrs Miller who is coming to

18

St Jago was married to this Mrs Miller who was in Miss Tulloch's shop's son Tommy! That's a proper Reachfar reachfar!'

'What do you mean?'

Twice smiled at me. 'Sorry. That's a bit of private mental idiom to describe those involved phrases Tom goes in for. I have always called them "reachfars" inside my head.'

'And you never told me until now? I think it's a splendid name for them. And Reachfar has a way of reaching far too. It sent us up to New York last year and here it is again sending us this Mrs Miller.' I went back to Monica's letter and began to read again. 'I haven't met Mrs Miller but I saw her from the car one day when I was in Achcraggan – a pretty woman of about sixty or so. She is a widow and her son is a minister who is going out to St Jago to take charge of a church at a place called, Tom and George said, Fountain Bell. This seems to be an oddish name to me, even for St Jago, but that is what they called it. Mrs Miller had been up to Reachfar to visit them and was terribly pleased to know that you were out there. Torquil and I went down to Beechwood —'

I read on to the end of the letter and when I had finished Twice said: 'Fountain Bell! It's Fontabelle! That church on the gorge road that all the row was about in the Island Presbytery!'

'What row?'

Another of my failings is that I am never up with the hounds of local news. I seem, always, to be interested in things that other people do not even notice so that I have no eyes or ears to spare for the events that are claiming the attention of everyone else. My reading of the island newspaper, *The Island Sun*, tended to concentrate on the macabre In Memoriam notices on the back page and the equally macabre advertisements such as 'Large stocks finest imported high-up and low-down water closets. Opportunity of a lifetime.' There is an analogy, I think, between my newspaper-reading habits and my attitude to life in general. I tend to read all the odd corners of the newspaper and forget to notice the big black headlines on the front page.

'They passed over half a dozen Negro applicants for its

pulpit and decided to import a white man. This Mrs Miller of your's son must be the said man.'

'Oh. When was all this row?'

'About three months back. It was quite a do – near-riot and the tear-gas squad called out to one of the congregational meetings down there. Well, what about the rest of the mail?'

We went on reading the letters until we came to one at the bottom of the heap that bore the Cairnton postmark.

'I don't like the look of this one at all,' I said. 'It's from that ghastly hole Cairnton.'

'Flash, don't be an idiot! It's simply frightening the way you carry forward all sorts of impedimenta in your mind.'

'Why is it frightening? Surely everybody establishes associations with places and things? There's nothing odd in that.'

'But you do it to such an extraordinary degree! You don't seem to realize that your memory for Reachfar is quite fantastic – all the minute detail of every flower and tree and stone. And I don't think you realize how you literally live by Reachfar. The moment anybody or any situation puzzles you, you go right back to Reachfar and work things out by Reachfar standards.'

'Well, why not? All one has got to go on in this life is one's experience and —'

'But I think your every experience has been seen in the light of Reachfar. It's a sort of philosopher's stone with you. I'm not saying this is a bad thing, Flash. But the reverse of the medal, like this morbid thing about Cairnton when you dislike even the sight of the postmark, does strike me as a bit absurd.'

'I suppose it is,' I agreed. 'I suppose I did form a sort of obsessive hatred for Cairnton and all obsessions are absurd.'

'Most of the time it isn't an active hatred or obsession – it is more that you seem to have made up your mind to forget that you ever knew Cairnton or lived there at all and I must say you succeed remarkably. I bet all the people here, like Madame and Sir Ian and the Macleans, think that your whole young life was spent at Reachfar. It isn't a wilful deception on your part. It's simply that Cairnton doesn't seem to exist for you.'

'It doesn't, most of the time,' I said and stared down at the letter.

'But it does exist really and has a post office with a franking machine!' Twice said. 'Now, open that damned thing and be done with it!'

Twice is very good for me in many ways, I think. Obediently, I slit the envelope, took out the two small sheets of paper and looked at the signature.

'Frances B. Hadley!' I said. 'Twice, it's from my old headmistress at the Academy! She was the nicest woman!'

'I've a good mind to write and tell her that you would hardly open her letter,' Twice said, 'and that's another one for you to answer. I wonder how many thousand words you write in a week?'

'It must be a fair number. I am just realizing that I am practically a one-woman pen-pals club. Lord, when I was a youngster and was mixed up with old Madame X and Muriel in that Chain of Friendship pen-pals thing, I used to think it was the silliest thing in the world but now I am not so sure. Since we came out here, the mail is a very important part of our lives.'

'But your mail is a natural development. It's letters from home and from people you actually know and like – not people you've got in touch with through an agency. And then, your ties with home are terribly strong – it goes back to what I was saying about your feeling for Reachfar. You seem to have Reachfar all about you here in a curious way – I suppose the letters from there are a sort of channel of communication between you.'

'I can't imagine life with no communication between me and Reachfar. Mind you, I repeat it – it doesn't mean that I am homesick or unhappy or anything. As for communication, you can't call George's and Tom's letters much in the way of communication!'

'At their age, it's jolly good that they write at all,' Twice defended them.

'Dad is older than George and he writes a decent letter.'

'He does. It's a specialized gift he has. In fact, I suppose you inherit from him – you have a flair for it too.'

21

'If I have a flair, my mother may have had something to do with it. She used to write all the family letters and when I was small she was the one who always saw that paper was available for me to scribble on.'

'Sometimes I grudge all the time you spend sitting at that desk in there writing letters. You ought to write a book.'

'A book? Me? Are you off your nut? What sort of book?'

'You once told me in an unguarded moment that when you were young you would have liked to write.'

'I told you that as a sort of not very funny joke. Most youngsters go through a soulful phase of thinking they can be epic poets like that lovely bit in Daudet when the little boy got the exercise book and headed it "Canto One" and wrote down:

"Réligion! Réligion! Mot sublime mystère!"

– and that was as far as his epic ever got. The only poetry I have ever written was scurrilous doggerel about people I didn't like.'

'I wasn't thinking about poetry. I was thinking more of those monthly letters of day-to-day things that you send to Reachfar – the diary, as you call it. Those descriptions you write of what goes on very live and completely individual. That one you wrote about the night we acted *The Varlets* at the Great House was a humdinger.'

'Any ass could make that interesting, with attempted murder and all the general mayhem that went on. That's mere reportage.'

'Not quite,' he argued. 'You told it well, it came alive and even when *I* read it and although I was there when everything happened practically, I felt as if I were seeing it all for the first time through different eyes – your eyes. That's where the gift lies – in getting that individual vision across.'

'Oh, rot! I'll stick to the letter-writing. I wonder who that Mrs Miller can be?'

'Listen, what was that about you letting a ferret loose in Miss Tulloch's shop? I've never heard about that.'

'Oh, that happened away back about 1918. And *there's* individual vision for you if you like! I don't remember any Mrs Miller wanting to have me arrested that day. All I remember is that the Miss Boyds clung round George's and Tom's necks to get away from the ferret and Tom was so embarrassed that he shouted at me and swore. Davie the Plasterer and I were catching rats in Miss Tulloch's back yard and Angus, my ferret, went down a hole outside and came up in the shop among all the women. I've never seen a woman yet who wasn't terrified of a ferret – I don't think I'd care for Angus myself now – you've never seen such a shambles. Women were climbing up the walls and over each other and the Miss Boyds were climbing up Tom and George. *You* met some of the Miss Boyds once, with their spiv of a nephew. Don't you remember?'

'Oh, yes. One of them was dotty.'

'That's right. But I don't remember this Mrs Miller. It's your individual vision thing. George and Tom probably remember her that day especially because they'd have had to pacify her about getting Davie and me arrested but I only remember being furious with the Miss Boyds for clinging to Tom and making him swear at me. Let's go and have lunch.'

When Twice had gone back to the factory for the afternoon, I sat down at my table to write to Miss Hadley and this first letter after a gap of many years was of necessity of the kind that was dull to me because I seemed to have written it so often before. With the second paragraph, the phrases that came into all these letters to the friends and acquaintances who kept on coming out of my past began to recur: 'In 1947 I married an engineer, a Scotsman, called Alexander Alexander but I call him Twice for short and at the end of 1948 we came out here although we have been home in Scotland twice since then. St Jago as you probably know is a sugar island and this house is on the largest sugar estate in St Jago, an estate owned by Madame Dulac, a widow who is over eighty and who lives here, at the Great House, with her son, Sir Ian, who is in his late sixties. We are not part of the estate staff. Twice is actually Caribbean Area engineer for his firm which is Allied Plant Limited but we live here because Twice is engaged in the third year of an expansion programme at the Paradise Sugar Factory. Madame and Sir Ian are so kind to us that

23

we might be part of their family instead of strangers in their midst.'

As I wrote words from the forepart of my brain, as it were, the deeper part at the back of my head was engaged with this Mrs Miller, teased and taunted by the fact that George and Tom thought I must remember her. It was only now, when I began to search for some specific thing among them, that I realized how numerous and how clear were my memory pictures of Reachfar, Achcraggan, the whole district of my childhood, its people and its events. Reachfar was a small croft on the top of a flattish hill and I think my earliest memory of all of it as a place as apart from its people was of looking through the bars of the gate that separated the farm-yard from the heather moor, dotted with fir trees, that lay to the south of the house, and with the memory I could feel again the desire to get through the gate and explore the moor. I could also feel again the tug as Fly, the trained Shetland collie who was my nursemaid, took a fold of my woollen dress in her mouth and pulled me back through the bars. This must have happened shortly after I learned to walk for, by the time I was four years old, Fly and I knew intimately every tree that grew on the moor and every inch of all the rest of the Reach-far ground as well. I know this because, one beautiful warm day in August, when I was four, Fly and I went away on to the moor and stayed there long past supper-time and when George found us – which he would never have done if Fly had not barked when he whistled, because we were hiding – I got a dreadful scolding from my grandmother. My grand-mother, who was really Mrs Sandison but was mostly called Mrs Reachfar, did all the scolding in our house and, indeed, a lot of the scolding that was done in the whole district as well. She did not scold my grandfather or my mother but all the rest of us, my father, my Aunt Kate and especially my Uncle George, my friend Tom and myself were often in trouble with her. And when she was scolding you, she was not very patient about listening to any explanation you might have and be-sides, somehow, Tom, George and I were the sort of people who often did things for which there *was* no explanation that could be offered to my grandmother. She could never understand, for instance, that if the parlour window was open in summer, George simply had to nip off two pairs of twin flowers from the fuchsia plant that stood on the sill, hang a pair over each of his ears and pretend to be old Lady Ishbel for the entertainment of Tom and me. And on this evening in August when I was four, she could not understand why I had run away to hide in the moor and I could not find any words to tell her why, but it was because my father and George had come home from work too early, which was frightening in itself and then my father said: 'Germany has invaded Belgium and war has broken out.' These were words I did not understand but they made everybody suddenly go very quiet and unhappy and not like my family at all – even George and Tom were quiet and grave. I knew, of course, that it was a terrible nuisance if sheep or cattle broke out into the corn or turnips and it made my grandmother scold, but whatever this was that had broken out, it was worse than the time the scarlet fever broke out in Achcraggan for my grandmother was not scolding now, and it was so unnatural and frightening that Fly and I went away to the farthest corner of the moor and hid.

It was easy and pleasant to drift away into these memories of Reachfar, a bright hilltop above the even brighter Firth that came in from the North Sea between the two great cliffs called the Cobblers and stretched away west almost to the foot of Ben Wyvis. Ben Wyvis, the great mountain to the west and slightly to the north, was the arbitrator of our weather at Reachfar and no important operation like sowing the seed in spring, mowing the hay in summer or beginning the harvest in autumn was ever undertaken until my grandmother had gone out to the gable end of our house and had had 'a look west at the Ben'. I loved Ben Wyvis but I also feared him a little.

He was, in my mind as a child, indubitably a male – a giant of a male, of stupendous strength and strength of two kinds, differentiated in my mind as 'ordinary' strength and 'pulpity' strength, which was quite a different thing, a sort of power, a soul-stirring, fascinating yet frightening power like the power that gathered round the Reverend Roderick Mackenzie the

Minister when he stood in his pulpit on Sunday, his arms raised so that his black gown made great wings about him, and said in his deep resonant voice: 'Hear, now, the Word of the Lord!'

I liked to go to church with my family and I liked the Reverend Roderick who was tall and handsome and smiled down at me through his long black beard when he met me coming home from school; I knew that God was Love and not anything to be afraid of, for it said so on the cross-stitch text on the wall of my grandmother's bedroom but, in spite of all that, there were times in church when the pulpity feeling came over me so that I wanted to run away and creep into some small cosy place such as a 'cave' in the straw of the barn with Fly for company. In a similar way, sometimes, I would get the pulpity feeling when I looked at Ben Wyvis. Most of the time he lay against the skyline, gay and smiling if it were a summer morning or drowsy with a reddish flush if it were a summer evening and the sun were sinking into its bed behind his broad back or, in winter time, he lay hidden and cosy under his blankets of white snow and puffy eiderdown of grey clouds, but once in August, I saw him angry and the pulpity feeling came over me and, after that, I never looked at him without respect and a deep sensibility of his power and mystery.

It was a very hot day and I was not quite five at the time, and after midday dinner my grandmother said: 'Janet, don't you go wandering away into the moor or far from the house this afternoon. It's going to rain.'

I had intended to go away up to the Picnic Pond after dinner, for I had two biscuits and two sweets saved for a picnic for Fly and me but I did not argue with my grandmother. Nobody – not even the Minister or Sir Torquil the Laird or anybody – argued with my grandmother. So, instead of going to the Picnic Pond, I went along to the Stone Dyke Corner which was no distance at all from the house but at least concealed from it by a thorn hedge, and there I sat down and we had our picnic while I brooded darkly on the devilish power vested in my grandmother for foiling the desires and designs of everyone and of me in particular.

'Her and her rain!' I thought and then repeated aloud to Fly: 'Poop to her and her old rain!'

Fly had clear amber eyes and, putting her head on one side, she stared at me rather unsympathetically, I thought.

'How does *she* know whether God is going to make it rain or not?' I asked Fly crossly.

At that moment, there came a growling rumbling noise from the sky and Fly crept in close beside me and pushed her head against my chest. It was only a rumble of thunder, I knew, and Fly was afraid of thunder because she was only a dog, after all, although so clever in her own way and not sensible like a person, really. Still, it was quite comforting to put your arm round her neck and take a handful of the strong wiry hair under her chin while the sky sent down another ominous rumble.

'Janet!' came my grandmother's voice from the door of the house. 'Janet!'

'Coming, Granny!' I called back and stood up.

As I stood, Ben Wyvis came into sight above the dry-stone wall in front of me. He seemed to have grown in size since I had last noticed him and he was as black as midnight, although it was August and only that morning he had been wearing his best cloak of royal purple which he wore only in the heather-honey season. But now, deep black himself, he cast all about him an even blacker shadow and hanging over his frowning brows was a crown of black clouds, a high crown, pile upon pile of plumed cloud like the great sombre ostrich feathers that formed a bunch on top of Mr Maclennan's funeral hearse. And, as I looked at him, there was a small angry rumble, then from his crown of clouds there darted out a long green streak of fire which snaked across the sky like a whiplash, was reflected in the waters of the Firth and, as if from out of the great mass of the Ben himself, came a very loud, very angry bang followed by a long, reverberating, growling rumble as if, driven by rage, Ben Wyvis were about to move from his eternal place, throw himself upon me and crush me to death. I stood transfixed, Fly cowering beside me, waiting for the onslaught when, once again, came the voice of my grandmother: 'Janet! Come here at once!'

27

I jerked my eyes away from Ben Wyvis and took to my heels.

My grandmother was waiting for me at the little gate at the west end of the house and as I ran towards her she said: 'Come into the house at once! Have you no more sense than that Mrs Miller down there?'

# 3

I SUDDENLY realized that I was sitting in the drawing-room at Guinea Corner, Paradise, St Jago with my elbows on my writing-table, one on each side of a completed letter to my old schoolmistress, Miss Hadley, and staring out through a window screened with mosquito mesh at a tropical garden, its lawns burned brown by the harshly merciless sun. Ben Wyvis under his crown of clouds, the lightning over the Firth and the stern tall figure of my grandmother faded away for a moment but I still heard her voice coming down the tunnel of memory from the past: 'Have you no more sense than that Mrs Miller down there?' I deliberately laid aside my pen, pushed the letter to Miss Hadley to one side, put my hands under my chin, stared out into the dark clump of hibiscus beyond the mesh and conjured up once more the picture of my grandmother.

She shooed me ahead of her into the big, warm, safe kitchen as the first heavy drops of the storm began to patter on the corrugated iron roof of the milk-house. On one side of the fire, my mother sat sewing while my aunt baked scones, and my grandmother, in an irritable way, now took up her knitting from the little table in the corner and, sitting beside my mother, she began to click the needles.

'Granda and Tom will get a proper soaking away east on the hill there,' she said. 'I told them this was no day to go out there to mend that gate.'

The clicking of the knitting-needles was drowned in another roar of thunder that rolled like heavy iron wheels along the roof ridge of the house.

'And *you*!' my grandmother said to me. 'Standing west there at the dyke looking at the sky as if you had no more sense than a tethered goat!'

She finished the row she was knitting, dropped the work into her lap and then, when she raised her head and spoke to my mother, her face and voice and all about her became quite different. As I put it in my own mind, she had changed from my grandmother into my granny, a change that she could make in the wink of an eye.

'Your head is sore with the thunder, *m'eudail*?' she asked my mother. 'You would be better lying down on your bed, maybe?'

My mother raised her big grey eyes from her sewing and smiled. 'The headache is gone now, Granny. It always goes after the thunder breaks. Goodness, what a storm, though!'

We all looked towards the window as another peal of thunder went rolling over.

'It will go on for hours, likely,' my aunt said, as she dusted the flour from the girdle with the brush that was a bundle of hen's wing feathers bound together with white string.

'It always does when it comes from the west,' my grandmother agreed. Then she took up her knitting again and looked at me over the needles. 'Don't stand there like a horse at a gate, Janet! Have you nothing to do?'

My grandmother could not bear to see anybody idle. The only person who could do nothing in her presence and be praised for it was my mother, for in the eyes of my grandmother, my mother could do nothing wrong, unfitting or unbecoming, but one of the first contradictions I noticed in life was that my mother, who was at liberty to be idle all day if she pleased, did not seem to want to idle. She was always busy with the light gentle jobs that were her part of the Reachfar world. She was always sewing, knitting, mending, writing letters or attending to the flower garden and she was the only one of us to whom my grandmother ever said: 'Come now, lassie, stop your work for a little. Come and get a droppie tea.' The rest of us were dragooned from morning until night.

Now, with her eagle eye upon me, I took the scarf I was knitting from the little table – in spite of my good memory I cannot remember when I learned to knit or to read – and retired with it out of sight into the scullery. The scullery had the only window in Reachfar that looked to the wild north and it was, really, only a little door of glass about eighteen inches square in the thick wall, with a broad sill, and in front of it stood the white-scrubbed scullery table. My grandmother did not approve of people sitting on tables but I knew her well enough to know that, in her present mood of worry about my mother who was always upset by thunder, she would not seek me out as long as I did not thrust myself on her notice. So, with my knitting, I climbed upon the table but I did not knit. Kneeling, I put my forearms on the broad sill and my face close to the glass and from here I could see the whole sweep of the Firth and the hills to the north and, by poking right into the corner and twisting my neck, I could also see Ben Wyvis, black and angry under his crown of grey clouds. He was not so fearsome and pulpity, seen from here, from the warm shelter of the house where the big fire blazed in the next room and the smell of baking scones was all around.

The rain fell in long slanting shafts, straight as my grandmother's steel knitting-needles, and the Firth and hills lay patient under the onslaught of the fury from the Ben, everything still, as if afraid to move so that, in the nearer distance just beyond our march dyke, the figure that moved along the top edge of the Poyntdale Long Ley, shoulders hunched against the slanting rain, seemed incongruous, almost sacrilegious. In our own fields, on the nearer side of the dyke, the black Aberdeen Angus cattle stood by the gate, their hindquarters against the slant of the rain, their heads hanging low, like naughty children who had been stood in shame in a corner for their sins. In another field, Dick and Betsy, the plough horses, stood close together, also in the corner by the gate, Betsy looking very dejected while Dick, pretending to be manly, brave and comforting in spite of his own misery, nibbled a little, between the rolls of thunder, at a spot on her spine near the end of her mane. I had the feeling that for all his pretence of nibbling to comfort Betsy, he was really doing it because it was a comfort to himself, as I sometimes rubbed my mother's hands when they were very cold in the frosty weather, pretending it was for *her* when it was really a comfort to myself to feel them grow warmer again. And still, along the top of the Poyntdale Long Ley, the little hunched figure moved along, south-westwards, amid the slanting rain.

'That foolish Mrs Miller is down there, making for Dinchory as usual,' came the voice of my grandmother from the kitchen.

'Oh, of course, this is Wednesday,' my mother said.

'She'll get a right good soaking before she gets to Dinchory in this,' said my aunt.

'She'll put between that young couple before she's done!' my grandmother's voice was fierce now. 'Why can't she let the laddie be, him and his young wife?'

'She is bound to find it lonely, Granny,' my mother said gently, 'left down there at Achcraggan by herself. She has just lived for Tommy since Mr Miller died.'

'And a fine mess she made of Tommy too!' said my aunt who, to me, was part of the far-off, grown-up world but who was really, at this time, only about sixteen and, if you listened to my grandmother, a 'flighty young madam'.

'Tommy Miller is just a proper big sapsie,' my aunt continued, 'and he was lucky to get that girl from the south to marry him. None of us round *here* would have taken him.'

'All you around here,' said my grandmother scathingly, 'had better wait till you are asked before you choose who you will take. Hold your tongue and make some tea.'

'Well, *I'm* not for any Tommy Miller that wants to cry into his mammy's apron every Wednesday and Sunday!' said my aunt defiantly.

I heard my grandmother's angry indrawn breath and then the gentle tones of my mother in her role – a very frequent one – of peacemaker.

'A man can like his mother, Kate, without being a cry-baby,' she said, 'and a daughter-in-law can be very good friends with her husband's mother too.' She gave a small laugh. 'After all, Granny and I don't quarrel.'

'Ach, that is quite another thing!' my grandmother said and I heard her get up and put away her knitting in her impatient way. 'There is no comparison between Tommy Miller and his little wifie and Duncan and you, lassie! It's not the same thing at all! It's —' Words failed her, a thing that did not happen often and she made one of her savage attacks on the fire with the poker for she always had to have an outlet of some kind. My mother's little laugh became a definite chuckle, a very gay sound.

'And I wouldn't say there was much resemblance between Granny and Mrs Miller, would you, Kate?'

'Not a great deal,' said my aunt and gave her lovely laugh that was like a happy chime of contralto bells that made the old rafters of the kitchen ring.

'That's quite enough from the two of you!' said my grandmother. 'Well the rain's clearing a little. Janet! Come and get your tea and then you'll have to carry some east to Granda and Tom. Put your moor boots on. Look sharp now!'

Twice came home about five o'clock with his usual greeting of: 'What sort of afternoon?'

'Very lazy,' I said, 'but I've caught up with Mrs Miller.'

'Mrs Miller? Caught up? How d'you mean? Oh, *you* mean the Reachfar Mrs Miller?'

'Of course! Didn't we agree to call the other one Mrs Miller of Hope as they do in the island?'

'Yes, but I meant to tell you there's another.'

'Another what?'

'Mrs Miller.'

'Now, look here, Twice Alexander —'

'Look here yourself! *I* can't help this sudden plethora of Mrs Millers. She is a stenographer in the office at the Bay – the best stenographer we've got – and I've just been on the phone to her, and naturally when I come in here and you say Mrs Miller, I think of her because I've been talking to her only a moment ago.'

'What's her name?' I asked, which, I now see, was pretty stupid.

Twice glared at me. 'MRS MILLER!' he bellowed.

'Sorry. I meant her Christian name.'

'I don't know.'

'I thought it might have helped,' I explained humbly. 'We'll have to call her *your* Mrs Miller for now.'

32

'Actually, I am hoping to make her my own secretary. She's the brightest thing we've got in the office down there and I'm having a go at nobbling her for my work exclusively.'

It was only about a year since Allied Plant had opened their new Caribbean headquarters in St Jago Bay, the capital town of the island, and Twice, who was much more of a practical engineer than what he called a 'paper wallah', spent as little time as possible there and seldom spoke of what went on in the offices. When he was not at Paradise or at some of the other sugar factories or industrial plants in St Jago, he was at similar places in the other islands of the Caribbean, for his area extended over all the British islands as well as British Honduras. The office in St Jago Bay was under the management of a colleague, a non-engineer, called Lionel Somerset.

'You'd better see that Somerset doesn't nobble her first, if she's good,' I said now.

'She is not his type. Besides, he is very happy with Miss Wong.'

'Chinese?'

'Not pure-bred but a bit of a glamour-puss. Goes in for the Miss St Jago beauty contests and all that. She's more interested in what she calls her vital statistics than in any statistics of the Allied Plant sort but she seems to suit Somerset.'

'The things that go on down there! And what is your Mrs Miller like?'

'A really nice woman and unusually intelligent. She's been very well educated.'

'A Negress?'

'Dark *café-au-lait*, and a funny thing – she's got a lot of little jet-black freckles on her nose. But her features are true Negro. She's got two children – a little girl of about seven with tight black pigtails that stick out and have red ribbons on them – she's cute. And a little boy who is younger, with great big Negro eyes and a very fat stomach and a big head. He looks a bit like a specially nice sort of tadpole.'

'Why have I never heard of Mrs Miller before? When did she come to the office?'

'About two months ago. I never noticed her much except that she produced a very nice-looking letter and she spelled "helical" with only one "l" in the middle. The Wong always puts two in it which makes a letter look extraordinarily impolite, somehow. Then, last Saturday morning when I ran down with that specification to catch the mail, I went along for a beer before I came home and met Mrs Miller out shopping with her two children.'

'What does the husband do?' I asked.

'He was in government service of some kind – Customs and Excise, I think – but he died a couple of years ago, I believe.'

'I'd like to meet Mrs Miller.'

'That's easily arranged. Come down to the office with me some day.'

'I don't mean like that. I'd like to invite her here. Twice, do you mind?'

'Me? Of course not! Madame and Sir Ian may not entirely approve but what of that?'

'Yes. What of it?'

It was easy to say this but in my mind there was a hankering feeling that the approval or disapproval of Madame and Sir Ian did matter and in rebellion against this, I said: 'You and I were brought up too strictly in some ways. This business of always taking our lead from our elders and betters is an example of it. After all, we are forty-two now – we're not children. It's possible that we are elders and betters ourselves now, even the elders and betters of Madame and Sir Ian in some ways, although they have sixty years' experience of this island and we have only three.'

'That could be true. Experience isn't a matter of time so much as of intensity and Madame and Sir Ian have spent their sixty years resisting real experience of the island when you think of it. To speak the truth, they are an exasperating pair when you come to grips with them.'

'I'm glad you said it first,' I told him. 'It is only since Marion Maclean went away on leave that the full irritation potential of Madame has been borne in on me, but I've never mentioned it because I thought you had enough to do without listening to me grousing.'

'Then from now on we can grouse in unison.'

Hitherto, in the course of our three years at Paradise, Twice had not been in immediate working contact with Sir Ian and Madame, for Rob Maclean, their Scottish estate manager, had always stood between, just as Marion, his wife, had stood in the social hierarchy of the place between me and Madame. Rob and Marion Maclean at this time, however, were on long leave to Britain and Twice, at the end of the first month, was beginning to show some signs of nervous wear and tear.

'Say what you like about Rob Maclean, he must have the patience of a saint to have run this outfit for over thirty years,' he now said bitterly. 'Madame is absolutely exasperating. And somehow I wouldn't be so exasperated if I didn't basically like her so much, if that makes any sense.'

'What is she up to now?' I asked.

Twice is seldom ill-natured and when he is it does not, as a rule, last for very long if he is given a chance to 'talk it out'.

'She sent for me this afternoon, just at the very moment when we were casting that cement platform with all the holes for the foundation bolts in it. It was urgent, the boy said. So I drop everything and go steaming over to the Great House and she announces that she has thought of a terrific plan. We are to start an apprentices' school at Paradise and train Negroes to be shift engineers! An apprentices' school at this moment in the history of Paradise!'

I saw what he meant and could think of nothing very helpful to say. The period from now until December was the Out-of-Crop period and the factory which, from January until June, had been a humming hive that produced sugar day and night was now more like the yard of a scrap-metal dealer than anything else. This was the third and final year of an expansion programme with a great deal of new equipment to be installed in new buildings before December and certainly it was no time to think of establishing any extraneous schemes like apprentices' schools.

'She couldn't have chosen a madder moment to produce the idea,' I said, 'but in point of fact I myself have heard you say that that is exactly what should be done on an estate like this in this stage of the island's development – train the Negroes, I mean.'

'Oh, I know! It was just that she should pick on today and

35

that particular moment of today. The school is a first-class idea – I would think so because it's my own. I've been pumping it into Sir Ian to pump into Madame for months, hoping that eventually it would be pumped out as an idea of her own.' He began to laugh. 'I suppose being dragged off to the Great House to have it pumped out at me today is my own fault for bad timing!'

'You can stave it off until after Crop starts. If things go well, you'll have lots of time after the factory is running and you can start organizing the school. You know you'll love it!'

'Yes, I *would* love it if —'

'If what?'

'What's the good,' he burst out, 'of me and the others training young Negroes if, when they're qualified, Madame won't let them rise above the rank of mill-hands? It'd be just like those five island ministers. They're trained, they're ordained, but Fontabelle Church is not for *them*, thank you very much.'

'But surely —' I began and paused. I thought of the engineering structure of the factory and was defeated. In charge of each eight-hour shifts round the clock were Mackie, Christie and Vickers, three young, imported white men.

'It's a pity there is such a cleavage between theory and practice,' Twice said. 'In theory, Madame and Sir Ian are all for helping the Negro, education of the Negro and all that, but what's the good if, in practice, you merely frustrate him?'

'I don't see how Fontabelle Church didn't go to one of the island men,' I said after a moment. 'After all, it comes under the island Presbytery, doesn't it?'

'Lord, yes, but only of later years since the Presbytery got going. It's one of the oldest churches in the island, founded by that redoubtable old Mistress Kirsty that Sir Ian tells all the yarns about – Mistress Kirsty Beaton of Craigellachie Heights, old Miss Sue's great-grandmother.'

'That church was one of Mistress Kirsty's works? I thought her great thing was hospitals.'

'So they were but it seems she had a spare moment one day and had that church built and then she sent home to Scotland and imported a minister for it. He lived to be nearly a hundred

– Sir Ian can remember him. Anyway, a tradition got established. There has been a Scotsman in that pulpit ever since but it's not tradition that carried the day this time – it's Beaton money. Craigellachie Heights has an endowment on that church – it pays half the minister's stipend. The effect of the endowment is to *double* the stipend – a white man couldn't live on what any of the other country churches in the island can pay. One has to accept the fact that money talks, I suppose, but I have a deep-rooted dislike of it talking in church, although I'm not a very religious bloke in the orthodox way.' Twice stared across the room with his dark brows drawn down over his blue eyes which were made more blue by the almost mahogany-coloured tan of his skin.

'You seem to feel much more strongly about this church thing than I had realized, Twice,' I said. 'Why?'

'I think a big mistake has been made or, rather, it's not so much that I think it as that I *feel* it, to use your sort of parlance. And at the same time I'm conscious of being a new boy in this island compared with an old hand like Sir Ian who was born here, so I can't come out into the open and say very much. I'm only a visiting consultant here, after all – the church is none of my business – but since Rob went away and I have been in more immediate contact with the men up at the factory and in the fields, I have begun to notice things I hadn't noticed before. This Paradise community doesn't seem to me to be the secure, feudal, friendly affair that everybody likes to think. There's a change working – a great big change, and I don't think Sir Ian or Rob Maclean are aware of it. It is possible, isn't it, that they have been too close to Paradise for too long to notice it?'

'It's highly possible. What sort of change do you mean, though, Twice?'

'The sort of change that's working all over the island – just a sort of general unrest. It's difficult to pinpoint symptoms or incidents – it's just something in the air and behind the eyes of the men. Remember last Crop when the workers struck down at Cambuskenneth and burned out a thousand acres of cane in the end? Remember how Sir Ian and Rob reacted? Sort of uppity and superior and how old Royde had never been clever at handling his labour and all that? An attitude that such a thing could never happen on Paradise? Well, I think it *could* happen on Paradise. It could happen at the drop of a hat. And things like importing an unknown, untried white minister into our own district for a church that a lot of our people attend and turning down five island applicants makes the hat just a little readier to drop, that's all. Sir Ian and Rob tend to regard Paradise as a kingdom separate from the rest of the island. Maybe it was once, but it isn't any more.'

'I'm no good at politics or economics. They're too big and complex for me but this separate kingdom thing is the root of the whole trouble. Look at this separate kingdom of the white community – it's so basically stupid. We're a hopeless little white minority, that's all, hanging about on the fringe of the life of the island like a little froth at the edge of a great black whirlpool.'

'The trouble is that we have got the money – not you and I personally.' Twice laughed a little. 'But the whites in general are the capital interest. And in the past we have had most of the skills as well – the doctors, the lawyers, the ministers, have all been white.'

'And the engineers.'

'And the engineers,' he agreed. He took thought for a moment. 'But there comes a time,' he said then, 'when one has to accept that a cycle has been completed; that things have changed almost imperceptibly slowly, but they'll never be the same again. It's one of the most difficult things to accept that. We seem to be constructed in the most extraordinary way – the thing we hate most to accept is the thing that we really know to be inevitable. Miss Sue Beaton must be more aware than any white in this island that the old order is changing. Craigellachie Heights is a pimento property – it used to be one of the richest places in the island when the Negroes were willing to turn out for a few pence a day and climb trees and throw down branches to their wives and children who picked the berries off into baskets for a few more pence. Fontabelle used to be a small township but it has faded away to a few ruins and a few old people and the church in the short time we have been in the island. The Negroes have moved down to the Bay where they can get more cash more easily than by shinning up pimento trees. They've left the Beatons sitting on the heights with their trees neglected so that the disease has got in and they don't fruit any more. It's time Miss Sue came down out of the clouds and got her feet on the ground but oh, no. She has to maintain the old dead order, so she gets five island men shoved aside and imports a Scotsman for Fonta-belle pulpit. Sorry to be talking a blue streak about all this, Flash, but I do wish these people would take a thought about it. They won't, of course. That's another inevitability that we've got to accept. Let's talk about something else.'

After a moment, I said: 'This isn't exactly something else but you mentioning blue streaks made me think of it. When you say "talking a blue streak" it always makes me think of the lightning that used to streak along the Firth at home when we had a thunderstorm. As I told you, I've remembered who this Mrs Miller is that George and Tom and Monica were going on about.'

'Oh, yes?'

'I don't remember her being at Miss Tulloch's the day of the fantod about my ferret but I remember her from much earlier than that and I remember a lot of rows about her at Reachfar one way and another. She was a small dark sour-looking old woman —' I began, and I told Twice of that first thunderstorm that I could remember and of how I had watched the lightning over the Firth from the scullery window while, in the kitchen next door, the women of my family discussed Mrs Miller who trudged through the rain on one of her bi-weekly visits to her son.

'My grandmother prophesied disaster,' I said, 'that Mrs Miller would "put between" as she called it her son and his young wife and as usual my grandmother prophesied true. I think it must have been 1917 or 1918 that the young wife left Tommy – it was the summer anyway because I was playing on the old mill-pole outside the scullery window this time, and the window was open and it must have been late on in the war, for there was a German prisoner involved. One or two of them were allowed out of the camp and were working with

39

the Newfoundland wood-cutters over in Ardgruanach wood. Anyway, I heard my grandmother and Aunt Kate going at it hammer and tongs.'

'I'm sorry in a million ways that your grandmother was dead before I knew you,' Twice said. 'I'd have liked to see Kate up against a foeman worthy of her steel.'

'Reachfar must be a pretty queer place without Kate in it.'

'Yes. A big change in the old order. But Kate deserves some happiness and she seems to be getting it with Malcolm.'

'Imagine her liking New York and living in a flat in Brooklyn! Quite a change from Reachfar, you might say.'

'Kate will take it in her stride. What more about this Mrs Miller?'

I was silent for a moment, still trying to visualize Reachfar as it would be now, for a few months before, at over fifty, my aunt had married her old admirer Malcolm Macleod and had gone away with him to the United States. Reachfar without my aunt there was something I could barely imagine for she had always been there, first as the youngest daughter who stayed at home to help my grandmother and, later, after the death of my grandparents, as mistress of the house herself. She was a woman of great beauty, strong character and fiery temper, and my childhood had been punctuated by lively exchanges between her and my redoubtable grandmother when they came to a clash as they often did.

In theory, I, the child, was not supposed to know of these clashes but, as Twice had remarked, theory tends to be a little different from practice and Reachfar being my child's world, I made it my business to know most of what went on within it. Now, as I talked to Twice, I could see my Reachfar world exactly as it had looked to me over thirty years ago and I could hear the voices that spoke in the scullery and came to me through the open window as clearly as if my aunt and my grandmother were immediately outside the window of the Guinea Corner drawing-room.

'What these young women are thinking about I don't know!' said my grandmother. 'And one of these German prisoners of all the men in the world! Tommy Miller's wife

40

must hold herself gey cheap. Poor old Mrs Miller, having a disgrace like this in the family and her always holding her head so high!'

'And always holding her Tommy to her apron-strings too,' said my aunt. 'Well, she'll get her Tommy back to herself now and good luck to her!'

'Hold your tongue! You should be ashamed of yourself!'

'You said yourself that Mrs Miller would put between Tommy and Lena in the end, Mother. Well, she's done it.'

'It wasn't Mrs Miller's fault that that loose-minded Lena began to carry on with that German!'

'How do you know whose fault it was?' my aunt flared. 'Lena is a nice girl and no more loose-minded than anybody else. If *I'd* been married to Tommy Miller and that old besom never out from between my feet, I might have gone for a bit of a walk with a German myself!'

'Kate Sandison!'

'You needn't shout Kate Sandison at *me*, Mother!' When my aunt's temper was up she had enough of my grandmother in her to give as good as she got, and Kate had liked Lena, Tommy's young wife from the south, and Kate was loyal to her friends. 'And you needn't go issuing orders to me not to speak to Lena either for I'll speak to her any time I get the chance. All this stuff about Tommy Miller putting her out of his house is a lot of rubbish. Tommy Miller hasn't the guts to shove a herring off a plate – it's that old mother of his who made the trouble, you can bet your boots. It's my belief Lena left of her own accord and took this job at the woodcutters' canteen and good luck to her and her German too if she likes him! And old Mrs Miller can skitter round her Tommy's tail till God blesses her for all I care!'

'Kate Sandison, stop blaspheming —'

'Blaspheming my Aunt Maria! I'm sick and tired listening to you all going on about Lena and sympathizing with that old bitch Miller!'

'Kate Sandison!' my grandmother thundered. 'Hold your wicked tongue this minute!'

'Well, then —'

'Goodness gracious me,' said the peace-making voice of my

41

mother who now joined them, 'what put you into such a tirravee, Kate?'

'Oh, nothing!' and I heard my aunt run out of the scullery, slamming the door.

Then came my grandmother's thoughtful voice, a little rueful too.

'What a passion of a temper is in Kate, Elizabeth! Och, maybe she is right in a way. Mrs Miller did interfere something terrible between the young couple, right enough. But I wish Kate wasn't so hot-headed.'

'Kate is all right, Granny.'

'These are trying times for the young ones, with this war and all the upheaval. But for this war, Lena wouldna have found it so easy to leave her man and her home – Mrs Miller or no Mrs Miller.' What my mother said next did not seem to me to make much sense, for it was all about my aunt and Granny was talking about Lena, not my aunt, but I knew that it must make sense for my mother was the wisest person in the whole world. It was a quieter sort of sense she had than my grandmother's but it was often an even more sensible sort of sense.

'Kate will be all right, Granny,' she said now. 'Kate is a wiser lassie than Lena for all her hot temper and she has a mother who is a lot wiser than Mrs Miller. Come through and see the new curtains in the parlour.'

Now, these thirty and more years later, I realized that my grandmother must have worried a lot about her beautiful, passionate, fiery-tempered daughter amidst all the upheaval of the Great War which brought the secure world we all knew tumbling about our ears.

'You know, Twice,' I said, 'the Great War must have been for my grandmother and Lady Lydia and all the people like them at home very much like what this emancipation of the Negro thing is for Madame and Miss Sue Beaton. I can remember Armistice Day in 1918 – nothing was ever the same afterwards and now, when I look back at it, the very day had in it the shadow and the implication of what came after.'

'How do you mean?' Twice asked. 'I remember the Armistice too. In our Berwickshire village it was typical, cold drizzly

November day, but we got out of school early and there were flags hanging out of people's windows on the way home. I thought this Armistice must be a fairly good thing because we missed the grammar class that day but that's about all the significance it had for me. What happened at Reachfar?'

'It wasn't at Reachfar – it was at Achcraggan. It was the first day of the coal boat's visit.'

That clear frosty day of thirty-four years ago came back to my mind with extraordinary vividness and I told Twice of its excitement, the excitement of the horses, even, as they danced down the hill from Reachfar in front of their clean carts. I told him of how the day worked up to its climax as the destroyer bringing the news of the Armistice came dashing into the Firth from the open sea, her siren blowing as she passed the pier where we all were, loading coal from the boat. I told him of how, when they heard the news, all the men with the Captain and crew of the boat went into the Plough Inn and drank all day until the Plough's cellars were empty and '– in the middle of it all,' I said, 'the tide went out and left the boat high and dry on the beach. Then, suddenly, the sun went in and it was a grey cold November evening. The brightness had fallen from the air. I didn't know at the time that that day in 1918 was the day that a sort of debauch began that left the whole of Britain on the beach – a beach we didn't refloat from until the 1930s and then only to float into the storm of another war. I didn't know then that a whole world came to an end that day, that the coal boat would never come in again. But that is how it was. It was a case of "never bright confident morning again".'

We were both quiet for a moment or two before I said: 'Anyway, to go back to what we were really talking about, the Mrs Miller who is coming out here is the one called Lena who ran away from Tommy and his old mother and was reported to be larking about with a German prisoner.'

'It seems that the larking about got no further,' Twice said. 'Her name is still Mrs Miller and her parson son's name is Miller too. Farewell Romance! She probably went drearily back to this Tommy that Kate thought so little of in the end.'

'I suppose so. Dad and I left Reachfar for Cairnton not so long after that and I don't remember hearing any more about either her or Tommy.'

# 4

EVEN the St Jagoan winter is hot to someone born and bred in Scotland. The summer is even hotter and that summer of 1952 had been a particularly trying one. Since the end of July, one hurricane after another had formed in the Atlantic to the south-east and in procession they had followed a north and more or less westerly course, some dying out off the coast of Florida and some expiring in the Gulf of Mexico. None of them came within eighty miles of St Jago, but the eye of a hurricane passing eighty-five miles away is near enough to bring two or three days of torrential rain, a low barometric pressure and an atmosphere so stifling, enervating and depressing that one might be living under a grey blanket which is being kept permanently soaked with boiling water. The weeks slid sluggishly by and it was the beginning of October before the blanket lifted, the sun came through, a fresh breeze began to blow from the west and we all felt that we could breathe again.

During the months of August and September, I do not think that I went out anywhere, except to go round to the Great House when Madame sent for me. All of us European women at Paradise were regarded by Madame as something in the nature of ladies-in-waiting to herself, and during these months most of the waiting duties fell to me because so many of the other women were on leave to England. At all times, too, I was her principal aide in her various charitable and committee activities because, unlike the other wives, I had been trained and had worked as a secretary in my time and could cope with paper work more readily than the others could. Also, during this period, I had comparatively few visitors at Guinea Corner, partly because the weather robbed everyone of the energy for social intercourse and partly because so many of the white people were on leave during these months.

But with the first breezes out of the west in early October it seemed that everyone began to sit up and look around themselves, and one of my first visitors was Sir Ian of whom I had seen remarkably little for two months. As a rule, he was in and out of Guinea Corner every other day.

'Hello,' I greeted him. 'I thought I had offended you.'

'Good Gad no, me dear! Been busy one way an' another an' the weather's been somethin' hellish.'

I went to the kitchen to ask for some tea, came back and said: 'I hear the new minister has arrived at Fontabelle at last.'

'That's part o' what I came round about, me dear – that an' Mother.'

'Madame? Is anything wrong?'

'No, no. At least, nothin' we can do much about. She's got Mrs Buckley an' one or two other women round there 's afternoon all gabbin' at once so I took my chance an' came away. Ah, thank ye, me dear,' he said, accepting his cup of tea and helping himself to cake. 'Just came round to have a chat about Mother in a general way. Don't know if you've noticed it, but she's gettin' blind.'

'In point of fact, Sir Ian,' I said slowly, 'Twice noticed the other day that her sight was failing and mentioned it.'

'Twice don't miss much. Well, there it is. Mother won't admit it, of course. Says I'm talkin' a lot of nonsense. Ye know Mother. She always was a pretty cussed sort o' woman an' she gets more cussed with every day that goes over her head. Not that I'm criticizin' her or complainin', mind,' he admonished me, 'but I could wish she was a little less cussed about gettin' blind. I mean if ye can't see, ye can't *see*, dammit!' He took a large gulp of tea. 'As if life wasn't difficult enough, we've all got to start kiddin' ourselves an' each other *an'* Mother that her eyes are better'n they ever were.'

'I see,' I said, which was a fairly silly remark when you think of it. 'Sir Ian, when did you first notice that her sight was going?'

'It seemed to start quite suddenly at the beginnin' o'

45

August or so. Oh, she's been usin' glasses for years but this is a different thing. I think all that carry-on with Roddy Maclean an' Cousin Emmie had a lot to do with it. Shock, ye know. That may seem silly to you but Mother got into such a temper over the whole thing that she was fit to be tied for about a fortnight and at her age ye just can't go on like that. I had Bradley the eye man up from the Bay – Mother was fit to be tied about that too but I got him up all the same. He asked me after he'd examined her if she'd suffered a shock o' some kind. At her age, he said, even a slight upset might cause it. Funny, ye know. I've always known Mother was an old woman – dammit, I'm gettin' on for seventy meself so me mother can't be a chicken – but I never thought of her as *old* if ye see what I mean. It just seemed to come over me in a sudden flash when I was talkin' to Bradley that day.'

I knew what he meant. In a similar way, in a similar heart-piercing stab, I remembered, I had suddenly come to the knowledge about twenty-five years ago that my grandmother had grown old. Viewed in retrospect, the evidence that she was failing in power had been piling up for years, just as it had been piling up in the case of Madame, but in my grandmother's case the actual moment of realization had been a sudden sharp stab at the heart and mind, just as it had been for Sir Ian with Madame.

'Anyway, there it is. Bradley's goin' to get her a pair o' these glasses with the thick lenses – an' she won't wear them, likely – but there's nothin' more he can do. He says if she goes quietly she may not get any worse for years but, as I told him, it's just stoopid goin' sayin' a thing like that. Mother's never gone what he calls quietly an' she ain't goin' to start now so that's what brought me round here partly, me dear. People like Bradley ain't got any damn' sense. Oh, they're clever enough about shinin' lights into your eyes an' tellin' you you've got the lord high cockalorum o' a mastigation in them or somethin', but to tell me to keep Mother quiet an' not let her go out an' see people an' all that is just plain stoopid. Mother'll go on goin' out an' havin' people in an' tickin' people off an' interferin' with them until she's in her grave an' that's all that's to it. Only, she can't see well enough to pour out people's tea any more an' although she's all right round at the house where she's been all her life, it ain't too safe to let her go visitin' other houses – she might miss a veranda step or somethin' an' there you are. What she needs is a sort o' companion to be with her an' pour out the tea an' that but when I sort o' suggested it she nearly went through the perishin' roof – asked me why I didn't bury her an' be done with it. Marian an' Janet, she says, are all the companions I need. Sometimes, she says, my neuritis is troublesome in my elbows and knees and I can't lift even the teapot and sometimes I stumble a little, but I don't need a keeper as if I were in my dotage, she says. Neuritis my foot! She's never had neuritis in her life. However, there it is, me dear. She's got neuritis an' she wonders if, when she has a tea party, you'll come round an' do the pourin' out for her.'

'Of course, Sir Ian!'

'That's very good o' you, me dear. An' when Missis Marion gets back it won't be so bad. You can take it in turns an' maybe I'll get her persuaded into the companion thing before too long.'

'And when she goes out, you would like one of us to go with her, I suppose?'

'Well, I had that in mind but this is where you've got to hand it to Mother, cussed old woman as she is. There are times when she reminds me o' the time when I was at Sandhurst, learnin' soldierin'. We used to have classes in strategy – all about knowin' how to pick a position an' maintain it an' that. Mother had an invitation from old Miss Sue yesterday to go up to Craigellachie Heights an' meet the new minister an' what d'ye think she said?'

'I haven't an idea,' I said, nor had I.

'She said: Ian – ye know that commandin' way she has o' sayin' my name – Ian, I have decided that I am not going to go bumping round these island roads in my car any longer. It aggravates my neuritis. If people wish to see me, they can come here.'

'Well done, Madame!'

'But that ain't all. At the same time, she's too damned inquisitive to know there's a tea party at Craigellachie Heights

47

an' not know who was there an' what went on so she says: I shall write to Sue Beaton and say that Janet will represent me. After all, someone from Paradise ought to greet the new minister. So I came to ask if ye'd go up there, me dear. It's next Friday, at four o'clock.'

'Of course I'll go, Sir Ian.'

'That's very good o' you, me dear.'

'It isn't really. I'd like to see the new minister and especially his mother – she lived near my home for a bit when I was a child.'

'D'ye tell me that? Have ye met them already then?'

'No, but my people wrote to tell me they were coming out here.'

'Well, bless my soul! Mother'll be very interested in that. She's always interested in people meetin' people an' knowin' people before an' all that. That's splendid. Well, I'll tell her you'll go to Miss Sue's party for her. It's a hell o' a place to get to, the Heights. Ever been up there?'

'No.'

'Better leave here about three o'clock. I'll send the car at three anyway. Fine place when you get there, though, but it's in pretty poor repair now. But a devil o' a road – like goin' up the side o' a house.'

The topography of St Jago was always extraordinary to my eyes and I never became used to it in all the years I lived there because it was so different from my native highlands of Scotland. St Jago had mountains almost twice the height of Ben Wyvis but, to me, they were never so impressive or majestic as the Ben, partly because they were clothed almost to the summits with bright-green rioting vegetation and partly for another deeper reason. The bulk of Ben Wyvis had, in my eyes, an air of primeval inevitability, as if on the very day of creation, it was there, a solid lump of rock, deeply rooted in the very heart of the earth, as if it had been there when the earth was an inchoate shapeless mass, and which the Creator wisely forbore to interfere with so that it was left with its shoulder humped against the sky, making an irregularity on the curving rim of the newly made world. By contrast, the mountains of St Jago had a new look and, indeed, geologically

48

speaking they are much newer than the rocks of the Scottish Highlands, as if they were an afterthought on the part of the Creator, a caprice whereby He had decided that the Caribbean Sea looked a little bare, so He caused a submarine earthquake which threw up these islands out of the blue water. The mountains looked as if they had been thrown up in mighty spadefuls of wet rock and sand from the ocean bed, rising shoulder on sharp shoulder in great heaps and pinnacles which were then left to bake and harden in angular shapes in the heat of the blazing sun.

From the east to the west end of St Jago ran the Sierra Grande, named by the Spaniards when they first discovered the island, and it was a long twisting ridge of rock like the spine of a dinosaur, dropping away into the sea at each end, where a line of pointed vertebrae still showed above the blue water as small rocky islands. Craigellachie Heights, about seven miles inland from the west end of the island and towering above the town of St Jago Bay, might be described as the westernmost of these vertebrae that was connected to the rest of the spine by land. To reach it, you climbed from Paradise, which was an upland plateau, by tortuous roads to the still higher plateau of Coffee Plains and from there by a road like a spiral staircase round the peak of the vertebrae itself until you emerged in front of the house, near the top, on what I can only describe as a large shelf cut into the rock of the pinnacle.

There is a West Indian saying: 'Man should build his house where cattle sleep,' for cattle always make for high ground before they lie down to sleep, but the early settlers who built Craigellachie Heights must have, I thought, gone a little farther and have followed some mountain goats. How the actual building of the house was engineered is another matter – it was probably built from the rock which was taken out to form the shelf on which it stood – but the mechanics of it I could not bear to think about. It had certainly been built by slave labour for the stones were massive and hand-hewn and as I reeled out of the car, my ears buzzing from the climb, I felt that it was so old that it might easily crumble to pieces and roll down the mountain, taking me with it like a grain of sand in an avalanche.

It was grey, with ferns and vines growing between its stones, the vines blowing in the wind like a series of grey beards, and it was literally crumbling at the corners with age and weather, reminding me of the old tea caddy on the mantel at Reachfar which had once borne a picture of Queen Victoria but which had been handled so much and dusted so often that, when I was a child, all that remained of Queen Victoria was a hand holding an orb. She had no head. The place where her head had been was plain shiny tin, this plain patch being exactly the shape of the ball of my grandmother's left thumb. Craigellachie Heights even had the equivalent of this thumb-mark on its façade in the form of a great roughly boarded aperture near one end of the upper floor. I discovered later that it was the entrance to the loft where the pimento was stored in the former wealthy days.

In the big old drawing-room which housed far too much valuable old furniture and far too many ornaments, Miss Sue Beaton had assembled some twenty people, but among them all the most noticeable was the Miss Sue herself. The first time I met her at Paradise, in my early days in the island, I knew that she was the largest woman I had ever seen and since then I had not met one more massive. I myself stand five feet eight or nine inches – perhaps a little more in my highest, dressed-up, going-out-to-tea heels – but I have never been very fat. Miss Sue, in flat heels, was at least two inches taller than I was and Twice, who has an engineer's eye for measurement, was prepared to stake his reputation that her circumference was equal to her height, if not greater. She had a large face, so red that it was almost purple, a cascade of chins and a very daring taste in dress with a penchant for brilliant colours and what is known as costume jewellery, so that between each two chins and between the rolls of fat on her arms there seemed to be a glitter of rhinestones or a few barbaric chunks of gilt metal. She was quite frightening at first sight but a very pleasant kindly soul when one got to know her a little. 'Here you are!' she greeted me. 'Lottie wrote that she's too old for tea-parties – what a lot of rubbish – and you would come instead. Glad to see you. Andy, for goodness' sake don't just stand there. Bring a chair for Mrs Alexander.'

50

'Yes, of course,' said Andy, pushing forward a chair.

'Be quiet, Andy. Not that one – you know it's got a shaky leg. Push over that big one with the hole in the seat that that fool Nancy burned with the candle. You can't see the hole if somebody's sitting in it. Sit down!' she commanded me and I sat down obediently on the hole. 'I'm not going to go leading you round shaking hands with everybody. You know all these people or you ought to and if you don't you soon will and anyway it doesn't matter for that's not what we're here for. This is Mrs Miller and that man over there is her son, our new minister. Andy, tell them that jug of hot water isn't big enough and to bring another and then pass the sandwiches.'

Miss Sue was the apotheosis of the St Jagoan white woman of the old school. The white society that had developed in the island over some two and a quarter centuries tended to be matriarchal, as was the society in my own part of Scotland in the earlier days. Many things in Miss Sue Beaton, Madame Dulac and other island women reminded me of my own grandmother. I do not know how the white society in St Jago had tended towards matriarchy in this way but I think it possible that it may have begun because many of the early male settlers were family black sheep, remittance men with some weakness of character who were sent out to the fever-ridden islands to sink or swim. As opposed to this, any women who went out in the early days must have been women of considerable physical strength, redoubtable determination and indomitable courage, and they probably, by the sheer urge towards survival, had to take over the management of the lands in addition to the management of the households and at the same time keep within some bounds their drinking, gambling, roystering menfolk. At all events, women of Miss Sue's type were the rule rather than the exception among them, although most of them – even Madame Dulac who was fairly downright – took the trouble to dress the mailed fist in something of a near-velvet glove. Miss Sue, however, never wore gloves and perhaps just as well, for gloves in the form of any kind of feminine charm would have looked very incongruous on her.

It may have been that the early Beatons who built the house upon Craigellachie Heights were devil-may-care drunken

51

roysterers as I have imagined – I think they must have been at least devil-may-care to have built a house in such a place – but Andy Beaton, if this was so, was not true to his male ancestors. On the contrary, he was the product of generations of bullying by matriarchal bullies. He was a small man, about half the bulk of his sister, fair and pale where she was dark and purple, and instead of her cascade of chins, he had little chin at all but his upper lip was garnished by a thin but long, drooping pale moustache which hung down at either side of his mouth and gave him an air of extreme dejection. He had pale eyes with a few fair lashes on lids that blinked very often and when Miss Sue gave tongue with her two most frequent phrases which were 'Be quiet, Andy' and 'Not at all, Andy', his whole frame seemed to shudder and shrink and he would throw a flickering glance over his shoulder like a tortoise in search of its lost carapace. Out of doors, he wore always a khaki pith helmet and when at tea parties and other functions to which he was sucked along in the wake of Miss Sue, he would take off his helmet on entering the house but never be parted from it. He placed it upside-down on his knees and stared blinkingly and wistfully down into its green lining, as if he were wishing that he could crawl inside it, curl down and be safe from the storms of the world. Today, in the Craigellachie Heights drawing-room, the helmet was not even in sight and poor Mars Andy as he was known, for he had never been allowed to outgrow the 'Master Andy' title of his childhood, seemed to me to be very naked and vulnerable. Miss Sue, I should say, would be about sixty-five at this time and Mars Andy little more than fifty, for I had been told that there was some fifteen years between them, and Mars Andy's fifty years had quite obviously been spent in total thrall to his domineering sister.

'All right,' said Miss Sue, glaring round at us all as she stood by a table in mid-floor wielding a massive silver teapot with a spread eagle as a handle on its lid, 'why don't you all talk about something?' Naturally, this had the effect of striking us all speechless. 'Or talk about some*body*. I'd always rather talk about people than things. Andy, don't hand the milk to Mrs Buckley – you know she hates anything to do with

52

cows. Myra, I saw Maud Poynter in the Bay the other day and she told me Paul Peterson has divorced that awful wife of his up in the States. I always said he was a fool to marry her in the first place. I bet she's cost him a packet. Andy, take this cup of tea and sit down somewhere out of the way. Has everybody got something to eat?'

Due, probably, to her colossal weight, Miss Sue wheezed as she breathed and each sentence she spoke was divided from the next by a series of wheezing puffs like those emitted by a faulty steam engine, but this did nothing to limit her flow. A wheeze and a puff or two and a sip of tea and she was off again: 'All the Peterson men went mad at the sight of a flighty petticoat – no wonder when you think of all these anaemic skinny sisters they had. I remember at the Paradise Cropover Ball back before the war – not this last affair but the first one – all five of them wore dresses the same and believe it or not they were yellow – muslin yellow. They looked like a row of quarantine signs. Andy, pass the cake.'

Under cover of Miss Sue's barrage, I turned to Mrs Miller who was sitting just to my left and looking a little bemused and no wonder, I thought. She could be no older than fifty-five and was still very pretty, with faded fair hair that still showed a goldy glint, blue eyes and pink cheeks and a particularly sweetly-folded, half-smiling mouth. She would look in solemn wonder at the mountainous Miss Sue, gaze a little fearfully round the wide circle of strangers, glance at the decayed magnificence of the room and then her eyes would seek out the handsome figure of her son in his white linen suit, black vest and clerical collar. Then, her eyes would soften, the smiling folds round her mouth become more pronounced and her chin would rise and she would turn to Mrs Buckley who was on the other side of her and venture some small remark.

When Mrs Buckley had turned the other way, I said: 'I am so happy to meet you, Mrs Miller. You won't remember me but I think you know some of my family.'

'Are you George Sandison's niece?' she asked. 'Yes, you must be. I can see something of Mrs Reachfar about your face.'

'Yes, that's right. I was Janet Sandison. To be honest, I don't remember you at all, Mrs Miller. I don't think I ever saw you, but George and Tom wrote to tell me you were coming out here and that I was to look out for you.'

'Now,' she said, 'that was real good of them. I *am* pleased to meet you here, Mrs – Mrs —'

'Janet will do nicely, Mrs Miller, but my name is Alexander.'

'Janet Reachfar!' she said and smiled her strange sweet, oddly patient smile. 'I can remember you when you were only a little wee thing coming to Dinchory sometimes with your uncle on a Sunday afternoon. I am right glad you are here. This island is a queer kind of place. Have you been out here long?'

'About three years. It isn't so bad when you get used to it.' I glanced at Miss Sue. 'Some of the people are a bit queer at first but you get used to them too.'

'I can't keep away from the windows at the manse – I can't get used to nobody but black people going past. Tommy says I'll get used to that too, in time, but I am still finding it very strange. Mind you, they are very nice, the black people. Miss Beaton and the church committee found two servants for us and when we arrived at the manse everything was ready as if we had just been away for a holiday instead of coming there for the first time. Very different, as I said to Tommy, from the time we went to his first manse in Aberdeenshire – a great big dirty cold barn, it was, on a perishing night in January and all the pipes frozen.'

'You won't find anything like that here,' I assured her. 'And I am glad you are finding the coloured people so nice. They are very very kind if they get a chance to be. Where is your manse? I'm afraid I don't even know.'

'Just at the bottom of this awful hill. What possessed them to put a house up here, I wonder?' she asked in an undertone before going on: 'You'll pass it – the manse I mean – just before you get to the main road. I hope you'll look in on your way by and see the children.'

'The children?' I asked. 'Is your son married? I didn't know.' I looked vaguely round the room for another Mrs Miller but could see no woman who was a stranger to me.

'He is a widower,' she said. 'His wife died at the birth of the second baby.' Her breath caught in a little sigh but then she smiled again. 'That's why I am here, an old granny like me coming abroad to a new country at my age. Karen – she is called after her mother – is six and going to school – I mean she was at school at home – but little Thomas is only three and I just said to Tommy that if his mind was made up to come out here, I was coming too, to look after the bairns, so here I am.'

'I am sure your son is very glad you are here, Mrs Miller, and so am I.'

'Mrs Alexander,' came a wheezy shout from Miss Sue, 'what's all this about Lottie not coming out today? What is she up to?'

'She has a touch of neuritis in her elbows and knees, Miss Sue,' I lied and, always being the in-for-a-penny-in-for-a-pound sort, I went on: 'And being shaken about in the car, especially on awful roads like yours, makes it worse and she says that if you want to see her you can come to Paradise.'

'And so I will! Neuritis! It's probably only this damp hurricane weather we've been having and living in that swamp-hole at Paradise. In this island, people should live on hills. What she needs is a good pepper-bush plaster on her elbows and knees and she'd never feel another twinge.'

'I have no faith at all in pepper-bush, Sue,' said Mrs Buckley. 'I believe in mustard.'

'Tchah! Imported rubbish! Island remedies for island ailments, I say. Andy, pass the cigarettes. I remember when our old headman broke his leg once, falling out of a pimento tree —'

I turned again to Mrs Miller. 'I am really here today in place of the lady who owns the sugar plantation we live on. Her name is Madame Dulac —'

'Oh! I had a letter from her this morning telling Tommy and me to come to tea with her a fortnight today.' I laughed and Mrs Miller said, naturally enough: 'What is it? Did I say something funny?'

'Something true, rather, Mrs Miller. You said Madame *told* you to come to tea, not that she invited you to tea.'

'I'm sorry. It's Tommy's fault. After he'd read the letter, he said: Well, that's an order. So it was, you know.'

'I am sure it was. But I think you will find her very nice. She is very old but a great lady.'

'They are all great ladies here. You never see people like them at home now.'

'No. This island is about a hundred years behind Britain in some ways.'

'And will you be at Madame Dulac's tea-party next Friday week, Janet?'

'I expect so.'

'Goodness, I'm glad! Meeting you here has just made all the difference. I wasn't homesick or anything but everything was so strange.'

'But I hope we'll meet again before Madame's party,' I said. 'Couldn't you and Mr Miller come to us some afternoon and bring the children?'

'That would be nice but I'd have to ask Tommy. He is very busy, you know.' She looked across the room. 'Tommy!' she called softly. Amidst the babble the young man did not hear, but Miss Sue did and at once said: 'Mr Miller, go to your mother!' in stentorian tones. A little startled, Mr Miller looked across the room at his mother who flushed, smiled at him and nodded, whereupon he came across to us.

'Tommy, this lady comes from Reachfar near Achcraggan. This is my son, Mrs Alexander.'

She was proud of him and little wonder, for he was a fine-looking man, fair and blue-eyed and well suited by the white drill and clerical collar.

'Achcraggan district has a great hold on my mother,' he told me, 'although she was there for only a few years of her life.'

'It seems to be the sort of district that takes a hold on people,' I said. 'I was born there and all my life, even out here, I never seem to have got away from it. I would be very pleased if you and your mother could come and spend an afternoon with us any day soon. I am sure you are busy but couldn't my husband and I be special because of Achcraggan?'

He smiled down at his mother and said: 'Oh, yes, Achcraggan is special. We could go any day, Mother, except Monday, Wednesday and, of course, Sunday.'

'And you'll bring the children with you?' I said. 'We have no children of our own but we have a very large mastiff dog who is known to almost every child in the island as a playmate.'

'It is very kind of you, Mrs Alexander. Mother is never quite happy when she's away from young Thomas.'

Miss Sue, with another wheezing trumpet blast, now called him away from us and Mrs Miller and I fixed the time of their visit to Guinea Corner, and then she began to talk to me about her grandchildren and went on talking to me until the party broke up and the procession of cars started off down the fearsome hill.

She talked to me much more intimately, I was sure, than she would have talked to me had she met me casually at tea at some house at home in Scotland, and I thought I knew something of how she felt. I had been less than forty when I arrived in the island for the first time and I found it a very strange and disorienting experience. This woman was in her fifties and with every year reorientation to a new environment becomes more difficult. Several times she said: 'It's wonderful to meet somebody from home' and she said it again as we parted outside Craigellachie Heights, for it was too late for me to call at the manse that evening. As I was being driven back to Paradise through the falling dusk, I remember thinking how extraordinarily pleasant it was to meet, on the other side of the world, a stranger who had actually walked across the moor of Reachfar.

## 5

IT was very shortly after my visit to Craigellachie Heights that Twice's Mrs Miller came to see me for the first time. Twice was now extremely busy at the Paradise factory and he had hit upon the idea of going down to the office in St Jago Bay, attending to all his mail there, then coming back to

Paradise, leaving Mrs Miller to come up with the letters, reports and specifications when they were ready for signature.

'I can't think why I never thought of this before,' he said.

'But how will she get here?'

'Drive, of course. She has her own little car. Non-drivers like you are practically a one-woman minority here as I keep telling you.'

Mrs Miller arrived at Guinea Corner in her small black car about four in the afternoon. She was short, plumpish but very shapely and wore a plainly tailored green linen dress and high-heeled white shoes. Her jet black hair was of the short, coarse, curly Negro kind but it had been to a good hairdresser who had straightened and oiled it so that it clung to her head in big sculptured waves. I noticed the scatter of jet-black freckles on the flat negroid but small nose. She had beautiful eyes and teeth, her smile had a sweet gaiety and her whole demeanour betrayed her confidence in the fact that, of her race, she was pretty.

'Mrs Miller? How nice of you to come.'

'How nice of you to invite me,' she said and her voice had the liquid lilting note of the island.

'Twice is still round at the factory but he should be here soon.'

'Twice?' She pronounced the word 'Twyce' with the vowel very deep and broad.

'His full name is Alexander Alexander,' I explained.

She laughed, a pleasant sound. 'A. Alexander. Yes, of course.' She handed me a basket she was carrying. 'I brought you a little fruit.'

Inside the basket were six shiny purple star-apples and six matt-brown nazeberries, two of the most delicious and delicate fruits native to the island but so difficult to transport and so perishable that they were seldom to be found in the markets.

'Mrs Miller, what beautiful fruit! Are they from your own garden?'

'The family garden at home, not from my little garden in the Bay. My family has a little piece of land on the river below Craigellachie Heights.'

I noted the characteristic Negro phrase 'a little piece of

land', the phrase that described the proudest possession of any Negro and which could mean anything from quarter of an acre to a minor kingdom.

'This is very kind of you,' I said. 'Sit down while I empty the basket.'

When I came back into the room, she was standing before a picture of Poyntdale Bay which is one of the bays in the Firth below Reachfar.

'This is a painting of Scotland?' she asked.

'Yes. Near my home in the northern part of Scotland.' I put her basket on a chair near the door. 'Thank you again for the fruit, Mrs Miller. It is one of the nicest things to happen to me in St Jago – such a neighbourly thing. When I was a little girl, I seemed to spend a lot of time carrying baskets of things from my grandmother to her neighbours down the hill that you see in the picture there. Not fruit, of course. We don't have much table fruit in my part of Scotland but honey and jam and eggs and cakes and things.'

'And it was always very cold?'

'Not always. In winter, yes, with snow everywhere quite often, but in summer on one of our best days only a little cooler than about five o'clock on Christmas afternoon here in St Jago. Your family property near Craigellachie Heights, is it a farm?'

'Yes. A few coconuts, a few bananas, a few cattle and some market vegetables and fruit.'

'How lovely. My people are small farmers too. My father and my uncle are still farming Reachfar.'

'My father is dead but Mama runs the property and my brother and sister are there with her and all the rest of us go out there most weekends.'

She pronounced the word 'Mama' with equal emphasis on each syllable. It sounded very pretty.

'You are a big family?' I asked.

'We were fourteen altogether but a brother and a sister died when they were babies.'

'And Twice told me you have a little girl and a little boy.' Her soft brown eyes became still more soft. 'What are their names?'

59

'Mary Louise and Edward John.' She laughed suddenly and then added: 'Edward John has just begun to go to baby school so every evening he furthers my education for me now.'

When Twice arrived and we had tea, a change came over her. She became much more formal, very much the efficient secretary and, having been a secretary myself in the past, I respected her for this attitude but when the various letters she had brought had been signed, the reports and specifications checked, Twice said: 'Well, that's that. Let's all have a tot as Sir Ian says,' she laughed and relaxed again.

Twice went to the kitchen to ask Clorinda to bring in the drinks and Mrs Miller who was putting the letters and papers back into her case looked up at me and said: 'Mr Alexander works at too high pressure, Mrs Alexander. This' – she indicated the letters and papers in the case – 'all dictated in a single afternoon would represent the average Jago Bay businessman's output for a week.'

'He has always been a rapid worker,' I told her. 'I worked with him before we were married so I know.'

'Yes. He told me. He said you were the best secretary he had ever come across – a great compliment.'

'I didn't tell you she was also the worst-tempered,' Twice said, coming into the room again. 'She once hit me over the head with a file of papers, Mrs Miller.'

'Twice!' I protested. 'Don't listen to him, Mrs Miller. I wasn't in my secretarial capacity when I clouted him with the file. That happened in a quite unprofessional way.'

'It was quite a professional clout, though,' said Twice. 'What will you drink, Mrs Miller? There's whisky, gin, rum or beer.'

'Oh the wine of the island, please, Mr Alexander. Rum with a little soda.'

'And ice?'

'Yes, thank you.' She sounded a little surprised and Twice noticed it.

'I always ask. Janet won't have ice in anything. I don't like it with whisky myself.'

'Oh?' She looked down into her glass for a moment and seemed to make a decision to say what was in her mind. 'I think, sometimes, that ice is a sort of snobbery with us St Jagoans. When I was a child, it was a great great luxury and it still has an aura of luxury in our minds.' She rocked her glass a little and the lumps of ice tinkled. 'That is a sound that came from a prosperous veranda, usually a white people's veranda.' She looked up at us. 'I don't think we use a lot of ice as we do now – we St Jagoans, I mean – because we like the taste it gives our drinks or for coolness. I think we like to have it because of what it meant when we were children.'

A shyness came into her expressive face, as if she were now a little ashamed of so much self-revelation.

'I can understand that so well!' I plunged in, trying to reassure her. 'Ideas absorbed as a child stick for ever. Mrs Miller, this will make you laugh, I think. Do you know part of the reason why I was so keen to meet you? Twice spoke of you as Mrs Miller. When I was a child, there was an awful old woman in the village at home, a Mrs Miller, and I wanted to get her image out of my mind. Every time Twice said "Mrs Miller" I would think of her, trudging across the hill in the pouring rain and I wanted to be rid of her!'

'And are you?' she asked with her gay smile, the shyness quite gone.

'She ought to be,' Twice said. 'You are the third Mrs Miller she has met in the last month or two.'

'Oh?'

'The new minister at Fontabelle Church is a Mr Miller and he has brought his mother out to the island with him,' I explained, but went no further as I saw Mrs Miller's eyelids fall over her eyes so that the short, black up-curled lashes made two crescents of jet above her high cheekbones.

'Oh, yes.'

She drank what remained in her glass and rose to her feet. As Twice and I also rose, she raised her eyelids and the big brown eyes looked up at us. 'Yes. Our new minister. My brother was one of the applicants for the church but he was not successful.'

'Have another tot before you go!' Twice said hastily.

'Do you attend Fontabelle Church, Mrs Miller?' I asked in the same moment.

'Yes. Fontabelle has always been our family church.' Twice had poured a drink into her glass and he now handed it to her. She took it. 'Mr Alexander, I shall be tight!'

'Not on a couple of wee ones. Sit down and have another cigarette.'

She sat down again.

'So you are Presbyterians like us?' I said in an awkward attempt to recover the suddenly lost ground.

Her chin came up and a smouldering light appeared in the big dark eyes. 'Yes, we are a Presbyterian family but we are not exactly like you and Mr Alexander, I think. My great-grandfather was born into slavery at Craigellachie Heights. The Beatons of the Heights are a Scottish Presbyterian family – the slaves followed the religion of their masters, as a rule.'

The words struck me as a challenge. 'Most of the people in my home district of Scotland followed the lead of Sir Torquil Daviot, the local landowner or laird as we call them in just that sort of way,' I said. 'Mrs Miller, I think it is terribly interesting that your family home is still in the Craigellachie Heights area. So many people must have been uprooted in the disruption and rioting that went on at the time of the emancipation of the slaves.'

Some of the tension went out of her. She took a small sip from her glass and when she looked up she was smiling a little. 'My great-grandfather did not run away or take part in the rioting at the emancipation. He stayed put and eventually became cattle headman to the Beatons and when he grew old the Mr Beaton of the time gave him his house and ten acres in the valley bottom as a gift. Ginger Grove our home is called.'

'And you still have the same house that was given to your great-grandfather?' Twice asked.

'Yes, but it is now a little larger and so is the property. We have about two hundred acres now.'

'You must all be very proud of it, aren't you?' I asked.

'We-ell —'

'My wife is thinking of her native hilltop in Scotland,' Twice said. 'Reachfar, it is called. It is pretty barren and rocky, soil reclaimed from virgin moorland —'

'Most of Ginger Grove has been reclaimed from the bush —'

'I see. So it is the same sort of history.'

'I think my ancestors must have wandered up the hill to Reachfar and settled there because nobody else wanted that lump of rock,' I said. 'But that doesn't stop me being proud of it. Proud of it isn't the right phrase – it is more that it is built into me. I can't imagine myself without Reachfar behind me.'

'I think people must feel so of their country and must be proud of it too,' Mrs Miller said. 'We St Jagoans are proud of St Jago and I do not feel that this can be wrong. And we regard it as ours. I do not think that this can be wrong either. It is our work and the work of our people that have made St Jago what it is.'

'Mrs Miller,' Twice said, greatly daring, I thought, 'do you believe like the Progressive Party that all of us white people should clear out?'

She looked at him and her eyes smiled. 'I am a woman, Mr Alexander, and women do not think in broad sweeping terms. My answer is that it depends on the quality of the white people. This island, like all the islands of the West Indies, has suffered from many second-rate white people, white people who would be failures in their own country but come here and enjoy all the privileges of their race.'

'You couldn't be more right!' I said.

She smiled again. 'I do not know a great deal about politics and parties and their policies. For women, everything is much more personal, isn't it, Mrs Alexander?' I nodded. 'I felt the injustice of the appointment to Fontabelle Church because my brother was one of those who had been thrust aside. If my brother had not been involved, I should have taken less notice, I suppose.' Her big eyes looked at us with courageous honesty. 'But we Negroes are patient people. My brother may have failed to get Fontabelle Church but my son or one of my nephews may get it if they go into Holy Orders. Time is long and we can wait.' She finished her drink, laid the glass aside

63

and clasped her small brown hands on her pale-green linen lap. Then she looked from one of us to the other and smiled. 'But you must not think that St Jagoans like me want to send you back to Scotland.' She looked into my eyes. 'We still have a great deal to learn and people like Mr Alexander can teach us.'

'Have you heard of the project for an engineering school at Paradise Factory?' I asked her.

A light seemed to glow behind the dusky skin of her face and to gleam in her eyes. 'An engineering school?'

Twice outlined the project to her and when he had ended she expelled a deep satisfied breath.

'That is what we need! Not political parties or patronage! That is wonderful.' She was thoughtful for a moment. 'And when the boys have served their five years' apprenticeship, will Madame Dulac continue to import her engineers?'

'In five years, Madame Dulac too may alter her mind, Mrs Miller,' Twice said. 'Madame is a very intelligent and generous-minded old lady.'

'But old,' said Mrs Miller, rising to her feet. 'My mama is old too. Mama does not approve of how we do our hair' – she patted her smooth coiffure – 'or of the lipstick and, la, how Mama hates it when we girls wear shorts or slacks, especially on Sundays! It is difficult for old people to make a change in their minds even about little things and about the big things I do not think that their minds can change at all. Mrs Alexander, I must go home to my children. Thank you so much for – for everything.'

'I am so glad you came, Mrs Miller. You will come again?'

'Thank you. And one day you might care to visit Ginger Grove?'

'I'd love to!'

Twice and I watched the little car go down the driveway, the brown hand waving as she made the turn at the gate into the road.

'Twice!' I burst forth, 'that one has just about everything – beauty, brains, the lot, and buckets of human kindness!'

Twice stared down the drive. 'She didn't half come out of her shell today – I knew she was a good secretary but I didn't

64

know she was such a personality. It must have been your effect on her.'

'Me, nothing! Her whole face melts when she looked at *you*! Many women wouldn't like it but I am big-hearted.'

'Don't be a fool. That was an ugly moment about the church.'

'I know. Awful. But I thought she took up her position with great courage and dignity. And she is right. My brother may have failed —'

'But my son won't —'

'Yes. Time is long and we can wait. Yes. She is right. The time of her race is coming. She is right in every way. For women, everything is personal, she said. And she is right there too. I've never seen the Negroes so clearly marching forward to claim their own as I saw it in that little woman's face today. She is an inspiring little person, Twice. I am so glad I have got to know her.'

'You are very easy to please, Flash. A few Mrs Millers and you are happy for hours.'

'Three Mrs Millers, and I happen to like them all very much. It isn't often that you meet three people that you really like within the same few months.'


6


PARADISE ESTATE lay in a saucer-like valley among its own surrounding hills which made of it a private world, shut away from the rest of St Jago, where all sorts of events could take place without the knowledge of the world outside; but inside the Paradise valley itself there was no privacy. It could be approached from outside by only two roads, one coming from the north coast of the island, a road that climbed up and over the lip of the saucer and then came gently down on the shallower inner incline into the valley. The other way in was from the south by a road which followed the winding gorge of the Rio d'Oro which rose in the hills above Paradise and debouched, after pursuing a tortuous course, into the sea south-west of St Jago Bay. Both these roads had been built long ago for one purpose, which was to give access from the Great House to the outer world, and in the days when Paradise Great House was built, every white man's house in the island was a minor fortress. The House, like all its kind in St Jago, stood on a slight eminence, looking out over its acres of sugar-cane fields, and from its west upper veranda, where Sir Ian had what he called his 'house office' as opposed to his 'factory office', it commanded a view of the whole length of both approaches from north and south.

In later times, other minor roads had been constructed, stemming off like veins from this main artery, to serve the staff houses of the Compound and all the other buildings and to join Guinea Corner and Olympus, where the Macleans lived, to the Paradise system. Guinea Corner and Olympus were houses nearly as old as the Great House itself, but they had once belonged to other separate estates and had been acquired by Paradise as it had grown and swallowed up its neighbours in the struggle for survival down the years. It was easy to see, historically, why the Great House stood where it did and why the main roads to it followed the course they did, and historically it was all very interesting to me, but the effect of this local geography on day-to-day living was that no car could drive up to Guinea Corner without Madame and Sir Ian being aware of it.

It reminded me, in a way, of my home at Reachfar where the only approach by road – and a very rough road at that – was from the north and where we could always see a stranger coming from a mile and a half away. As a child, I would run into the house and say: 'Granny, there's a trap turning on to the hill above Poyntdale!'

'Now, who can that be?' she would say and go to the scullery window and look down the hill. 'Och, it's only Jockie Mackay, the pig-dealer. I see him at that trick of opening the catch of the gate with his whip, the lazy lump. Run west to the Little Parkie and tell Granda that he is coming.'

Or, another time, it would be: 'Now, who in the world would be coming up so early in the forenoon? Mercy, it's that old Mrs Miller with her head down between her knees as usual. She will be on her way to Dinchory. Kate, I will not be bothered with her girning gossiping tongue this day. Put on the girdle and start to bake. Elizabeth, go ben to your room and lie down for a while. Janet, you come with me and we'll go up to the moor and see can we find where that turkey is hiding her eggs. Chust you tell her I am out, Kate, and you don't know where, for I am not going to listen to her complaints about her neighbours and Tommy's wife. Come, Janet.'

It was all very well, I often thought, when one was in the commanding position as at Reachfar or the Great House but when one was in the position commanded, as I was at Guinea Corner, it was a different matter, and this thought crossed my mind again when, on the forenoon following Twice's Mrs Miller's visit, Sir Ian drove up in his Land Rover and stepped on to the veranda.

'Mornin', me dear. The weather's coolin' nicely. A blessin' – people feel a little more like movin' about.'

Sir Ian was endlessly inquisitive, although in a very benevolent way and always very interested in even the smallest human events, but as a diplomat he was a little heavy in the hand. I was sure he had taken quite a little time to work out this diplomatic approach to inquiry as to whose car had come to Guinea Corner the day before and I smiled a little inside myself.

'Have a glass of beer,' I said.

'Thanks, me dear. Got nothin' much to do this mornin' an' thought I'd come round for a chat. Mother's got one o' the girls from the office round doin' her letters. An' Twice an' them are so perishin' busy at the factory that I thought I'd better get out o' the way . . . Well, I see you had some visitors yesterday. That's nice. Don't like you to be dull.'

'It wasn't visitors exactly,' I said.

'Oh?'

'No. Only Twice's secretary with some stuff for him from the office. She is a very nice woman, though.'

'A coloured girl, of course?'

'Yes. Twice says she is a remarkable good secretary.'

67

'What's her name?'

'Miller – Mrs Miller. She is a widow. Her husband was a government servant of some sort.'

'What was her own name, do ye know?'

This interrogation was not caused by the facts that Mrs Miller was a coloured woman or a secretary or a widow, but by the fact that Sir Ian knew a great deal about the island and its people and was very interested in families and their genealogies.

'I don't know but she told me that her home is near Craigellachie Heights – her people have a property there called Ginger Grove.'

'Oh, now I know where you are! She's a Lindsay – must be a granddaughter of old Josh Lindsay. What sort of age is she?'

'Around thirty, I should say, but I find it very difficult to tell with the coloured people, especially the women. They either seem to be young girls or old grandmothers. She is a very pretty woman.'

'Pure Negro?'

'In features, yes, but her skin is more *café-au-lait* than really black.'

'That'll come from the mother's side. Old Josh and young Josh, her father, were absolutely pure-bred and jet black. Great big men – good blood in them somewhere. Most o' the Negroes that were caught in Africa by the slavers and brought out here were very primitive bush people but the odd one or two were from the more developed tribes, probably prisoners o' war an' sold to the slavers, ye know, or found wounded an' thrown on board the slave ships.'

'There's a big family of them – twelve in all, she said.'

'Yes. I knew there was a tribe o' them. Saw them all at the funeral when young Josh died a year or two back. One o' them is a doctor down at the hospital at the Bay. They're a smart lot. Another o' them is mixed up in politics – a proper hot-head – hates our lot like stink. The doctor fellah don't care for us either, come to that. Works entirely among the coloured people. Poole, the SMO at the hospital, tells me that if he was a white man he'd be a big shot in London or New

68

York – brilliant fellah, apparently. Specializes in hearts an' livers an' he's the main drive behind the anti-malarial campaign.'

'I think it all wrong that a man like that should be limited because of the colour of his skin, Sir Ian,' I said.

'He ain't really. He'd be accepted in London or New York all right if he'd go but he won't. Ye see, me dear, he'll be a man of forty-five to fifty – a year or two older than you – that's the first generation o' the highly educated Negro in these islands. They had to go to Britain for their trainin' – they got it pretty rough over there a lot o' them. They were odd-lookin' ye know.'

'I don't see that,' I said. 'When I was at Glasgow University in the late 1920s there were lots of Indians and people. Nobody thought anything about it. I never knew any of them personally but —'

'There ye go! You never knew any o' them personally. That's the whole point! How many o' you youngsters did know them, do ye think? What sort o' time did they have? Goin' to Glasgow from a climate like this an' livin' in digs in that perishin' fog with some sour-faced landlady? No, me dear. That generation o' them had a poor time of it. A lot o' them came back qualified as doctors an' lawyers an' that but they were soured an' ye can't blame them. I don't know about the doctor fellah o' these Lindsays – except that I do know he refused to treat Charlie Montgomery's wife, just because she was white, they said, although he didn't say so in so many words – but the political one, I heard somethin' about what happened to *him*. He was the brightest o' the bunch – got some big scholarship an' went over to Oxford or was it Cambridge? Not that it matters because the trouble happened in Edinburgh. He'd got up there with some friends and they were at a dance an' some trouble broke out about a girl. It came to a fight anyway an' half a dozen o' these undergraduates were arrested in the end for breach o' the peace. They'd have been drinkin' a bit, likely. The point is that the rest o' them got off with a fine but Lindsay was clapped inside for seven days – so the story goes. Whether it's true or not don't matter much. What does matter is that Lindsay came back here an' he's never stopped raisin' hell an' trouble for us whites since the day he landed in the island.'

'Has he a profession? Did he qualify at his university?'

'I'm not sure – it wasn't for lack o' brains if he didn't. Dammit, yes, he must have done. He's a lawyer! He's the one that took ten thousand pounds o' damages off that American for killin' that drunk fruit peddlar with his car a couple o' years ago. Proper scandal the whole thing, but Lindsay worked that Negro jury and good-for-nothin' Negroes have been throwin' themselves under people's cars ever since, hopin' to lose a leg an' get a thousand or two. Haven't heard o' him in the courts much lately, though, since he took to politics. He's a clever devil. All that family o' Josh's were clever.'

'Another brother is a minister, Mrs Miller told me.'

'That's right. That's the reason there was all that row about Fontabelle Church. Young Lindsay applied, was passed over an' then the political agitator brother got started on it. *Kevin*, that's the political fellah's name. He's an impressive-lookin' customer, ye know. Big, strong, handsome – the livin' spit o' his grandfather, old Josh, and bein' well-educated he can talk a blue streak as Twice calls it. A proper rabble-rouser. It ain't that I don't sympathize with the Negro, my dear, but men like Kevin Lindsay don't help things in my opinion. When things are difficult an' people have got grievances, that's the time to be most reasonable, but Lindsay jumps on the nearest soapbox an' before you know where you are, there's a riot. That's what happened down the gorge there over Fontabelle Church. Old Sue made a mistake, shoutin' for a white minister at every meetin' like that an' given a little time the rest o' us could have talked her round, but this Lindsay gets up on his hind legs, collects a followin' o' idlers from the Bay an' marches on the church that Sunday and frightens the hell out o' that visitin' American preacher so that *he* calls out the riot squad. Then old Sue sticks her heels in an' says that no nigger is goin' to dictate the policy o' *her* church an' cables to Scotland for a minister. Put that poor fellah Miller in a very poor position, she did, but he's a fine-lookin' chap an' looks as if he's got his head screwed on an' he seems to be managin' things very well.'

70

'I like him,' I said. 'I think he is a proper minister.' I then realized that I had defined my opinion in the words of my childhood when, by a 'proper minister', I meant a man who seemed to be in exactly the place to which he had been called.

'I mean,' I clarified, 'that I don't think he is a minister because it is a clean job or gives him social status or because he likes talking from a pulpit so that nobody can argue with him, like a lot of so-called ministers these days. I think he is a minister because he has a true vocation of the right kind for it.'

'That's the impression I got meself, me dear, and I liked the mother – Mrs Miller, ye know. A nice quiet sort o' person without bein' stoopid either. Have ye ever noticed that the white women in this island are mostly clever an' the damnedest bullyin' harridans that ever lived or else very pretty an' so perishin' stoopid they don't know their elbow from their you-know-what?'

'Yes. I have.'

'But that little mother o' the minister's ain't stoopid although she is a pretty little woman. She comes from your part o' the country, you said?'

'No. Her husband was an Achcraggan man but I think she was born somewhere near Edinburgh.'

'Sensible little woman, anyway. An' doesn't seem to have any ideas o' interferin' an' runnin' the church like some o' them.'

'She definitely has no ideas of that sort. She told me she would never have left Scotland but for her grandchildren. I think it was a very courageous thing to do at her age.'

'She ain't that old!'

'She must be about sixty.'

'You think so?'

'I am going by the age of her son as much as anything.'

'Maybe you're right. She don't look it though. She's a pretty little woman. She seems to be very fond o' *you*, me dear.'

'I think that is because I come from a place she knows, largely,' I said. 'She has never been out of Scotland before and that tea-party at Craigellachie Heights must have been a bit of a shock to her. Miss Sue seemed specially outrageous

71

that day too. I suppose I looked like an oasis in a desert or something. In Scotland, I don't suppose she and I would have much in common but out here we seem to have a great deal.'


# 7


DURING the months of November and December, all the European members of the Paradise staff who had been on leave overseas returned, the last to arrive, in early December, being Rob and Marion Maclean. Rob released Twice from some of the tyranny of the final work at the factory before Crop and Marion released me from some of the tyranny of the Great House, but Twice could not rest on his oars because, during Rob's absence, his projects in the other islands had been neglected and immediately after Rob's return he announced his imminent departure to Trinidad.

'So,' he said to me, 'get a letter off to Mrs Miller at Hope.'

'Twice, do you think I should? All Madame's Christmas appeals and things are at their height and —'

'If our plans work out, muddle-head, this is your second-last Christmas in this island if not your last. The sooner Madame and Marion get used to counting you out of their list of retainers, the better. And this summer has knocked the stuffing out of you. You're as thin as a rake. Now, just sit down and invite yourself to Hope for a week.'

I duly wrote the letter and had a reply by return which told me that Mrs Miller would be in St Jago Bay on the day of Twice's departure and that she would pick me up at the airport after I had seen him off, and this was the plan that was carried through.

By this time, I had seen a number of the Great Houses of the island, but never had I seen one that was as beautiful as Hope. It had a great natural advantage in that it stood so high above sea-level, on one of the spurs of the Sierra Grande, on a green eminence that was dotted with pimento trees, so that it had something of the nature of an English country house standing in parkland. At two thousand feet, too, it was well above mosquito level so that none of its windows were screened and verandas, an essential feature of houses at lower altitudes, were here unnecessary. Pure Georgian in character, it rose out of the green grass, coolly dignified yet warmly welcoming, and the pasture land rolled away below it down the hill to the boundary where the rioting bush was held back by a strong wall of grey stone.

'This is the most – most civilized house I have seen in the whole island,' I said. 'It makes me think of Poyntdale at home except that this is of a more beautiful period.'

'I am very fond of it,' Mrs Miller said. 'And I am glad I don't have to have verandas stuck out all round it. They ruin the character of a house.'

'And this is the only Great House I have driven to, except Paradise, without feeling both sick and frightened with the corkscrew of the road.'

'That *is* an advantage. We are only four miles of our own road away from the Central Highway, you see.'

The Central Highway was the main north to south road across the island, a good road that had first been engineered for military use and, although it climbed sheer over the Sierra, the sharp backbone of the island, it did so by a series of long smooth curves that were barely noticeable in a car.

'I imagined something like the Mount Melody or Craigellachie Heights roads, only worse!' I told her and she shook her head.

'Those places are not for me. Here, the island and I come to terms but Mount Melody has always simply terrified me. As for Craigellachie Heights, I'd be afraid that it – and I – would fall down the mountain some night. . . . Let's go in here. I use this little sitting-room in the evenings – it faces south and the evenings can be coolish up here.'

The windows of the sitting-room looked up over a green tree-dotted slope to the high Sierra, the slope intersected by fences and walls until it ended with the grey stone wall, behind which the tropical bush grew, thick and seemingly impenetrable. Beyond the wall, the Sierra rose, ridge upon bush-covered ridge to the sharp vertebra-like points of the summit.

'I like how your boundary wall seems to hold the bush back,' I said.

'That isn't our actual boundary on this side. It's the limit of our pasture, but what the Negroes call our "mountain" goes up to – do you see that little house on that ridge that shows just above that coconut?'

'Yes.'

'That is our southern limit. There is some quite good pasture in the valleys – quite a lot of timber, good hardwoods and a fair amount of mahogany and cedar but most important of all, our water comes from up there. We have two springs.'

'Does someone live in the little house?'

'Not now. We used to have a cattle headman up there in the old days but people won't live there now. It's too remote. The children use it, though. They furnished it with a lot of odds and ends and throw-outs from here and use it as a sort of summer camp when they are in the island. Not so much now. It was when they were in their teens that they loved it so much but Marcia still has spells of wanting her own society and goes off up there.'

'I think I know exactly how she feels. Down at Paradise, I often get the feeling that the island is rioting over me and that I can't breathe. It's a claustrophobic frightening sort of feeling, very difficult to describe.'

'I think I understand what you mean though – I had it myself in a very nasty form that night my car broke down and Twice found me on the Mount Melody road. It was in that wooded part between Mount Melody and the gorge – do you know it? And it was dark. I was terrified.' I shuddered at the very thought of being alone in the dark in that creeping whispering forest where plant seemed to feed on plant and vine to strangle vine. 'I have never taken that short cut since – not that one can now, since Mount Melody opened as a hotel. What an odd pair of girls those are who own it. Do you know them?'

I laughed. 'I brought Dee Andrews to the island, I'm afraid.

Or rather, Twice and I did. I was her governess for a time when she was little.'

'I'm sorry, Janet. I didn't know they were friends of yours.'

'They're not special friends in any way. And they *are* an odd pair. You are perfectly right.'

She smiled a little. 'One should know better than to make a remark of that sort, especially in this island. Or, indeed, anywhere. People's relationships are private affairs.'

'But an all-female one like that is still remarkable and they don't go to any trouble to keep it private,' I said. 'I don't know if Dee and Isobel are lovers but they have an air of it. And they seem to be very self-sufficient. We hardly see anything of them now, since they've gone up there. Just as well, really. Twice finds them embarrassing.'

She smiled more broadly. 'Twice and I have much in common. So do I. You don't?'

'I found it odd at first,' I admitted. 'My experience of these things is very limited. I had never seen anything of a Lesbianite nature before except for one or two suspect types when I was in the Air Force during the war. But happy relationships are very scarce – they have enough scarcity value for me to accept one, even welcome one, that is out of the normal run.'

Mrs Miller poured more tea from the elegant silver pot. 'So you believe primarily in relationships?' she asked.

'I think I do,' I said slowly. 'The relationships in my life seem to constitute the only importance it has. You see, I have never achieved anything in a material sense. I have never been ambitious – I have just bumbled and muddled along, and when I look back over the years I see nothing but a network, a sort of tapestry, even, of relationships with people, their lives all interwoven with mine. All the happiness I have known, all the good things that have happened to me have depended on these relationships, have grown out of them. Yes, I do believe in relationships as you put it. It seems to me that communication between people is the most important thing in the world. "In the beginning there was the Word" you know . . . Mrs Miller, I think I have just discovered something. This thing we were saying about the bush on the Mount Melody road being frightening – my fear of that bush is what my professor of moral philosophy called numenous fear – the fear of a sort of presiding spirit, a spirit that is beyond my means of communication. I feel this sort of fear about the whole island and about the whole Negro race. I don't hate the Negroes because their skins are black or because they are uncivilized as some people claim. I don't hate them at all. But I fear them in that numenous way. You see, I can't establish communication with them; I am living in the midst of mystery all the time. This is really why Twice and I are going home for good in another eighteen months.'

'You are? I am sorry to hear that,' she said. 'But you are probably wise. I think Twice works much too hard in this climate for one thing. But to go back to what you have said about the Negroes, I can understand exactly what you mean. And I think you are so right, but people as a rule will not admit that they are afraid of the mystery of a different racial spirit. Instead, they take refuge in prejudice and all sorts of artificial growths which have developed down the centuries. By the way, did you tell Madame Dulac that you were coming to stay with me?'

'Yes.'

'And?'

Puzzled, I looked into her face and she looked back at me with bright blue eyes. I then recalled my few words with Madame as I was leaving the Great House the day before.

'She seemed to be surprised that I knew you,' I said now. 'I felt rather proud in a catty sort of way because Madame rules us all at Paradise and sometimes I think she has the idea that we can't make a friend without her being there to introduce us.'

Mrs Miller laughed, went to a side table and picked up a cigarette box which she offered to me. Beside it, there stood a silver-framed photograph of a very good-looking dark-haired young woman.

'Is that your daughter?' I asked.

'Yes. That's Marcia.'

'She is beautiful. Has she got blue eyes like you?'

'No. Dark brown.' She picked up another photograph from another table. 'This is my son, Wilmot. He is dark too.'

'They work in the States? What do they do?'

'Wilmot is a surgeon. Marcia is a speech therapist – she works with deaf and dumb children.'

'Neither is a farmer like you?'

'No. They take after their father.'

'Your husband was a doctor?'

'Yes.'

She put the photograph of the young man back on the table, came to her chair and sat down again.

'So you and Twice have decided to go home?' she said next. 'I shall probably do the same, the children not having turned into farmers, as you said.'

'You mean that you would sell all this?' I looked round the elegant room and out over the green pastures beyond the windows.

'I think so. Not quite yet, of course. But I *am* an English-woman and I think I'd like to end my days in Wiltshire – things being as they are. If my husband had lived, it might have been different. Relationships are important, as you said, my dear. But this island must in the end belong to the Negroes and I can afford to retire now that the children are educated and out on their own. And it is lonely here, without them. When they were overseas at school, it was different. School cost money and the drive of running the property to make the money mitigated the loneliness, as it were.'

'Doctor Miller died when the children were young?'

'Marcia was three and Wilmot only eleven months old.'

'It must have been hard.'

'I was more fortunate than many. I had Hope, after all.'

She now looked away out of the window and up the long green slope to the darker green mountains. 'I had Hope and the children but' – she turned suddenly and looked straight at me – 'no other relationships. Janet, I had a very happy moment when I found you in the airport restaurant this morning. You see, I did not expect you to be there.'

I looked at her, aware that I was frowning. 'But why ever not? Didn't you get my letter?'

77

'Yes. Yes, I did. But I expected Paradise to intervene.'

'Intervene? In what way?'

'I thought that Madame Dulac or Sir Ian or Mrs Maclean would have told you that my husband was a man of colour.'

Involuntary, I looked at the photographs of the beautiful dark girl and the handsome young man and then I looked into Mrs Miller's blue eyes and her faintly smiling face.

'They didn't,' I said. 'If they had, I should have been at the airport just the same.'

'Probably they knew that,' she said quietly, 'and that is why they did not think it worthwhile to tell you. I have told you now because I don't believe it will make any difference to you, but I wanted to give them every chance to tell you first. However, it explains why no tea is taken between Hope and Paradise.'

'I think that's simply abominable!' I burst forth.

'It isn't really,' she said quietly. 'To a large extent, people are at the mercy of history, Janet. One can't cast off the past completely. You can never cast off your early days at your lovely Reachfar or all that tapestry of relationships you spoke about. People like Madame Dulac can't cast off the early prejudices that grew on them when they first came to the island here. Her husband was of an old island-white family and she came under his influence as a young bride. Those people, socially, just did not know the coloured people, just as my people at home – a Victorian church family as I told you – did not know the brewer's wife in the local town. My mother would never have had a brewer's wife to tea; the Paradise Dulacs don't have coloured people to tea.'

'I think that's —' Indignation silenced me.

'Nonsense, my dear. It isn't a matter of indignation – it is merely social prejudice. Oh, I was not always as cool and reasonable as this about it. I didn't take kindly to being ostracized. After all, Wilmot wasn't a negro like Josh Lindsay of the Farmers' Federation – I didn't know that Wilmot had Negro blood until he told me and by then it was too late. What you would call a relationship had been formed' – she smiled at me – 'between us and I wanted to marry Wilmot or nobody. Wilmot had one coloured grandmother – his people otherwise

78

were white. He and I met during the war – the 1914-18 war. I was nursing and he was in the Medical Corps. He was badly gassed in France – that is what killed him.'

'I am so terribly sorry.'

She smiled again. 'It's all past now. He and I didn't have very long – only six years altogether. We came out here in 1919. We hoped that the climate might help his lungs but he died early in 1922. But the six years were happy in spite of everything.'

'And have you relations by marriage in the island?' I asked.

'No. Wilmot was an only child – his parents were dead before I knew him and he was brought up by an aunt in England. Why did you ask, Janet?'

'Partly for a selfish reason – one's reasons are so often partly selfish,' I said. 'I do so want to get to know some real St Jagoan people. Not that your nearly white St Jagoan people are what I mean.'

She began to laugh, and when I looked a question at her she said:

'I am sorry that my relations, if they were alive, are not St Jagoan or coloured enough to please you!'

'I apologize, Mrs Miller.'

'Don't be silly, Janet. I was teasing you. You looked so very solemn and serious.'

'I *am* solemn and serious about it. The only island person I know is Twice's secretary – she is a Mrs Miller too, by the way, and she is a widow too – and she is very nice but she promised to invite me to her home and she has never done it. She is a sister of that Josh Lindsay you spoke about. I'd love to get to know that family but they just don't *want* me, I feel.'

'Poor Janet!' Mrs Miller mocked me. 'And it's so nasty not to be wanted! My dear, if you want to meet Josh Lindsay, I can arrange that sometime when I am in the Bay. He and I are founder members of the Farmers' Federation.'

'Have you been to Ginger Grove?' I asked.

'No. Not in a social way. I have seen the cultivation, of course. It's an island show-piece in its way. No. Josh and I are business friends. Frankly, I think it unlikely that you will

79

penetrate to the house at Ginger Grove, Janet. Negro families can be as exclusive as the Dulacs, you know.'

'So I am finding out,' I said.

I enjoyed every moment of my visit and I think it is truthful to say that Mrs Miller enjoyed it too. During the days she was very busy, for there were cattle to be sprayed against ticks, cattle to be injected with serum against disease, coconuts to be picked, limes to be gathered and a thousand and one things to be done, all of which she supervised personally. She drove about the pastures from cattle-pen to cattle-pen in a Land Rover and for the first few days I went with her, interested to see how a property of this sort was managed, but I was careful to keep out of the way, as I had been taught to do when I was a child and privileged to go to Poyntdale or Dinchory with my father or George. At the end of the day, on the way back to the house, I would ask questions about the work I had seen in progress until, one evening, it occurred to me that I might be displaying overmuch curiosity.

'I ought to tell you,' I said then, 'that there is a phrase to use to me when you are tired of answering questions. George and Tom always used to say: Och, be off, Janet, with your ask-ask-asking!'

Mrs Miller laughed. 'I won't use it until you ask me something I can't answer.'

'Gosh! That never occurred to me before. It was always at the how-did-the-calf-get-inside-the-cow sort of question that Tom and George used it!'

Later on, one lot of cattle being sprayed for ticks being very like another, I began to explore Hope on foot on my own, and in the end I found and followed a track through the bush on the upward side which, after a long steep climb in this winding tunnel of green where the sky was obscured by the dense foliage overhead, brought me out at a little wooden gate at the bottom of a small garden that lay below a little empty house. It was only when I went through the garden, up on to the wooden veranda that ran along the front of the house and turned round to look down the hill that I discovered that I had come up to the cottage I had seen from the sitting-room window on my first evening at Hope.

Only at one other place in the world that I had visited had I seen a view like this and that place was Reachfar. Looking from Reachfar, you could see Ben Wyvis to the west, the Firth and the hills of Ross and Sutherland to the north and, away to the east, beyond the Cobblers, as the cliffs that guarded the entrance to the Firth were called, the vast expanse of the North Sea. Looking out from this hill above Hope, you could see Craigellachie Heights and below it St Jago Bay on the shore away to the west, eastward a little and inland the valley of Paradise and due north and away to the east the seemingly limitless blue of the Caribbean. Hurricane Point, the easternmost rocky tip of the island, with a little imagination, could be turned into the South Cobbler.

When I got back to the house in time for tea at the end of Mrs Miller's long working day, I told her where I had been. 'And I must write to George and Tom about it!' I ended. 'It's a St Jagoan Reachfar!'

'I'd like to see that letter,' she said.

'Then you shall. I'll do it on the typewriter when I get home and send you a copy. Mrs Miller, it's lovely up there. Has the house got a name?'

'It's called High Hope.'

'Perfect!'

'You and your names and words!' she said. 'But that's a promise? I get a copy of the High Hope letter?'

'That's a promise.'

It was after tea that she said to me: 'Janet, a thing has occurred to me. Do you and Twice get local leave?'

'We are having a month's leave next August. Why?'

'If you would like to come to High Hope, you have only to say. It's as comfortable as any of those hill cottages that people rent, I think.'

'Mrs Miller, that's terribly kind of you.'

'Not a bit. You could come here, of course, but I hope to go up to the States next summer and I'd like to close this house and let the servants go home for a bit. And High Hope is really cool, even in July and August.'

'Thank you very much. I am sure Twice will love it – we both will. Oh, can we get into it with the car?'

'Oh, yes. You carry on up the Central Highway through Hope Town and you come to a signpost for High Hope. It's only a track – seven fairly rough miles – but it's passable.'

On the day of Twice's return, Mrs Miller drove me to the north gates of Paradise where we met Twice's car, driven by Sir Ian's chauffeur, which took me on to the airport to meet the plane, and almost at once I began to tell Twice about High Hope.

'Well,' he said when he could insert a word, 'you've got a real bubble on, my pet. You sound as if you'd spent the time at Reachfar itself.'

'It was a lovely holiday, Twice, while you were away slaving in Trinidad. But wait till you see High Hope! It's not a bit island-ish. There's no steam or fug or bush or exotic flowers or anything. It's all clear and bright and beautiful and – just High Hope!'

'It's very kind of this woman to lend it too.'

'Twice, I like her more, almost, than any woman I have ever met. She – she *thinks*, Twice.'

'Does she now? Isn't that remarkable?'

'Don't be so snooty! Most of them don't think, you know, even the forceful characters like Madame. They all live by a sort of code but it isn't an original code that has welled up out of themselves and their experience. It's a thing they have put together piecemeal – a bit from the Bible, a bit from a book on etiquette, a bit that was a habit of thought they learned from their old Aunt Fanny and various bits that are expedient for this and that. I've rather gone off these *grandes dames* like Madame.'

'Oh? I should have said that Mrs Miller of Hope was even grander than Madame,' Twice said. 'Madame, after all, is just a fat little Edinburgh housewife with a dictatorial manner and a *penchant* for good works. Mrs Miller is a far grander, more dignified character, I should have thought.'

'You are quite right. And yet Madame had the gall to cut her socially!' I exploded, and told him of Mrs Miller's marriage. 'I've read of these things but I didn't really think they happened. It's monstrous!'

'They happened all right. They can happen still.'

82

'Well, it's all wrong!' I said in a general burst of indignation, for I can never be coherent when I am deeply concerned and yet I have to seek relief in words. 'It's like all the other things that are so wrong in this island, like the white people living on the tops of mountains as if they were gods and the Negroes being relegated to the valleys as if they were less than human!'

'Naturally, the white people built their home on the coolest spots,' Twice said reasonably.

'Oh, I know. It's the opposite of Scotland – the dominant people in Scotland took over the fertile valley and the poorer people were relegated to the poorer land higher up, like Reachfar. But here, somehow, the Madames and Sue Beatons sitting on their mountains geographically, socially and every other way seem to me to have been tempting Providence for years – the higher they are, the harder they fall, as you are so fond of saying.'

As the car turned into the south approach to Paradise Twice, looking thoughtfully out of the window, began to hum a tune that was vaguely familiar to me but I could not identify it.

'What's that you are humming?' I asked after a moment.

'Huh?' He looked at me, thought for a moment, then hummed the few bars over again to himself and said: 'Oh, it's one of the things from Handel's *Messiah*. It must have been your talk of mountains and valleys that brought it on.' He began now to sing in his pleasant voice the words: 'Every valley shall be exalted and every mountain and hill made low —'

# PART TWO

## *The Mountain*

# 1

MY return to Paradise from Hope marked the final moment of my disenchantment with the island of St Jago. By this, I do not mean that from that moment I began to hate the island – indeed, the reverse would be more true of my meaning for I use the word 'disenchantment' in its literal sense. Until the time of my return from Hope, I had been in a state of enchantment, under a spell which the island had cast over me at my first arrival and from which it had been a long gradual process to break free. Until this moment, St Jago had never been entirely real for me. Even although I lived there, I looked upon Britain as the 'real' world and upon this island as a figment of the imagination or romance, a tangle of literary associations with treasure islands, pirates, the Hesperides, doubloons, Robert Louis Stevenson, pieces of eight and Gauguin, all seen in the light of eerie mystery that haunts poems like *The Ancient Mariner* and *Kubla Khan*. The island had taken hold of me as the Ancient Mariner took hold of the Wedding Guest and it had woven a web about me thrice – I had even literally drunk the milk of Paradise. I had been, until now, what the psychologists would call an acute case of cultural shock.

The process of disenchantment had been working for a long time, probably since a few weeks after my arrival, I thought when I looked back, but on my return from Hope it seemed to be complete. The mystery had gone. I felt that at last I might come to know this island.

One of the main barriers between St Jago and me, I saw now, had been Madame Dulac and her son Sir Ian, not from any intention of theirs but because of their impact on Twice's life and my own. By sheer kindness, they had prolonged my enchantment by removing from my path many of the day-to-day difficulties of living. They had found us our house and our servants, and so well-established and efficient was the administrative machinery of Paradise that the milk came into the house morning after morning and it was several months before I discovered the process by which it came. Paradise, for me, had been a land of milk and honey and, with my type of mind, it was natural that the controllers of this land, Madame and her son, should take on something of the character of gods. I had certainly never, until now, regarded them as normally human. They had been fantasy characters and the fantasy had been intensified by their own eccentricities. They had been to me like mythical creatures – creatures from an amusing myth, it is true, but mythical none the less – but part of the disenchantment was my belief that mythical creatures do not go blind, as Madame was doing now, and mythical creatures do not become huffy with mortals like me for leaving Paradise for a week to visit someone of whom they do not approve, as Sir Ian was huffy about my visit to Mrs Miller.

'Not that I care a damn,' I said to Twice. 'It's all so silly. This thing of not knowing Mrs Miller is just a habit of thought with him and I think that deep down he is ashamed of it but he can't break out of it. Then he is peevish in a feudal way because we have broken out socially on our own. Any slight break we have made before has been among people who were acceptable to Paradise. Not that Mrs Miller isn't – I believe that Madame would invite her here tomorrow, but she knows that Mrs Miller wouldn't come. She won't set foot on the place.'

'And I don't blame her for that,' Twice said.

'No. It's all right Madame and Sir Ian wanting bygones to be bygones at this stage but I don't blame Mrs Miller a bit for standing off. She's got nothing in common with Madame now.'

During what remained of December, in the final stages of the preparation of the factory for going into Crop, Twice went very seldom to his office in the Bay and it was almost a daily routine that his secretary, whom I was now addressing by her Christian name, Freda, arrived at Guinea Corner at about four in the afternoon, had tea with us and then she and Twice attended to his mail. Sir Ian did not greatly approve of this either but the issue was not merely one of Freda's colour. No issue turns completely on a single factor. Madame's blindness was increasing; her temper was consequently worsening. Guinea Corner had always been one of Sir Ian's refuges from the trials of life; he had been welcome at any time for what he called 'a beer and a chat' and he was still welcome, but Freda's presence, although she worked with Twice in another room, seemed to cause him discomfort. I think too that another operative factor in the decrease of his visits was this state of disenchantment of mine. I no longer accepted, as I had done formerly, his every pronouncement about the island and its life as being infallible. Sir Ian was sufficiently the son of Madame to be something of a dictator while he was sufficiently old-fashioned to have a deep-rooted belief that women of my age should not argue with men of his. When I would question some of his pronouncements, he would draw down his bushy brows and glare at me and I could see in his mind the thought: 'She is different from what she used to be, dammit!' If I was less enchanted with the island now, Sir Ian was less enchanted with me. This did not make me unhappy. I had had enough of enchantment.

It was during this December that Freda brought her children to Guinea Corner for the first time. Since my first meeting with her, I had reminded her once or twice of her promise to bring her children to see me, and, after that, I did not mention the matter again. I thought the reason for the delay was partly the importance to herself of her children, her feeling that she was placing a great deal of herself at my mercy by allowing me to meet them, and partly that the staff children had returned from leave, so that she saw these little whites about the place and might have been nervous that her own children would be snubbed by them in the cruel way at which children can be so adept. However, one Saturday afternoon, to my real delight, she arrived in her little car, a basket of fruit beside her on the front seat and, locked into the back, a little girl with short black pigtails that stuck out and had red ribbons on their ends and a little boy with great big Negro eyes and a very fat stomach and a big head who looked a bit like a specially nice sort of tadpole.

While the children sat staring at me from their enormous and beautiful eyes, Freda got out of the car, greeted me and then saying, 'Come, children,' she opened the back door. The little girl stepped out first, in a bunchy white muslin dress with a red sash, white socks and small black patent-leather shoes. She wore a silver bracelet on one fat little arm.

'Mrs Alexander,' Freda said, 'this is my daughter, Mary Louise.'

I am very fond of children, very interested in them, but a little afraid of them because their large eyes always seem to be so wise and penetrating. I feel that, when they look up at me, I am being subjected to a very important test that I must pass. And this little Negro girl seemed to me to be all eyes. I held out my hand and said: 'How d'you do, Mary Louise?'

I was completely unprepared for what happened. She put her small, very soft right hand in mine, with her left she took hold of the side of her muslin skirt and putting one patent-leather foot behind the other, she curtsied with great grace and dignity and said: 'How d'you do, Miz Lecksander.'

As a child, I myself had been taught to curtsy in this way when meeting grown-ups and as I looked down at the black head of Mary Louise with its red bows at the ends of the three-inch pigtails, my entire childhood of before my mother's death seemed to pass before my eyes in one lightning but vividly detailed flash. The little boy had now climbed fatly down from the car and Freda said: 'And this is my son, John Edward.' Again I held out my hand and with great solemnity he put his heels together, put his fat left hand on the round fat front of his white shirt and bowed his big black cannon-ball of a head before saying: 'How do, Miz Lecksander.'

I was overcome with their charm to the degree where I could only stand staring at them and might have stayed there in a transfixed state for long enough had not Mary Louise said: 'And we are not 'fraid of the dog.'

87

Dram, my big mastiff dog, was not even in evidence, for he had gone up to the factory with Twice, so when the child spoke, I looked at Freda who looked down at the children and said: 'Go now and play in the yard,' which was the island name for the garden. The children ran away at once and she and I came into the house.

'The children are nervous of dogs,' she said. 'All we Negroes are, especially of large dogs like yours. I suppose you know the reason for that?'

I did know the reason and I was very ashamed of it but I was learning through Freda that the price of friendship in some cases can be the admission of bitter and ugly shame.

'Yes,' I said, 'I know. Bloodhounds and mastiffs were used to track down runaway slaves, weren't they?'

'Yes. And many of the large dogs bred here in the island still have in them some of the instincts of these slave-tracking dogs. You cannot blame them – they were born so. And you cannot blame us for being nervous, I think, for we were born so too.'

'Freda, were you nervous of Dram when you first came here?'

She smiled. 'Terrified. So terrified that I could hardly come out of the car.' I stared at her. 'Then I thought that Mr Alexander was not the man to have a savage dog in his home and I came out. Then, next time I came you gave me tea and I saw him take a piece of cake from your fingers. Then – you remember – he expected me to give him a piece too?'

'And you did give him a piece!'

'Yes.' She gave her sudden liquid laugh. 'I prayed – I really prayed as I held it out to him.'

'Freda, you have the greatest courage. And I am a thoughtless fool. You should have told me! I could easily have shut Dram up, you know.'

'That would make no sense,' she said downrightly. 'Dram is part of your life. You cannot be expected to shut away part of what you are in order to please your – your friends.'

'But I could be expected to try to understand my friends a great deal better,' I said. 'Freda, I am ashamed of myself.

And this is why you have not brought the children to see me until now?'

'No. Not entirely. But I did want to take a little time to tell them about Dram so that they would not scream when they saw him.'

'If they are in the least nervous, Freda, Dram can stay in the garage until you go. I am terribly sorry about this but Twice and I were both brought up in the country in Scotland and dogs were part of our lives. We simply don't think of them as being capable of hurting anybody.'

'And we cannot think of them except as our enemies, especially those large ones, and many of the island-bred ones know we are afraid by instinct and that makes them dislike us, I think. I have read that horses and dogs can smell human fear and that they do not like it. But I am not afraid of Dram any more – you must not worry. In fact, I can see now that he is beautiful, although at first I thought he was the ugliest living creature I had ever seen – uglier than an alligator!'

In spite of all my determination to understand and my attempts at understanding, my feelings were hurt in a childish way at this, in the way they used to be hurt when people shuddered away from Angus, my ferret, when I was a child, for I loved Angus and saw him through the eyes of love, although in reality he was a white weasel with pink eyes and not at all beautiful in normal sight. But Dram, I felt, was a different matter. He was a well-bred mastiff, a magnificent, deep-chested creature weighing about eighty pounds of bone and muscle, deep golden-buff in colour with a black muzzle and tail-tip, and 'Dram' was a shortened version of his kennel-name 'Drambuie of Kilcarron'. That anybody could look upon Dram and find him uglier than an alligator was, to me, almost inconceivable but the eyes of Freda had seen him so, in her honesty she had made me understand why, and I could only be grateful to her for her physical courage, firstly, in facing the animal at all and for her moral courage, secondly, in telling me that she had determined to accept him as part of my life. That she had succeeded to the point of seeing beauty in him seemed to me to be a tremendous conquest of the waste of misunderstanding that separated her race from mine.

The two children now appeared at the open french window and John Edward shook his big head from side to side and said: 'Mama, no dog!'

'No,' Freda said. 'The dog will come back with Mr Alexander.'

'Mars Lecksander soon come?' Mary Louise inquired.

'Very soon,' I said. 'Do you want to see Dram?'

'The dog,' Freda explained.

'Him called Dram?' John Edward asked. 'Dram his name?'

'Yes. Just like you being called John Edward.'

'Me didn't know dogs got names.'

'Oh, yes,' I said. 'Just like people.'

It was about then that I heard the car and ran out to meet it so that Twice would not open the door and let Dram come bounding in his exuberant way into the room.

'Keep him in the car,' I called, 'until I fetch his collar and lead,' and I came into the house and said: 'Come, children, and see the dog in the car.'

They went close to their mother who took their hands and led them out to the veranda steps. Dram was sitting up on the back seat looking out with interest through the open window and as soon as he saw the children, he smiled in the foolish way that some dogs can smile and said 'Uff!' in a deeply pleased voice. The children, their enormous eyes more enormous still, shrank close to their mother but with a 'Come, children,' she led them firmly down the steps and close to the car.

'I am going to put his clothes on,' I said and held out the big brass-studded collar.

'That him clothes?' John Edward asked, but did not take his eyes off the dog for more than a second.

'Yes. Dram, put your head out,' I said and Dram, always obliging, pushed his big head out of the window so that I might put on the collar with the chain dangling from it.

'Him know to put him head out!' John Edward said suddenly and both children went off into a paroxysm of laughter.

'He knows all sorts of things. You wait a minute,' Twice said. He took hold of the lead, then got out of the car from the other side and Dram jumped from the back to the driving-seat and then to the ground.

'Dram, sit down,' Twice said and the dog sat down, looking happily at the children while they stared uncertainly back at him and little wonder, I thought, out of the new insight given to me by Freda. Sitting as he was, Dram's head was still further from the ground than that of the four-year-old sturdy John Edward. Freda now loosed her hand from Mary Louise's, leaned forward and said: 'How d'you do, Dram?' And Dram, of course, raised his large paw and put it in her hand.

'Him do it to me?' John Edward asked when he and his sister had stopped laughing.

'Yes, of course,' Twice said and John Edward held out a very timid little hand. 'Dram, shake hands.'

With great goodwill, Dram raised the paw again and clapped it down on the boy's small hand so that its sheer weight bore the hand down and the child with it, whereupon Dram took the opportunity to lick his big tongue right up the small black forehead. John Edward was so startled, yet not afraid, that he held on to the paw and looked into the dog's face and Dram looked back at him and said: 'Uff!' with great satisfaction once more.

'Him didn't bite me!' said John Edward with utter amazement, still holding the paw.

'He doesn't bite people,' Twice said. 'Do you, Dram?' and he pushed his fist into Dram's large mouth.

'Me!' said John Edward.

'All right.'

The child put forward his small fist but Dram drew back and began to lick it, which made the boy giggle in a helpless way.

'I want to shake hands!' Mary Louise said in pouting protest and I felt as if a great and important battle had been won.

The children played with the dog all the afternoon but always within sight of Freda, for I wanted her to be assured that they were perfectly safe. They took the collar off and put it on a dozen times, led Dram round the room, made him stand, sit, lie and roll over and fed him a whole pound of the small dog biscuits which he knew as 'sweets' and which, normally, lasted him for a fortnight. And, of course, they shook hands about a hundred times until even Dram was bored with it so that, in the end, he got up and took himself off to the kitchen. The children were desolate but Freda said: 'He has played with you for a long time. Go into the yard now,' but before they could go, Dram returned, carrying his friend Charlie the cat in his mouth to deposit her at their feet.

'No man could do more than that,' Twice said to Freda. 'That cat is the love of Dram's life,' which was true. Charlie, a female in spite of her name, was a very ordinary striped grey cat but Dram seemed to see in her a beauty and grace that were not of this earth.

When Freda and the children were going away, I asked her to be sure to bring them again before Christmas which she agreed to do and she kept her promise on the Saturday immediately before the holiday. They had only arrived and the children were shaking hands with Dram for the first time when Mrs Miller from the manse drove up and released her two grandchildren from the back of the car, whereupon they, too, fell upon Dram as upon an old friend which, indeed, he was to them by this time. When I introduced one Mrs Miller to the other, however, Freda shook hands with her usual charming smile but I noticed the mask of reserve drop over her face, stiffening a little her very mobile features. I had seen this happen before, when Sir Ian chanced to come in one evening and again one afternoon, when she was sitting with me, waiting for Twice to come home from the factory and Mrs Cranston, the agronomist's wife, called. It saddened me to see this change in her but there was nothing I could do. Sir Ian was of an age and a class with which she could never come to comfortable terms, for any intercourse between them would always be haunted by ghosts from the past, and Mrs Cranston, whom I myself disliked, was a woman whom I would not recommend as a friend to anybody. When I thought about Mrs Cranston at all, which I did as seldom as possible, it was only to wonder whether I disliked most in her her pseudo-intellectualism or her conviction that, as a small-town English-woman, she belonged to a master race whose mission it was to lead the lesser breeds such as Scots and Negroes towards the light with an air of sad patience and gracious patronage towards their unameliorable inferiority.

We left the four children in the garden and I brought the two women to the veranda from which we could all see the children play, and when Mrs Miller had sat down, she turned to Freda and said: 'I've noticed you at church, wearing an awful bonnie hat.'

Freda smiled but glanced at me, not quite understanding what Mrs Miller meant.

'That's a Scottish idiom for you, Freda,' I said. 'It means a very pretty hat.'

'Oh!' She smiled again at Mrs Miller.

'It was the bairns – the children – I noticed first though,' Mrs Miller went on. 'I've never seen a wee laddie behave better in church than your John. Thomas is just a little nickum and I've stopped trying to take him.'

When this had been translated for her, Freda said: 'But John Edward is older than your Thomas, surely?'

'Thomas is three and five months.'

'You see? John Edward is four and a half. He must behave better than Thomas.'

'I'll be very surprised if Thomas ever behaves as well as your John,' said Mrs Miller. 'Now, you are just the very person to help me,' she continued. 'Where do you buy John's clothes? I went down to the shops to get shirts and trousers for Thomas and I've never seen anything like the prices! It's a perfect scandal, that's what it is! And yet I see people with their wee laddies looking very nice so it seems to me that I'm just not finding the right shops. With Karen, it's different. I can make things myself for a wee girl but I'm not clever at the boys' things. Do you make John's things yourself?'

'Oh, no.' Freda laughed. 'I go to work all day and haven't much time. No, my Aunt Baba likes to sew and she makes all the children's clothes to amuse herself.'

'Oh, I see.' Mrs Miller was disappointed. 'Oh, well, I'll just have to learn to make wee trousers and shirts for Thomas for I can't afford these prices down in the Bay, that's for certain.'

'Would you – would you care for me to speak to Aunt

Baba?' Freda asked very tentatively. 'She might be able to help you.'

'Mercy me, I couldn't think of that!' Mrs Miller said. 'A lady sewing for her own amusement is one thing but she doesn't want to be bothered with the like of me!'

'I think Aunt Baba would be very happy if she could help you but you must please yourself,' said Freda, the mask of reserve, which had lifted a little before Mrs Miller's homely manner, dropping into place again.

'Is that the aunt who is a cripple, Freda?' I asked.

'Yes, that is Aunt Baba.'

'A cripple? Dear me, what happened?' Mrs Miller's warm interest and sympathy flowed out like a wave.

'She was run down by a car in town when she was a young woman. Her spine was injured. She cannot walk.'

'My goodness, what a terrible thing!'

Mrs Miller inquired into all the details of how Aunt Baba lived and who looked after her with genuine interest and great warmth of feeling. Talking of her aunt, of whom she was obviously very fond, Freda lost a little of her reserve again and ended: 'But Aunt Baba is not a saintly invalid, I'm afraid. Sometimes when we go to see her, she tells us to go away because she is too busy and next time we go she tells us that we should have sent her our photographs in advance so that she would recognize us and that we don't care whether she is alive or dead. Then we have to bring all our friends to see her and when the girls bring young men, quite often she is rude to them or she tells them what the girls did when they were babies, which is worse. Of the family, I think she really likes only the children but under it all she does love to be visited.'

'Where does she live?' Mrs Miller asked.

'Right at Fontabelle, in the small bungalow at the corner.'

'The pink house with that great big tree with the red flowers?'

'That's right.'

'Well! Do you know what I think I'll do? I'll get my son to take me calling there and ask her about making boys' trousers on the sly!'

Freda laughed. 'There is no need to do that, Mrs Miller. I

could take you there this evening on our way home if you like.'

'Well, that's real good of you. Apart from the sewing, I'll be delighted, for you said she is sixty now and that's just about my age. I'll be very pleased to talk to somebody that's about my own age. It seems to me that all the women in this island are either very old or very young. There don't seem to be any about my time of life.'

'Oh, but there are many!' Freda assured her.

'Then I'm not meeting the right ones. That Miss Beaton up the hill must be about seventy-five and Madame Dulac is over eighty and Janet here is only about forty and you are younger still. Your auntie sounds just like the right thing for me.'

Mrs Miller went on chatting, quite unaware that Freda's big eyes were fixed, round with amazement, on her pretty genial face, and I smiled inwardly at what to Freda was a revolution – to hear Miss Beaton, Madame Dulac and her own Aunt Baba lumped together by Mrs Miller as, quite simply, women of different ages, among whom Mrs Miller chose Aunt Baba as the companion for herself who was likely to be the most congenial.

'You must have found our island way of life very strange at first,' Freda said to her while we were having tea.

'Well, the funniest thing was it being fine weather all the time,' Mrs Miller told her, 'and then seeing all the people going past the house with dark skin. For the first wee while, I was for ever looking out of the windows at them, especially the bairns, because they were so bonnie with their great big eyes. I was kind of worried at first because they wouldn't speak to me over the fence when they were going to school but it's just shy that they were. They all speak to me now right enough. And then, there were all the tea-parties. People like Miss Beaton having Tommy and me to tea and a lot of folk to meet us and all that old silver and everything. It made me feel kind of artificial and sort of unfriendly, although it's wicked of me to say that because it was up at Miss Beaton's that I met Janet here. My goodness, I was pleased to see somebody from some place that I knew. It's a funny thing and I can hardly describe it but folk like Miss Beaton are neither one thing nor the other somehow. They don't belong *here*, like the people in the village at Fontabelle, and yet they don't belong back at home in Scotland either, poor souls. Now Mr Barrett – you know Mr Barrett the grocer at Fontabelle? – when I go in sometimes and have a cup of coffee with Mr and Mrs Barrett, it's real homely.' Mr Barrett was half Negro, half East Indian and his wife was pure Negro and while Freda sat in amazed silence, Mrs Miller rambled on: 'And Mr Ching Lee that has the transport lorries and his wife are very kind people too but I have an awful lot of bother understanding what they're saying because their voices are so queer.'

The Ching Lees were pure-bred Chinese and their English, spoken in a strange idiom of their own and in a high-pitched sing-song, was almost incomprehensible.

Mrs Miller rambled garrulously along, giving her views of St Jago and its people without fear or favour, without prejudice from the past or any restraint born of present company and, all the time, unaware of the significance of her attitude to Freda. In the end, they collected their children into their two cars, the children clutching the small Christmas packages I had given them, and set off down to Fontabelle to call on Aunt Baba.

# 2

WITH the approach of Christmas, the pattern of my life at Guinea Corner changed a little, for Christmas and New Year were traditionally a very gay time at Paradise, beginning with Madame's dinner-party and dance at the Great House on Christmas night and continuing in a marathon of cocktail, lunch and dinner parties round every house on the Estate compound to end with the party given by Twice and myself at Guinea Corner on New Year's Day.

When Freda and I discussed our plans for Christmas, I said to her: 'Freda, it would give Twice and me the greatest pleasure if you would come to our party here on New Year's Day.'

She looked at me very solemnly. 'Thank you, Missis Janet. I believe you when you say that it would give you pleasure but I know you will forgive me if I don't come.'

'You really would rather not?'

'I would rather not, really.' She smiled. 'It would make for awkwardness and we both dislike that.'

'There would *not* be awkwardness!' I said, probably in a militant tone, for I tend to be over-vehement at times, I think.

Freda laughed. 'You are something of a Crusader, Missis Janet, but you cannot force me down all the white throats in the island, you know. For one thing, I should find it very uncomfortable.'

'I'm sorry, Freda. I do get my feet off the ground sometimes about some things. The last thing I want to do is to make you feel uncomfortable in any way.'

'I know that. And there is another thing. You must not let me spoil your friendship with Sir Ian Dulac.'

'You're not,' I said firmly. 'Sir Ian and I have never seen eye to eye about the race problem.'

'Perhaps so. But I think that, before, you differed only in theory and now you are practising the difference.'

This was a very acute observation which astonished me not a little. I did not speak and she went on: 'You are older than I am, Missis Janet, and much wiser about many things, but I think I know more about St Jago and the colour question than you do. You must not be angry with people like Sir Ian. He does not approve of my presence in this drawing-room but he is not truly hostile to my race. Socially, he may not wish to know us but I think he has some respect for us as people.'

'That is true, Freda. He has.'

'But Sir Ian is like my mama in one way – the only thing they have in common probably is that they are both growing old. He has always looked upon the whites and Negroes as belonging to two different worlds and he cannot change now even if he wants to. It is too late, just as it is too late with my mama. Long ago, I suggested to you that you and Mr Alexander should come to Ginger Grove. I have not mentioned it again but I have not forgotten. I have been working on Mama. You must not be offended. You see, Mama does not want white people at Ginger Grove, just as Madame Dulac does not want coloured people at Paradise Great House. These are things that have never been. Mama simply cannot believe that such things can be possible. Mama cannot quite believe that I regard you as a friend. Missis Janet, I am a pioneer in my family – I am the first to make white friends – and the way of a pioneer is always hard.'

I smiled at her. I felt that she and I were a rather weak and silly two-woman conspiracy trying to overthrow a primeval tyranny of segregation. 'You keep on working on your mother, Freda. As you once said of your own people, I can wait. You are quite right. You are far, far wiser about all this than I am.'

And so the Christmas season came along and pursued its usual crazy course at Paradise, the only difference from other years being that Madame did not come out to any of our parties in the staff houses. The failure of her eyesight was not mentioned by anyone. By sheer force of personality, she caused everyone to accept the fact that henceforth it was her policy not to leave the Great House and she caused this policy to be accepted without question or even remark.

The dinner and dance at the Great House were as grand and gay as ever with Madame, on her own ground, very much the mistress of the occasion so that it was almost impossible to believe that her sight was so gravely impaired, and I am quite certain that many of the guests were utterly unaware of her disability. Mrs Miller from the manse, who had not before seen the Great House on a really festive occasion, was overcome by its grandeur and, in a quiet corner of the big drawing-room, while the dancing was going on, she told me what she felt with the customary artless candour which made her so lovable.

'I've never been at a party like this in my life before. Never in my wildest dreams have I thought of myself at an affair like this and to think of my boy being asked to speak one of the graces.' Her pretty eyes filled momentarily with tears of pride. 'It reminds me of the days when I was a housemaid at Poyntdale – that would be away back before you were born, lassie. I was only a lassie myself – third housemaid I was – it was my first post. You know, people can say what they like but it's sad to see Lady Monica and Sir Torquil of Poyntdale now with only one or two servants and a gang of women coming in by the hour. Seventeen of us there were when I was there, not counting Her Ladyship's French maid, Fenchel, and that terrible old Mrs Fergus the housekeeper or Mr Bruce the butler. And we were happy too! I can remember the nights when there would be parties, parties just like this and us girls used to be allowed to watch the ladies going in to dinner. Beautiful the dresses were in those days.'

'That is a very pretty dress you are wearing tonight,' I said.

'Do you like it? Tommy gave me the brocade for my Christmas present and Miss Baba and I made it.'

'Really? It's beautiful.'

'Miss Baba is very very clever with her fingers. . . . What a size that Miss Beaton is and in this heat too! It can't be healthy!'

'She doesn't behave as if she were sick.'

'No, indeed. And the way she bullies that poor brother of hers is something awful. He comes down to us quite a lot, always making excuses about Church business but I'm sure it's just to get away from her. He's a nice soul when he gets a chance. He reminds me of old Mr Macrae at Achcraggan – maybe you wouldn't remember them – although in a way Mr Macrae's position was just the very opposite for his wife never spoke to him for twenty years. Well' – she looked round the big room – 'this is a far cry from Achcraggan. You never know at the start of your life where you'll be at the end of it but although I've imagined a lot of things, I've never imagined myself as a visitor in a house like this.'

On New Year's Day, Mrs Miller and her son also came to the party at Guinea Corner which was not, of course, anything like so large and grand as the gathering at the Great House. Mrs Miller appointed herself, in a very helpful way, co-hostess with myself and shortly after everybody had arrived she turned to me and said:

'Freda's not here yet, I see. She must have mistaken the time.'

'Freda couldn't come, Mrs Miller,' I told her.

'Oh what a pity! Of course, they are a big family and

they will have all sorts of ploys on among themselves. How Mrs Lindsay manages to know them all apart just beats me. There's not a time I've been in that house when there's been less than twenty there, what with the in-laws and the bairns and everyone. A proper clan of them there is.'

I could hardly believe my ears. I am not a jealous-minded person as a rule, I think, but if I had not been so fond of Mrs Miller I believe I would have turned green with jealousy at that moment. In my mind rose the question: 'What has this woman got that I haven't got?' and as I tried to think of the answer, I came to something of a fitting humility. Among the many things that she had and I had not, Mrs Miller had a human kindness that was quite uncritical and generously open-hearted.

'I have never been to Ginger Grove,' I said.

'You haven't? It was Miss Baba that took me there the first time. It's not so far and I pushed her down in her wheelchair, but they wouldn't let me push her back up the hill again. One of the sons came home with us. It's right down beside the river at the very bottom of the valley. You wouldn't know it was there at all, looking down from the road. It's awful hot. No breeze gets in at all but as I said to Mrs Lindsay, she is made in a more sensible way for this climate than me so she doesn't notice it.'

'Is Mrs Lindsay a very old woman?'

'She is over seventy, she told me, and getting grey like my-self but she is very lively and interested in everything. She's always asking me about Scotland. Do you know she thought heather was a big plant as tall as a tree? When she told me that, I had a good laugh and then I told her that until I came here I always thought bananas grew in half-dozens like you get them at the fruiterers' and not in these great big long bunches and then we both had a good laugh. We have many a laugh, Mrs Lindsay and I. She called in at the manse one day when she was passing – I shouted to her to come in for a cup of tea. After she'd drunk it, she told me she had never drunk tea in her life before and had only taken it out of politeness. But she quite liked it and makes it at her own place now. All her children drink it, she says, but she had never taken to it but she'll soon be as much of a tea-jenny as I am myself. Och well, if I've taught her a bad habit, she's taught me one as well. I'd never drink rum until she got me to try it and it's quite good, especially with some lime-juice in it.'

'I would like very much to meet Mrs Lindsay,' I said.

'I thought you knew her long ago. I've often talked to her about you and she seemed to know you *and* your husband.'

'She may have heard of us from Freda,' I suggested.

'Oh, yes, that will be it. Well, you can easily get to know Mrs Lindsay. Could you get down to the manse tomorrow afternoon? She always comes in on a Friday when she's up in the village at the grocery. Come down for a cup of tea about four o'clock, the two of you.'

'Thank you, Mrs Miller. We'd love to,' I said.

When the last of our guests had gone, I told Twice of this invitation and ended: 'I accepted for both of us, darling, but if you can't come, I am going to be a nuisance and ask you for the car and a driver. I've got to get face to face with this Mrs Lindsay and if I get snubbed for my pains that will be that.'

'I'll drive you down myself,' Twice said. 'To the best of my belief, that factory should go into Crop next Tuesday and if it doesn't, nothing I can do tomorrow afternoon will make any odds. Besides, I like that bloke Miller. I've never had much to do with parsons but I take to him because he seems so damned interested in his job and he's interesting *about* it, too.'

The next afternoon, we drove the few miles down the road that followed the river gorge to Fontabelle and were welcomed at the manse by Mrs Miller, her son and her grandchildren.

'You've never been to see us before,' she said, 'but I've been to see you plenty, goodness knows. You'll have to learn to drive, Janet. Come away in. Mrs Lindsay's up at the shop – I noticed her going by – but she won't be long. Karen, take Thomas out to the garden and you'll get picnic tea out there with Matilda.' The children went away. 'Those bairns have just had one long picnic ever since we came here. I must say it's a grand climate for the bairns. There's Mrs Lindsay now. That's fine.'

Twice had gone away with Mr Miller to his study and I sat

101

alone in the drawing-room, listening to the two women chatting like old cronies in the hall. I began to feel desperately nervous and told myself that this was the worst thing that could happen which made me feel more nervous than ever, if anything. They came into the room and I stood up.

'This is Mrs Alexander – Janet Alexander – Mrs Lindsay. I've often spoken to you about her.'

I held out my hand, looked into the face of Freda grown much older and saw the mask of near-hostility drop over it like a visor.

'How d'you do, Miz Alexander?' she said in a deep languid drawl and I felt that she was purposely exaggerating the Negro accent and idiom in her speech.

'Your daughter and I are very good friends, Mrs Lindsay,' I said, 'and she is a tremendous help to my husband which makes me very grateful to her as well.'

'Freda is not a bad chile,' said the old lady with an affectation of carelessness, sat down and, ignoring me in a pointed way, said to Mrs Miller: 'Mr Barrett tol' me to tell you the fresh bacon come,' and I was more certain than ever that the island accent and idiom were being exaggerated.

They talked for a little time between themselves until the tea came in and Mrs Miller said: 'I've something new for you to try today, Mrs Lindsay. I made some pancakes although I thought I'd melt into a pancake myself with the heat in that kitchen. Janet here had a grandmother that made the best pancakes I ever ate so maybe she'll not think very much of mine.'

Mrs Lindsay looked at me, as if trying to assimilate the fact that I was human enough to have had a grandmother, and all I could do was to look back at her and smile, hoping that my nervousness did not show. Matters had worsened for, by decree of Mrs Miller, Twice and the minister were to have tea in the study. I felt very much alone.

'Yes, Janet's grandmother was a great old lady – a bit like yourself, Mrs Lindsay, to tell the truth. All us young ones were quite frightened of her. You put me in mind of her the other Sunday when yon two lassies were giggling in church and you gave them a scolding afterwards.' Mrs Lindsay continued to stare at me out of brown eyes whose whites were growing a little yellow with age. 'Oh, yes, Mrs Reachfar was a great old lady. We called her Mrs Reachfar after her place, you know, just as if we called you Mrs Ginger Grove.'

A faint smile, the first flicker of a smile lit the old eyes.

'Reachfar – it was a property?' she asked me.

'A very small infertile one on the top of a rocky hill,' I said.

'Like Craigell'chie Heights?' she asked, the accent exaggerated again as the smile died and the eyes hardened.

'Goodness no! It's a very small house and a very small hill.'

'You still have this property in Scotland?'

'Yes. My father and my uncle are there.' She seemed to me to be thinking of asking me why I too did not stay at Reachfar where I belonged instead of coming here to her island of St Jago, and I decided to forestall her. 'But I had to leave it when I was young in order to earn my living. Our little piece of land could not keep us all. In Scotland, we cannot grow food enough to live on all the year round as you can here in St Jago. Scotland is not as fertile a country as this.'

'No?' She studied me for a moment. 'You like San' Jago?'

'I think it is very beautiful but I have seen only a few places.'

'And mostly white people's places, aren't they?' Mrs Miller said, saying what I did not dare to say. I do not know how she did it and without causing even a flicker of comment from Mrs Lindsay. 'I must say I don't like most of the white people's places I have seen very much. Oh, *your* house is all right, Janet. I mean it's not too big and quite homely but I could never feel at home at Madame Dulac's – it would be like living in Buckingham Palace. And as for this old barn up the hill here where the Beatons live, it fairly gives me the creeps. But Ginger Grove's a different thing altogether and that's a real nice wee bungalow Freda has down in the Bay, Mrs Lindsay, so neat and convenient. How d'you like the pancakes?'

'Not so much,' said the one candid friend to the other. 'Not sweet enough. We St Jago people like sugar,' and they both laughed in hearty good fellowship.

The more I listened to the talk between them, the more conscious I became of my own exclusion from any intimacy with Mrs Lindsay, and the fact that Mrs Miller was unaware that I was excluded made that exclusion all the more marked from my point of view. They were like two people close to a warm fire while I sat at a distance in a cold corner, one of them unaware that the corner was cold, the other aware of its discomfort but regarding it as fitting for me. I was indignant as well as hurt and thought that Mrs Lindsay was utterly unreasonable. If she wanted to keep distant from white people, why choose to make a friend of Mrs Miller, the white woman whose son had taken the place that her own son had wanted? If Mrs Lindsay had a grievance against white people, surely Mrs Miller would be a natural focal point for that grievance? And while I thought in this way I was aware that I was suffering from wounded pride as much as anything, for about the only gift I have is a slight flair for making friends with people and it hurt my pride badly that Mrs Lindsay did not give a fig for me and my friendship and would, indeed, prefer that the manse was not infested with my presence at all. I was very sorry for myself and possessed by a grim sense of failure when Mr Miller and Twice eventually joined us, just as Mrs Lindsay got up to take her leave.

'When does Joshua go off on his travels?' Mr Miller asked her and then to Twice and me: 'Mrs Lindsay's son has been elected to go to Jamaica to represent the St Jago Farmers' Federation at the Caribbean Conference.'

'Indeed?' Twice said. 'That's very interesting.'

'Joshua is always mixing in with something,' the old lady said. 'He don't go off till May-month I think it is. I don' know if all these meetings do much good. Joshua can dream up plenty queer ideas without going to meetings. He's talking now about planting Irish potatoes for the hotel trade. You stick to yams and sweet potatoes, I tell him. You stick to the things you know, black boy, an' let these over-the-water crops alone, I tell him.'

'My wife grows very good Irish potatoes at Paradise,' Twice said.

'Huh?' Mrs Lindsay's mouth fell open and she stared from Twice to me, her face so changed that I seemed to be seeing a different woman. 'You grow Irish potatoes?'

'Yes, but only a few, in the garden. I started doing it just for fun.' I heard myself speaking as if I were apologizing for some liberty I had taken with this island of Mrs Lindsay's. She sat down again, all her hostility forgotten in her interest in the Irish potatoes as she called them in the island way. During recent years, she told us, they had been grown in Jamaica and in some of the other islands as a commercial crop to meet the hotel demand created by the tourist boom, and Joshua Lindsay and his mother, it seemed, had been at loggerheads on the potato question ever since the last Caribbean Conference of the Farmers' Federations. Joshua wanted to experiment with this high-value crop but his mother would not hear of it, thinking that in St Jago, which was hotter than the other islands which had succeeded with potatoes, the crop would be sure to fail.

'Simeon Goode over to Copley Hill planted two acres an' got nothin' but green bush!' she told me indignantly. 'Copley Hill is higher'n cooler'n Paradise!'

'Isn't Copley Hill heavy clay?' Twice asked. 'I went up there once with Sir Ian Dulac and I seem to remember heavy red clay banks at the roadside.'

'Ye-es, it's clay dirt up to Copley Hill,' she agreed. 'But good dirt – ver' rich.'

'I think it's the clay the potatoes didn't like, Mrs Lindsay. What is your earth like?'

'Down to Ginger Grove, we're on river dirt,' she said. 'Good dirt. The best yams in San' Jago we can grow. An' up to our mountain it's still wash dirt.'

'Well, I should think you would be all right with potatoes.'

'If it's any help,' I said, 'I'd be pleased if you and your son cared to come to Paradise to look at mine. I've only got about twenty plants just now but if you have never seen them growing —'

'I thank you, Miz Alexander,' she said. 'I may not come – I do not go far from Ginger Grove now. But Joshua will come. What day, if you please?'

'Any day at all,' I said. 'Paradise goes into Crop next Tuesday and when Crop starts I am never out very much.'

'Joshua wastes no time. I thank you again.'

When she shook hands, there was still distance between us and I knew that with this old lady the distance would always be there, but the hostility had gone.

As Twice and I drove home, he said: 'And how did you get along with the old lady?'

'Not at all,' I told him, 'until the potatoes came up. She simply had no time for me. Twice, this black-white thing is very queer. The barriers are so subtle. A smattering of education, for instance, is a barrier and my slight knowledge of the history of slavery gives me a guilt complex and that forms a barrier. I don't think Mrs Miller has the consciousness of the slave thing that I've got. And then words even and the way we use them form a barrier. Did you hear her refer to the earth as "dirt"? I found it terribly offensive. To me dirt is the grease that clots up in a kitchen drain – it's filth, you know – not the good earth that grows the food we eat.'

'Your attitude to words is a little exaggerated in its detail, of course,' Twice said, 'but I see what you mean. I think the word dirt meaning earth is a usage that comes from the States.'

'And it is odd that all my goodwill towards that old lady wasn't worth as much as a few plants of potatoes. When I was a child at Reachfar, I hated potatoes – the potato crop from planting it to gathering it and all the pots of potatoes for hens, pigs and people that I always seemed to be filling for my grandmother but I take all that back. I'll never say another bad word about a potato. Big things like colour problems don't turn on big mass political movements – they turn on little everyday things like potatoes.'

JOSHUA LINDSAY arrived at Guinea Corner about ten-thirty the following morning and he remains in my memory as the biggest, blackest, most handsome Negro I have ever seen and yet, when he smiled, showing a double row of large shining teeth, his face took on a gentle gaiety that reminded me of his petite sister, Freda. Joshua, at this time, was a little over fifty, being the eldest of the family of fourteen.

In the back garden, he and I talked potatoes for over an hour and then I invited him into the house to have a drink before he left.

'And do you think you will persuade your mother into a potato project at Ginger Grove?' I asked.

'She is already persuaded,' he replied. 'She was persuaded last evening. Mama was very angry last evening.' He smiled at me.

'Why?'

'Because a white woman had grown a food crop in St Jago that she had been afraid to try.'

I was glad to find that he, like Freda, had none of Mrs Lindsay's restraint and reserve about the different colours of our skins.

'You must make her understand,' I said, 'that I am not a planter or a cultivator but only a woman with a lot of spare time who amuses herself by growing things. Surely lots of other people have tried to grow potatoes here before?'

'I don't think so. Perhaps some of the importees like you have done it in their gardens but in the Federation few of us have ever gone further than discussing it. We are all working farmers, you see, and a little afraid of wild experiments. However, we shall try this at Ginger Grove. You will come down to see our potato cultivation?'

'I'd be delighted.'

Over his glass of rum and water he began to talk of other things and I discovered that he had spent some years at the Tropical School of Agriculture in Trinidad and that, during the 1939–45 war, he had been in the Royal Air Force.

'For the first few months,' he said, 'I swept backyards. I did not know till then that there were so many backyards in England. Then I went on training in Canada and became a pilot. I was in Lancaster bombers. I made a lot of friends in England and we meant to keep in touch but you know how it is. I came back here to Ginger Grove to help Papa, then Papa died and here I am. In the island here, friends in England do not seem real. And we are an old-fashioned family in many ways.'

'And very modern in others. Freda told me that your doctor brother was educated in Edinburgh and the one who is a minister in Glasgow.'

'Yes, and Kevin went to Oxford. Kevin was a Rhodes Scholar.'

'Really?'

'Yes. Kevin is the clever boy of the family.' He became silent and grave for a moment, studying me intently, and then: 'There is a thing I want to say, Miz Alexander. It is this. A bad thing happened to Kevin when he was in England. We don't know what it was – I don't think even Mama knows all of it – but Kevin's mind is – is twisted, Miz Alexander, and he has made up his mind to hate white people and Kevin has a lot of mind. It can hold a lot of hate.'

It seemed strange that of his own accord he should speak like this to me of his brother and I made no remark but sat waiting.

'You will read of what Kevin is saying and doing in the newspaper but I hope it will not influence you against Freda. There is nothing of Kevin in Little Freda. I am not being disloyal to my brother, Miz Alexander, for every man must have his own thoughts and his own reasons for them. Kevin, I am sure, has his reasons and although I may think he has let these reasons take too much control of his mind, I cannot hate him for that. He is my brother. But Freda does not have reasons for hatred like Kevin and she has been drawn to you and your husband and you have become her friends. I am glad of this, Miz Alexander, and I have spoken so that you will not be influenced against her by anything her brother may say or do.'

'It is Freda herself who is my friend, Mr Lindsay,' I said. 'She is a separate person from her brother.'

'No person is ever quite separate from her family or her race, Miz Alexander. Everything would be much more simple if we were all separate as you say. And it is not only family and race that we are tied to. We are tied to the very dirt of our country, especially we cultivators.'

'Yes, that is true. I come from a family very much like yours. I was born on a small farm in the north of Scotland called Reachfar. It is only of late that I have come to realize how strongly I am tied to it. It is part of what I am.'

'And that was where you learned so much about Irish potatoes?'

'I suppose so but I was not conscious of learning about them. And from when I was a child until I came to St Jago, I lived mostly in towns and cities but if ever there was a piece of earth I could dig, I dug it. In the Air Force, I planted daffodils all round a Nissen hut in Buckinghamshire. Here, I planted potatoes and cabbages – there were plenty of flowers in this garden already. Once a crofter – what you call a cultivator, Mr Lindsay – always a crofter, it seems.'

'That is true.' He stood up and put aside his empty glass. 'You have been most kind and I can only say thank you. You will come to Ginger Grove soon?'

'I'd like to, but when we go into Crop on Tuesday my husband won't want to leave the factory for a bit and I can't drive the car.'

'But one of us will fetch you. That is simple.'

'It is very kind too. When you have got your seed and are ready to start planting, send me a message by Freda.'

'I'll have the seed within a week. I can get them from a friend in Jamaica by cargo plane. We must catch the cool weather.' He swung a long leg over the side of his open car, not troubling to open the door. 'Goodbye for now, Miz Alexander, and thank you again.'

During the next few days, I did not think about Ginger Grove or potatoes very much, for the steam trials were being run at the factory; Twice and Rob Maclean, anxious about all the new plant which had been installed, were working excessively long hours and I was afraid that Twice was brewing up one of the attacks of recurrent bronchitis to which he was subject.

'I wish to Heaven Crop had started and that beastly factory blown up if it's going to blow up!' I said.

'It's not going to blow up,' Twice assured me, 'not the factory, but I'm less sure about the labour. These Cambuskenneth men are a queer bunch.'

'You're wheezing like a grampus, Twice!'

'I know. I must have got a touch of cold when I went up there at three this morning. There was a heavy mist and dew. Cheer up. Rob's doing the night watch tonight. But I agree with you – I'll be glad to see us in Crop.'

On schedule, at six o'clock on the morning of Tuesday the sixth of January, the siren blew and the Paradise Factory went into Crop. I had seen before this awakening of the whole valley and its surrounding hills from their Out-of-Crop sleep, but this year there was a difference. Hitherto, the sugar cane had been hauled to the factory entirely by large tractors pulling trains of trailers, but this year one could see a constant cloud of dust hanging over the north approach road as the lorries from the Cambuskenneth area came from the west along the coast and drove south into the valley at whose centre the factory was situated.

Paradise Estate was the outcome of a long history of expansion from a small plantation to the enormous enterprise it now was and this latest extension of the factory and distillery that had just been completed had been undertaken at the dictate of the combined foresight of Sir Ian and Rob Maclean. Midway between Paradise and St Jago Bay, on the north coast of the island, was situated the sugar factory of Cambuskenneth, a small estate compared with Paradise, half of whose land was on the coastal plain and the other half on the foothills to the south. Cambuskenneth had been owned by a couple of English descent whose only son had been killed in the war, and in 1948, when other factories were beginning to modernize their plant now that new equipment could be bought, the Roydes began to sell their coastal land for tourist hotel development and their hill land to Negro farmers. These slopes had always grown sugar cane, the Negroes would continue to grow cane on them and it had to be processed somewhere. If it was not processed at Paradise, it would go to Yorke Factory on the other side of St Jago Bay, a factory owned by a big combine. Sir Ian and Rob Maclean decided to expand Paradise and contract for the Cambuskenneth cane, for Sir Ian's principle was that nothing stands still – if a sugar factory does not grow bigger, it can only grow smaller and eventually be squeezed out of existence as so many of the smaller St Jagoan enterprises had been.

The Cambuskenneth labour was an admitted risk. Cambuskenneth had a blood-stained history of burning and rioting and in modern times it had turned into a political hotbed, for it was within easy reach by the Coastal Circular Road for the politicians from the Bay in their big fast cars. Cambuskenneth had been the battleground on which the first sugar workers' trade union had been formed; it had been the scene of every strike about all sorts of grievances, some real, some merely manufactured; it had been the scene a year ago of the burning of a thousand acres of cane following the sacking of a mill-hand for being drunk at work in the factory. Rob Maclean blamed its proximity to the Bay for the trouble; Sir Ian blamed Mr Royde who certainly was a bad-tempered, cross-grained, illiberal old man, but there were other causes, I thought, since I had come to know Freda Miller. I had heard her say to her small son one day: 'Don't stamp your foot at *me* as if you were some Cambuskenneth bush man!' The Cambuskenneth people, it seemed to me, had a reputation among their own race that resembled more than a little the reputation of Kilkenny cats.

With Crop under way and the new machinery apparently settling down smoothly, Twice was able to work more moderate hours and the threatened attack of bronchitis did not develop. He now, too, began to give less of his time to the Paradise factory where his work of new installation was completed and more to his office in the Bay and to visiting other projects in the island where his firm had an interest, and it was about ten days after Josh Lindsay's visit to me that he told me that

111

Freda would be calling for me the next afternoon to go down to Ginger Grove to see the potato planting.

'George and Tom will die laughing when they hear of me travelling several miles to see a few tatties being planted,' I said.

'The Lindsays don't think it funny though,' Twice told me. 'I wish I weren't going away to the other end of the island tomorrow and could come with you. Little Mrs Miller was quite intense about it. In addition to asking to get off early – a thing she has never done before – she was so desperately anxious that you should be able to come. I think you have turned into a sort of luck charm for the crop, Flash – a sort of fetish, you know.'

'Oh rubbish!'

'It isn't entirely. You remember that time I put in the new little boiler at the little pickle factory last year? When the priest was called in to bless and sprinkle holy water on both the boiler and me? I got something of the same feeling of intensity when little Mrs Miller was talking today about Josh's potato project as they call it.'

The next morning Twice left early, and shortly after lunch Freda arrived at Guinea Corner. As we drove down the gorge road, it occurred to me that my feelings must be a little like those of old Mrs Miller long ago when she turned up the hill to Reachfar, for many a time she must have been as uncertain of her welcome from my grandmother as I was of my welcome from Freda's mother now.

'I am so looking forward to seeing Ginger Grove,' I said to Freda. 'It has taken shape in my mind as a sort of St Jagoan version of Reachfar and your mother reminds me in many ways of my grandmother – a sort of matriarch, you know.'

Freda turned her car at a sharp angle off the main road and on to a steep, rough, downhill track towards the river. 'Your Reachfar is on a hill, you have told me,' she said. 'Ginger Grove is at river level. All the cultivation is higher than the house.'

On either side of the road, I could see the cultivation, the land contour-terraced in long winding strips that ran along the hillside, parallel with the course of the river.

'This is beautiful,' I said. 'It's a show-piece of terracing.'

'It is rather. My father was one of the first cultivators in the island to terrace his land in this way and since then many people have come to see it and have copied it. Here we are.'

The house stood in the midst of a riot of vegetation. It was a rambling single-storey place with walls of stone and mortar for the first two feet or so and then wood the rest of the way and it was roofed with cedar shingles. It had obviously been built piecemeal, as another room or two were required, and with a fine disregard for any sort of architectural unity. In the course of building as few trees as possible had been felled, and at one place the wall actually curved round the trunk of a massive mahogany tree which spread its shade over the surrounding roofs. Other trees had been planted as close as possible to the walls – bananas, coconuts, mangoes, oranges and grapefruit screened every window so that, once inside the house, one had the impression not so much of being inside a building as of being in a small clearing in the midst of a fruit-bearing jungle. This, it suddenly came home to me, was one of the big differences between the Negro and the white man. The white, building a house, first cleared an open space which, eventually, he would turn into lawn and garden about his dwelling. The Negro cleared as little as possible and when his house was built he planted trees right up to his windows.

Along the front of what I took to be the original small house, there ran a wooden veranda, screened like all the rest of the building with creeping vines and fruit trees so that it was bathed in a humid green shade. Here, in front of the main door to the inner rooms, a little like a guardian in front of a temple, sat Mrs Lindsay in a large rocking-chair with her friend Mrs Miller from the manse beside her. As my eyes became used to the green shade, I discovered that this hollow among the vegetation was riotous with life. Among the surrounding bananas and coconuts which had been planted, as the house had been built, quite without plan, there must have been at least twenty children, darting about in their gay cotton clothes like brilliant little fish in a green pool, and among them, their white skins looking green in the filtered light, were Karen and Thomas Miller. In addition to the children, there were chickens, ducks, several goats tethered to coconut palms and two black piglets which rooted, grunting, among the brown earth. The immediate impression was of lusty abundance, an exuberant fecundity, and this was made more marked when Freda introduced me to two of her sisters-in-law, both of whom were heavily pregnant.

Mrs Lindsay, whom everyone including Mrs Miller addressed as 'Mama Lou', welcomed me with no hint of the hostile restraint that had been so obvious in her when I met her at the manse and then Freda led me to sit down at the end of the veranda with some half a dozen young and middle-aged women. They were all introduced to me and their positions in the family explained, but I am slow-witted and can take in only a little at a time. The only one I really noticed was a very large Negress, introduced as 'Sister Flo' and so addressed by everybody, who was the eldest sister of the family. All this teeming life and the quick patter of the island dialect, interspersed with loud liquid gurgles of rich Negro laughter, was too much for me. Bemused, I could only sit and look around me.

I was still in a state of bemusement and eating a most excellent sherbet made from some exotic fruit when what looked like a regiment of menfolk, led by the massive Josh, came through the trees and up the steps on to the already overcrowded veranda, and when they had sorted themselves out a little, perching here and there along the veranda wall and Josh himself sitting on the steps, I almost dropped my sherbet glass with amazement at seeing Mars Andy Beaton among them, very small, wizened and pale among all the big shiny-skinned Negroes. At some stage, in my mind, I had allotted to the Beatons the place of hereditary enemies of the Lindsays, making one of these clear-cut lines which seldom or never occur in human relationships, and I was astonished to see Mars Andy here and apparently on good neighbourly terms with people who were, after all, his immediate neighbours. Also in the party were Mr Miller, in off-duty dress of open-necked shirt and khaki shorts and another young Negro in clerical dress who was the Lindsay brother who had applied for Fontabelle Church, and he and Mr Miller confounded me further by retiring together into a corner and discussing earnestly and with obvious good-fellowship some project of their own.

In the month or so since the Christmas and New Year festivities had got under way and I had been seeing less of the Millers and Freda, it seemed to me that life had been evolving at unusual speed in this circle round Fontabelle. Freda, her sisters and sisters-in-law were addressing the minister as 'Mars Tommy' and Mrs Miller as 'Missis Lena' while they were both calling Mrs Lindsay by her family name of 'Mama Lou'. And Mars Andy, who was Mars Andy to the whole island except his sister, was being addressed by Mrs Miller as plain 'Andy', but in a smiling tone, quite unlike the bullying bellow used by Miss Sue.

About four o'clock, when the day was beginning to grow a little cooler, Mama Lou rose from her chair for the first time and Josh took her arm. Beside him, she looked small and frail and the red checked head-cloth which she wore over her hair that was like grey sheep's wool did not reach the level of his shoulder.

'Come, Missis Janet,' Freda said to me and, in procession, we all followed Josh and the old lady along a narrow path among the fruit trees and then we began to climb a winding track between the terraces which, in places, was almost a staircase. Then we passed through the shade of a banana 'walk' of about two acres which lay on level ground before we began to climb again and, after passing through some pasture ground dotted with pimento trees, we came to another level shelf in the hillside, an area of perhaps three acres, where the soil, eroded down by the rains from the hill above, had been worked to a fine brown tilth. At the corner of this area there stood, under a thatched shelter of coconut fronds, the barrels of seed potatoes.

'This is our potato project, Miz Alexander,' Josh said, and taking one potato from a barrel, he put it into my hand. 'I am asking you if you will please to plant this first one for us.'

I had a moment of stark panic. Twice had been right in what he had said. These people had vested some sort of belief in me. I looked round at them all. Counting the children, who

115

had followed us, there must have been about forty souls standing there but, to me, they looked like a vast multitude, a multitude waiting for and believing in some miracle. I thought of Reachfar and my grandmother and, quite suddenly and with confidence, I began to speak.

'When I was a little girl,' I said, 'my grandmother who was an old lady like your Mama Lou told me that God had promised that there would always be seed-time and that there would always be harvest and that if we believed in that promise, our crops would prosper. We all ask God now to bless this crop and to bring it to a good harvest for us.'

I then kneeled on the ground, made a small hole with my hands, put the potato in it and covered it while, round me, the liquid voices said 'Amen' and the lighter voices of the children solemnly echoed: 'Amen.'

By the time I stood up, everybody had passed with Negro volatility from solemnity to laughter and Mama Lou, taking a potato from Josh, planted it about fifteen inches away from the one I had planted. After that, one by one, everybody planted a potato, right down to the smallest child.

'That row isn't too straight, Josh,' I said, 'but when the crop starts to grow one crooked row won't be noticed.'

Josh then showed me his arrangements for water supply from a spring higher on the hillside and then we began to walk down to river level and the house again. The others had gone down ahead of us, the children running even further ahead, and as Josh and I walked through the fruit trees towards the house in the five-minute tropical twilight, when the crickets, tree frogs and water frogs begin their evening chorus and as the lights from the house winked at us through the thick surrounding vegetation, I had a momentary glimpse of revelation of the Negro world. Paradise, with its open lawns and European architecture, seemed so distant that it had no more reality than a dream for I saw it, momentarily, as a Negro must see it. And I saw this crowded low-built house of Ginger Grove, too, as a Negro saw it, with its intimate closeness to the breeding earth, with its fecundity so in keeping with the rioting up-thrusting vegetation that surrounded it and covered the chickens, the goats, the ducks, the pigs and

116

the children as, tired with their games of the afternoon, they lolled about on the warm ground in the falling darkness.

When we came up the steps on to the lighted veranda, the moment of revelation was over, for the difference between this house and the house in which I had lived for a lifetime was too marked. There was in it no attempt at grace. The naked electric bulbs hung unshaded from the roof, glaring down upon the scarred furniture and chipped paint, and threw into relief in the dining-room the big refrigerator which a white housewife would relegate to the pantry but which, here, was a proud possession, and showed the layer of dust on the pink plastic bowl filled with faded yellow and purple paper roses that decorated the centre of the brilliantly varnished table. It is not, the thought flashed through my mind, the big things that make the difference but the little things. Mama Lou, in her love for her family and for this earth around her, had the same instincts as had animated my grandmother but my grandmother would never have tolerated that plastic bowl and those paper roses. As if to echo my thought, into a moment of silence when even the crickets stopped their chirping, there came the voice of Tommy Miller: ' – these are all small things –' and it was answered by Jack Lindsay, his Negro clerical friend: 'But men's minds are small.'

And now, as if to emphasize still more the small things which govern life and as if to throw into higher relief the difference between me and the Lindsay family, the mosquitoes, those creatures which seem to me to be the very devilish spirit of the tropic darkness, warmth and humidity, arrived on the veranda in their humming thousands but they seemed to attack nobody except me. There is some rule about the mosquito's choice of a victim that is known only to mosquitoes and while I furtively tried to rub, slap and scratch a dozen different parts of myself at once, the Miller family from the manse, fresher to the island by years than I was, seemed to be perfectly at ease. Inside a quarter of an hour, my bare legs, arms and neck were stinging hot all over, huge red lumps were rising on my skin and here and there there were blobs of blood, and by the second the cloud of insects became denser and their vicious whining song more loud. I hated the sound of them but

117

it was none the less a relief to hear them, for the anopheles mosquito, the malaria carrier, travels on sinister silent wings. The stab of the anopheles, too, although deadly in its results more often than not, is a single sharp prick that leaves little mark or surface irritation, but the Ginger Grove mosquitoes were large black whining insects and inside minutes I felt that I was in one of the more refined torture chambers of hell. Then, as I waited for a break in the clatter of conversation to announce that I must go home, I felt a savage stab at my right eyelid and involuntarily I raised my hand and slapped at the spot. I killed the mosquito and dusted the black corpse off my hand but, 'What is troubling you, Missis Janet?' Mama Lou inquired.

'Only a mosquito,' I said and got to my feet. 'I must go home, Freda, if that is all right with you.'

'Of course,' Freda said and got up.

My eyelid, however, had begun to swell and when I came forward under the light to say goodbye to the old lady, she noticed it and she noticed also the bumps on my face, neck and arms.

'Look at she face! Look at it swollen, it!' she said, lapsing completely into the Negro idiom, even to the emphatic addition of the 'it' at the end.

'My goodness!' Mrs Miller said now, 'look at the blood on her legs!'

Sister Flo fetched some cologne and began to anoint me; everyone gathered round to sympathize; a new battalion of mosquitoes came swarming towards their evening meal and I thought that I would never get away, but at long last I was in Freda's car and headed for higher drier ground. But I felt oddly sick at heart. It seemed to me that these mosquitoes had taken from me all the ground I had gained in the course of the afternoon and I could remember little except the circle of astonished and horrified brown eyes, staring at my swollen face and blood-stained skin. For an hour or two, I thought, they had forgotten that this skin of mine was white but the mosquitoes, when darkness fell, came out of the humid shade to remind them that I did not belong to their island.

# 4

W HEN Freda had dropped me at Guinea Corner and had gone away, I told Twice that this was how I felt while I scratched and rubbed at my arms and legs and he held a cold compress against my now closed eye and he said: 'Now, that's just morbid rubbish, darling, because you are feeling ill. You must be, with this load of poison in you. Dammit, hadn't you the sense to get out of there before the dark came down?'

'I didn't think about it. I was too interested in it all. Don't be angry with me, Twice. I don't think I could bear it.'

'I'm not angry but you really are alarming, Janet. How you don't get fever, I don't know. Let me see that eye.'

'It's going down. And they were not anopheles – they were big black humming ones. And I haven't got fever and I'm not talking rubbish. Those people were *annoyed* with me for getting all bitten like this – it's natural, after all. You don't like people to be uncomfortable in your house and you do tend to blame the people and not your house. After all, the mosquitoes don't bite *them*, it seems, and they feel that if I get bitten it's my own fault somehow. And actually, it is my own fault although it's a fault in myself that I can't do anything about. I've just been specially created to be mosquito food quite obviously and I should stay away from mosquitoes' places if I don't want to be bitten. It's just as if this island was telling me I had no business to go to Ginger Grove. Those mosquitoes were just saying to me what Mama Lou would like to say: "Gwan home, white gal!" It's what I keep on saying – it's the little things that make the barriers.'

'Before the mosquitoes descended on you, what was it like?' Twice asked.

I tried to recapture for him the atmosphere of Ginger Grove but I was defeated to find the words and, seen from the big drawing-room of Guinea Corner with its atmosphere of two hundred years of white tradition, much of the quality of Ginger Grove disappeared and the memory became a muddle of messy detail, of goats too close to the house and chickens dust-bathing by the doorstep. In memory, it was no longer richly fecund but sordidly oppressive.

'I think,' I said in the end, 'you have to be in the ambience of the actual people and your liking for them to see their way of life truly and appreciate its qualities. Seen from here, it just looks like squalor.'

To go back in time a little, it was shortly after my return from Hope that Tommy Miller and Jack Lindsay between them carried through a plan for enlarging the church at Fontabelle which, in future, they would run together as co-ministers.

'It seems an extraordinary development,' I said to Sir Ian when I first read this news. 'I see from *The Island Sun* that they have launched an appeal for funds.'

'It's sound sense,' he told me, 'but if you'd told me this time last year that it would happen, I'd never have believed you. You've got to hand it to that fellah Miller – he's got that congregation solid behind him.'

'You know, I think his mother is a big influence,' I said.

'That little woman? She don't seem to go out much – never hear anything about her.'

'She has a great gift for getting on with people, especially the coloured people.'

'D'ye tell me that?'

'Where is this Hill of Zion where Jack Lindsay has been preaching till now?' I asked next.

'Away to hell an' gone in the valley behind Craigellachie Heights – an old church all fallin' to bits. No village up there but hundreds o' small settlers an' they formed a co-operative a few years back under the Farmers' Federation.'

'Freda, Twice's Mrs Miller, told me the idea is to use their co-operative lorries to bring the people down to Fontabelle Church.'

'Queer how things go, when you think of it. Our factory's centralizin' the sugar industry here – takin' Cambuskenneth cane now an' Miller an' Lindsay are centralizin' religion, takin' the Hill o' Zion lot. Next thing you know, the Mary Vale congregation will be coming down to Fontabelle as well, you wait an' see. Oh, well, I suppose that's the drift o' things these days.'

It was about the middle of April, shortly after Easter, that a car arrived at Guinea Corner one Saturday afternoon and disgorged on to our veranda the two ministers, Mrs Miller, Mars Andy and Freda, just after Twice had come back from a courtesy look round the factory and we were having tea. When extra cups had been brought and they were all seated, Freda came straight to the point in her honest way.

'This isn't a social call, Missis Janet,' she said. 'We are a deputation.'

'Oh?' I said.

'A deputation to Twice,' said Mrs Miller.

'Oh?' Twice said.

'Sir,' said Jack Lindsay, 'we want to ask you if you will draw the plans for the extension to our church.'

'Oh, come!' Twice said. 'I am an engineer of sorts, not an architect.'

'We don't want an architect,' said Tommy Miller. 'Architects have to be paid but we hope a friend might do it for nothing. Mr Alexander, what we want to do is very simple. We want to knock out the north wall and move it a bit farther north and put it up again, that's all, but we have to have a drawn plan to submit to the Presbytery and to the housing and building people.'

'How much farther north is a bit?' Twice inquired, smiling.

'That's part of what we want you to help us with, sir,' Freda said. 'We could tell you how many people have to sit in the bit and then you work it out, see?'

'After all, Twice, you planned these new buildings at the factory here,' Mrs Miller said and Mars Andy, sitting beside her, blinked in a persuasive way.

'But that's a sugar factory!' Twice protested.

'A mill,' I said. 'A sugar mill. If you can draw a mill, you can draw a kirk!'

'You keep out of this!' he warned me.

'That's right,' said Mrs Miller. 'You can make a kirk or a mill o't!'

In the end, Twice made notes of all they said, asked a lot of questions, promised to meet the two ministers on the site the next afternoon and then said to me: 'Flash, for pity's sake get

121

Clorinda to bring some drinks in. I never thought to see the day when I would be building churches.'

Work had begun on the extension to the church by the end of April, much of the building labour being by volunteer members of the congregation, even the women and children carrying buckets of sand and water and doing anything they could.

'It's an extraordinary outfit,' Twice said. 'It takes me back to the time we rehabilitated Crookmill except that that crowd down there go at it with even more hell and less notion than we had. I wish I could see as much enthusiasm and goodwill up at the factory here. Rob's getting worried. That Cambuskenneth lot are just waiting for the slightest chance and the balloon will go up.'

'Madame and Sir Ian are sort of uneasy too,' I said. 'No wonder. There is something in the very air that wasn't there before – it reminds me of the feeling at Achcraggan on the evening of Armistice Day in 1918, a grey sluggish feeling of impending menace.'

'Menace is right. I'm glad I'm not in Rob Maclean's shoes. I'd lose my temper.'

'But Rob's got a far worse temper than you, Twice!' I protested.

'Not really. Rob girns and grumbles about little things far more than I do and goes off with a loud bang now and again but when it comes to diplomatic things like this labour problem he has far more patience for going on from day to day without blowing his top. Anyway, don't let's talk about it. It doesn't help. I wouldn't say I was a very romantically-minded bloke, would you?'

'Romantically-minded?' I asked. 'What's come over you? Are you feeling all right?'

'Perfectly, but d'you know what I think? I think there's something brewing between Tommy Miller the minister and my Mrs Miller.'

'Twice, you're dotty!'

'Maybe I am but I don't think so. It's not the sort of thing I would think of just for laughs. After all, I stand to lose a good secretary.'

'But, Twice —'

I stopped because I did not know what I had meant to say. What I had been going to say had its origin in the colour difference between Freda and Tommy Miller but when I took thought, colour difference at Fontabelle seemed to be buried somewhere under the manse, the house at Ginger Grove or the rising edifice of the extension to the church.

'Well, bless my soul!' I said in the end. 'And their souls too. Twice, loss of a secretary or not, I hope you're right.'

Twice was right. The engagement was announced in *The Island Sun* at the beginning of May, the newspaper arriving at Paradise in the middle of a forenoon when I was round at the Great House helping Madame with the letters.

'Is that the newspaper, dear? Just glance through the deaths for me. I'm sure old Julie Shaw must go any day now.'

'No,' I said. 'Mrs Shaw isn't gone yet. Young Mrs Findlay's had her baby though – it's a girl.'

'Another girl? Dear me, old Jackie Findlay will be furious.'

And then I noticed Freda's engagement and said: 'Oh, Madame, listen to this!' and read it aloud.

'Freda Miller? *I* don't know of a Freda Miller. A St Jago Bay address, you said? She must be one of those American tourist girls.'

'Actually, Madame, she is Twice's secretary down at the office in the Bay.'

'*I* didn't know Twice had a secretary down there. I thought there was only that man Somerset. When did she come out?' By 'out' Madame meant 'from Britain'. 'Why have you never brought her to see me, Janet?'

'She is a coloured girl, Madame. Her father was Josh Lindsay of Ginger Grove.'

'A coloured girl?' Madame rose from her desk and moved to another chair in her agitation. 'Oh, *poor* Mrs Miller!'

'You know, Madame, I don't think Mrs Miller will mind. She is very fond of Freda and of all the Lindsays and she goes a lot to Ginger Grove.'

'How quite extraordinary!'

Outside, at the front of the house, there was the sudden sound of a car pulling up with a jerk and within a moment

Miss Sue Beaton was in the office, Mars Andy behind her, blinking in a frightened way down into the pith helmet which he held between his hands and level with his waist.

'Lottie, have you seen the paper?' Miss Sue exploded from a purple countenance.

'Yes, Sue, I've seen it. Sit down. You will send yourself into a fit.'

'That's what I —' Mars began.

'Be quiet, Andy! This is all your fault, taking the Millers down to Ginger Grove. It's all right you going there – you know your place and the Lindsays know theirs but the Millers apparently don't. Lottie, it must be put a stop to! That young Miller must be mad!'

'What's goin' on here?' Sir Ian demanded from the doorway. 'Sue, ye can't go drivin' in here at that speed in Crop, dammit! Ye'll break your perishin' neck an' some tractor-driver's as well!'

'That's just what I —' Mars Andy began.

'Andy, hold your tongue. Ian, *have* you seen the news-paper?'

With shaking hands, Miss Sue snatched the paper from me, crumpled it into a sort of roll with only the engagement announcement showing and thrust it under Sir Ian's nose.

'Miller, Miller —' he muttered. 'God bless me soul! It don't even mean a change of name for her. Very handy, what? Who is she? Newly out from home? Never heard of her.'

In strophe followed by antistrophe on a rising scale of fury, Madame and Miss Sue informed Sir Ian, with a wealth of genealogical detail, exactly who Freda Miller was and when they paused for lack of breath, Miss Sue wheezing like a grampus, he said: 'Now, then, Mother, there's not a damn o' good in you an' Sue goin' gettin' like this —'

'That's just what I —' Mars Andy began.

'Be silent, Andy!'

'I will *not* be silent, Sue,' said Mars Andy in a high shaky voice, staring down into his pith helmet and electrifying us all so much that we were all dead silent while he went on: 'Tommy is a fine young man and Freda Lindsay, Miller, I mean, is a fine young woman and – and —' He suddenly realized the enormity of his situation, that he was speaking and that no less than four people were listening to him, and he began to blink, seemed to be tempted to dive head-first into the helmet and then, with a terrific effort of courage, he clapped it on his head where he could no longer see it and be tempted by it and ended: '— and all this is none of your business, Sue, and I wish them good luck and every happiness!' whereupon the chin-strap of the helmet became entangled in his moustache which went up his nose and caused him to give a violent sneeze.

'Andy Beaton,' said Miss Sue when she could speak, 'have you lost your senses?'

'No, he ain't lost his senses!' shouted Sir Ian who saw, as I did, that Mars Andy had fought to the last drop of the blood of his courage. 'It's time that you an' Mother came to *your* senses, Sue, an' realized that you are old women! I ain't so young meself but I ain't so perishin' old an' stuck in the mud as you two. An' another thing while I'm about it, Sue. With this merger — that ain't the right word for churches but ye know what I mean — with this merger that's goin' on between Fontabelle an' Hill o' Zion — an' Mary Vale's comin' down there next month when their old parson retires — you've got nothin' to do with the management o' that church, Sue. I know your people built it an' your family's always taken an interest in it but these days are done. If you go stickin' your nose in there any more you'll get into proper hot water. Now, sit down an' we'll all have a tot an' some lunch an' come to our senses.' He gave a violent push to the electric bell beside the door. 'I've got enough trouble on me hands over at the factory without comin' in here an' findin' a riot goin' on.'

'What is the matter at the factory, Ian?' Madame asked.

'That Cambuskenneth crowd's questionin' the sucrose content reports from the lab. . . . They claim we're cheatin' them.'

'Rubbish, Ian! How dare they? Our laboratory people are entirely reliable.'

'I know that, Mother, an' so do they, come to that, but they've been lookin' for trouble ever since Crop started.'

I did not see Twice until that evening for he was down at

the office all day but over dinner I said: 'What is all this about sucrose contents reports?'

'Cane farmers are paid a deposit price on their cane loads in the first instance but a sample from every load goes through the lab and according to its sucrose content they get a bit more for the load.'

'And what is the Cambuskenneth grouse?'

'One of the Paradise cane pieces down at River Bottom showed the highest sucrose content for last week. Cambuskenneth has always been known as the "sweetest land in the island" so they say the reports from the lab are faulty. They're not. Cranston and Murphy and their chaps know what they're doing. They made damn' sure of these reports before they let this happen. Cranston's theory about the thing is very interesting and seems to me to make sense. It was the coastal plain lands at Cambuskenneth that always kept up their sucrose figures, he says. The plains were carrying the hill land as it were, and this cane that is coming to us now is all from the hills. Cambuskenneth never made separate analyses, field by field, as we do here. They hadn't the lab facilities anyway. They just took out a general figure for the whole estate – they weren't buying from farmers. Then the other thing Cranston says is that this cane piece down at River Bottom is on good land to start with but it is also trapping a lot of the fertilizer and stuff that's put on the pieces up at Riverhead and gets washed down by the rains. That's the science of it, as Tom and George would say, but the Cambuskenneth men are not too keen on listening to science. Cambuskenneth has always been the sweetest property in the island and they are challenging the lab on it.'

'What will happen?'

'God knows. There's a meeting tomorrow. Sir Ian and Rob may talk them round – or they may not.'

Sir Ian and Rob Maclean did not get a chance to come to terms with the Cambuskenneth representatives but I did not know this until later. The first concrete intimation I had of something being wrong was that at ten-thirty I went to my kitchen to talk to my cook about the lunch and discovered that I had no servants. Cook, Clorinda, Minna and Caleb the

126

yard boy seemed to have vanished into thin air. I then noticed that I could hear the orchestra of sound that came from the factory very distinctly and realized that the reason for this was that no transport was moving in the fields or on the roads and that no field workers were cutting cane. It was a most uneasy feeling, to stand alone on the veranda in the midst of this charged silence, in the brilliant sunlight, and I was glad when Dram came to my side and pushed his big head under my hand. I was glad and more uneasy all at once, for his head under my hand reminded me of Fly at home at Reachfar when I was a child and she was afraid in a thunderstorm. Dram was afraid now. I looked uneasily over my shoulder at the silent house behind me and took a deep breath, squeezing down a panic that seemed to be swelling into a scream at the bottom of my lungs. It was then that I saw Twice's car coming very fast, with a cloud of white dust rising behind it, along the road from the factory. As he came up the steps, I heard the bronchial wheeze from his lungs.

'Darling, you are feeling ill!'

'No. I'm wheezing a bit – it's nothing much. Flash – Flash, I ran away!'

He stood staring at me and I stared back at him. 'Twice, what are you talking about? What happened?'

'Kevin Lindsay is up there, talking to the workers, telling them what brutes and pigs Sir Ian and all of us are.' His voice shook. 'Rob was there – I couldn't stand it. I felt my gorge rising, my brain getting red. I – I jumped into the car and ran away!'

'Darling, sit down. You did the best thing you could. Come and sit —'

'If I'd stayed I would have felled him! Lindsay was talking about Sir Ian and people bleeding the workers to get soft beds for white whores. Janet, I – I ran away. If I'd stayed I'd have died of shame. I couldn't stand there and —' He was almost raving.

'Twice, be quiet at once! Sit *down*, I tell you! You'll make yourself ill with that cursed temper of yours.' He sank into a chair, his hands gripping the arms of it until the knuckle bones gleamed white through the tanned skin.

'The dirty —'

'Twice!'

'Sorry, darling. You're right. Call to Cook for some tea.'

'She's not there. None of them are.' I suddenly knew where the servants were, where all the transport and field workers were. 'They have all run away to listen to Kevin Lindsay.'

We stared at one another again, silent except for the bronchial wheezing from Twice's lungs.

'I am going to make the tea,' I said. 'Will you be all right?'

'Darling, I'm sorry. Of course I'm all right. I'll come to the kitchen with you. To hell with these bloody Negroes. We'll make our own tea!'

We made the tea, came back to the veranda with the tray and before we could sit down the factory siren blew.

'What's that?' I asked Twice over the tray I was holding.

He raised his arm and looked at his watch. 'Ten to eleven. It's taken Kevin Lindsay exactly thirty-five minutes to bring four thousand men out on strike. That's what that is. Oh well, darling, pour us out a cup of tea.'


5


THE next day, Twice went down with the worst attack of bronchitis I had yet seen, although he had been subject to such attacks ever since he had caught influenza when we were on leave in Scotland two years before. This time, however, when the estate doctor, a kind and clever young East Indian who had replaced the old European doctor a few months before, examined him, he said: 'This is not only chest trouble, Mrs Alexander. There is a malarial complication.'

'Malaria? Twice has never had malaria!'

'This high fever, this fit of ague you told me about — these mean malaria.'

I swallowed. 'What do we do?'

'I have given him an injection. The fever should come down shortly. Try not to worry.'

I tried not to worry; I tried very hard but I am a miserable weakling and coward in the face of illness and I crept about the house like a frightened rabbit, unable to keep away from the screened door of the bedroom where Twice lay. Even when he was asleep and there was a risk of waking him, I tiptoed to and fro, watching him, listening to his breathing, panic-stricken.

The servants had come back the day before half-shamefaced, half-defiant about their defection and they too crept about, bullied by me into terror of making the slightest noise and also uneasy because the peaceful tenor of their household routine had been broken and also suffering, like everyone else on the estate, from the uncanny silence that seemed to spread in active waves from the closed-down factory. I always remember those first four days of Twice's illness as a brilliant, glaring silence under the merciless sun.

On the fifth day, though, the terrible post-fever weakness abated and at the same time his breathing became much easier.

'Want a boiled egg,' he announced in the morning as I sponged him.

'Splendid, darling.'

'How the blazes did I come to get malaria?'

'Goodness knows.'

'Of course, why you and I should think we are immune when everybody else in the island has it is another matter.'

'That's true, I suppose.'

'Of the two, I'd rather have the malaria than the bronk — with malaria you can at least breathe.'

'Stop chatting,' I said. 'I am going down to see to your breakfast.'

'When can I get up?'

'*Shut* up.'

'Oh, all right.' He caught at my hand and looked up at me with solemn blue eyes from the pillow. 'Darling, I'm sorry to be a nuisance. I know you hate people to be sick.'

I looked down at him, his towel and sponge in my hands. I wanted to burst into tears but I knew that I must not. 'You are not a nuisance, Twice,' I said with difficulty.

'Sorry. I put that badly. Look, sit down for a moment.'

I sat down on the edge of the bed and he took hold of my hand. 'Listen, Janet, anybody can get a touch of malaria. Ninety-nine per cent of the people in this island have it in them. Rob Maclean has a go of it every other month. Madame has had it since she was twenty years old. Why do you look as if the world were coming to an end because I have had a go?'

I looked down at the sponge in my hand. 'It isn't only the fact that it's malaria, Twice. It's just the very fact of illness – it's a sort of phobia I've got, I suppose. I think it comes right down from my childhood. Nobody at Reachfar was ever ill except my mother. She used to have headaches; not go to church when it was cold or wet. She had delicate health but I did not understand that. All I knew was that the people in the village always seemed to be asking how she was and I used to be defiant about telling them she was very well. Then, suddenly, she died. Ever since then I have felt that illness is something that creeps up behind you and strikes when you least expect it. I get a haunted panic-stricken feeling when anybody is ill, a feeling that there is no telling what the end may be. It is not that I can't or don't want to do the things that have to be done for them' – I glanced at the bowl of water and the tooth-glass on the chair – 'I like doing the things, especially for you. But I am haunted all the time in a morbid way, as if there was a spectre behind me, the spectre of sickness which I just don't understand. Darling, it's all silly and you shouldn't be making me talk to you like this.'

'It isn't silly and I think it may help you to have talked about it. But we have to get the spectral thing out of it. After all, a human body is a sort of machine – a very complex delicately-balanced one at that. The more delicate and complex a machine is, the more easily it goes wrong. A malaria bug can't do much to a wheelbarrow which is a machine of sorts, but it can make a hell of a mess of Twice Alexander.'

'Twice, what a fool you are!'

'That's not entirely foolish, my pet. It brings out in a crude way the point I want to make which is that there isn't a ghost in the house because I've had what the Negroes call a chill and a fever. What has happened is that an anopheles

130

mosquito has flown quietly up to me and stuck his proboscis into me and injected some poison into my machinery, that's all. And fortunately the doctors know the antidote for it. Now, please go away and flush your ghosts down the loo along with that bowl of soapy water and ask them to bring me some breakfast. And is there anything new to read in this blasted house?'

Twice was a fairly reasonable patient as long as there was plenty to read, but reading matter was one thing that was scarce in the lavishly fruitful island of St Jago. There were no bookshops as such at that time. Some of the Chinese grocers carried among their stocks a small rack of very bloody, thunderous and sex-ridden paper-backed novels imported from the United States, but that was all. The Great House had a library of leatherbound classics which had not been opened for the last fifty years; some of the staff houses could produce the odd novel that had been sent from home at a birthday or Christmas; our own house had more books than any other on the estate but Twice, of course, had read them all and many of them more than once. We were dependent on the mail bringing weekly and monthly supplies of magazines from home, together with the few new books we had ordered, for even the only public library in the island, situated in St Jago Bay, could produce from its scanty shelves little that Twice had not already read.

He was in bed for three weeks altogether, for his temperature kept rising a little as each day crept on towards evening which, the doctor said, was a typical malarial reaction. But for the slight variation in temperature, he was very well and growing more and more impatient with every day that passed and I was glad and grateful to welcome every one of the many visitors who came to the house.

For the first ten days, Sir Ian and Rob Maclean could not come very often for the factory was still standing idle while protracted examination of the sucrose content reports went on, and round the estate there was a constant tension which mounted as Kevin Lindsay's inspiring speech faded in the volatile memories of the Negroes, especially after their first full week of idleness when there was no pay packet to collect

131

on Friday. At this stage, the centre of enmity shifted, as it were, and feeling was no longer directed from the labour against the management of Paradise but from the Paradise men against the men of Cambuskenneth, and there were sporadic outbreaks of fighting and near-rioting between the two factions.

'It can't take all this time,' Twice said impatiently from his bed to Sir Ian and Rob, 'to examine a few sucrose reports and cane samples! What are those arbitrating blokes *doing* up there in the lab?'

'As little as possible,' Rob told him. 'They know the records are all right but they don't want to get on the wrong side of Lindsay. They are all government boys in cushy jobs and Lindsay carries a lot of voting weight.'

'Let them take their time,' Sir Ian said. 'Give the whole perishin' lot time to cool their heels. But if they don't get through before the start o' June, Rob, we'll stick up a notice sayin' we're closed down till next Crop. I ain't goin' on millin' into July an' August – the cane won't be worth a damn. All the juice'll have run back down to the roots.'

Other visitors who came were Freda and her fiancé, Tommy Miller, but in spite of my best efforts, it was a restrained meeting between Freda and me while we sat downstairs and Tommy talked to Twice in the bedroom above. I congratulated her on her engagement; we talked about the St Jago Bay office, Ginger Grove and various other things but the conversation was broken by marked silences and each one of them reminded me of that silence on the day that the factory closed down, the day that Twice's illness had begun. In the curious and tortuous way that the human mind works, for I do not think that my own mind is unique in this, Kevin Lindsay was enmeshed in my thoughts not only with the strike at the factory but with Twice's illness, and with the best will in the world I could not forget Freda's blood relationship with this man who, to me, had about him the aura of a genius of evil.

'It is silly and pathetic,' I said to Twice after she and Tommy had gone, 'pathetic and silly. My reason knows that Kevin Lindsay had nothing to do with your getting ill; my reason knows that he is a lot older than Freda and that he

132

stands off from the rest of the family and she is no closer to him than the man in the moon. He hardly ever goes to Ginger Grove or sees the rest of the family. And Freda knows that I know he is a renegade from the rest of them. But all these things we know with our reason don't make any difference. His shadow lies between us now.'

'I know. And the shadow reaches out and colours all sorts of things round about,' Twice said. 'When the factory is started up again, there's going to be lots of bother. You can't close down a plant like that with a bang and do the equipment any good. Rob and I are going to be cursing Kevin Lindsay every hour of every day for a month and it won't do any good. It will only add to the ill-will floating about the world but we won't be able to help it. And when Miller was up here this afternoon, I found myself looking at him. I hadn't noticed before how fair and blue-eyed he is. And I found myself wondering: How *can* you marry one of them? I wasn't thinking of Mrs Miller, a woman I know and like. I was thinking of "one of them", of the same kind as Kevin Lindsay. I wonder what Miller's mother feels about it all?'

'I don't know,' I said. 'I haven't seen her since the engagement. One of the children has been sick, of course, so that would have kept her at home. I must go down and see about your supper, darling.'

'Oh, all right, but don't be long. Janet, isn't there *any*thing to read? I'm getting up tomorrow and to hell with the doctor! A little over ninety-nine isn't a temperature at all and I think I'm generating it from sheer boredom anyway.'

'I sent for that new book you wanted on steam regeneration – I cabled to Jock to send it by air —'

'That thing will cost a fortune by air, you idiot!'

'I can't help it. Anyway, it hasn't come —'

'Jock probably had a fit in the post office, you fool!'

'I'm not a fool, Twice Alexander! And anything is better than you getting into a frenzy of boredom and —'

'I'm not in a frenzy!'

'Stop shouting!'

'Stop shouting yourself! That's no way to go on in a sickroom,' he ended smugly.

133

There were no books in the mail the next day either and Twice lay in sulky impatient silence while I sponged him at mid-day.

'There you are,' I said, drying his back and shaking some talcum powder over it.

'What's that stink you're putting on me?'

'It's very manly. It's called Spice of Seven Seas. It's a present from Madame.'

'Spice of my Aunt Fanny! I smell like a wedding-cake. Wipe it off!'

'Twice, your skin will get sore if we don't put powder on you and it's beautifully fine powder and not a bad smell.'

'You could put a pink ribbon in my hair while you're at it,' he said sourly. 'I'll stay here today until that doctor comes and not one minute longer.'

'Darling, try to be patient a little longer. The newspaper will soon be here and maybe there will be some magazines in the afternoon mail.'

There were no magazines in the mail but the afternoon brought an unexpected visitor in the form of Mrs Miller of Hope, a visitor whose coming delighted me and made me very grateful, for I knew that only real friendship for us could have brought her on to the ground of Paradise.

'This is most terribly kind of you,' I said, 'and I appreciate it in every possible way.'

'I had hoped to come sooner,' she said, 'but what with cows calving and one thing and another. How is he?'

'Nearly better. He will be getting up in a day or two and I'll be more than thankful. It's nearly impossible to keep him amused.' Down the staircase floated the strains of Beethoven's Fifth Symphony. 'The young engineers came round from the factory and moved his record-player up there,' I explained, 'and that has helped a lot. You can hardly get into the bedroom with books and stuff but will you come up?'

We went upstairs and Mrs Miller laid a large flat package she was carrying on Twice's lap on the bed. 'I seem to have brought the right thing,' she said. 'It may seem rather an odd choice but the girl at Orrett's kept saying "Mr Alexander

134

already has that record" until I thought I'd go mad. However, she said that lot came in only yesterday.'

Twice opened his package and exposed an album of gramophone records.

'The *Messiah*! Mrs Miller, how splendid – thank you very much. Janet, look, what a wonderful present!'

'As I said, it is an odd choice perhaps but you did once tell me that you liked the sound of the human voice as much as any instrument,' Mrs Miller said.

'And you remembered?' Twice smiled at her and then looked down at the album. 'And you have even got one of my most favourite human voices – Kathleen Malone. I'm going to have a splendid time with this lot. It takes me right back to the first music I ever heard. Every Easter, our County Choir used to do *Messiah* and when I was six I was taken to hear it and after that I went every year until the choir broke up. You couldn't have brought me anything I could like more, Mrs Miller.'

'We might as well go downstairs,' I said. 'He's dying to play these records,' and before we were well out of the room the first notes of the oratorio were coming from the player. 'He might as well be up, really, with the amount of energy he expends reaching out to the player and loading himself down with books but the doctor says he is less likely to get a chill if he stays in bed. Mrs Miller, I *am* glad to see you!'

She could not stay for very long but her short visit did me more good than all the other visitors who had come to see Twice because I found her so completely sympathetic. She seemed to think in terms similar to myself, to work by similar mental symbols, so that two words spoken between us conveyed as much as fifty exchanged with any other person. And, of course, there was her interest in Reachfar and its people which made her say: 'And how are George and Tom?' almost as soon as she had sat down in the drawing-room. 'I enjoyed so much that letter where you told me about the road-block they made during the war. But then I enjoy all your letters. You have a gift for letter-writing.'

'It comes from lots of practice. I left home to go to work when I was twenty-one and I have written to my father every week from then until now except for the short spells when I have been on holiday at home. I suppose that is another reason why Reachfar stays so close to me always.'

'And how are your mosquito bites after your visit to the St Jagoan Reachfar at Ginger Grove?' she asked with the humorous light in her blue eyes.

'They are better now but I itched for about a fortnight.'

'I did laugh at that letter of yours, Janet. You were so rueful at all your diplomacy being ruined by a cloud of mosquitoes.'

'It's not a laughing matter, really,' I told her. 'It's typical of what this island seems to do to me. Just when I feel I am coming to terms with it, it pounces on me with some dreadful secret weapon.'

We gossiped together for about an hour, then she went up to see Twice again and then she had to leave.

'It was very very good of you to come,' I said as she got into her car. 'I know that you don't like coming here.'

She smiled. 'Well, it did take Twice's being ill to bring me and I don't promise to make a habit of it. As you yourself once said to me, we all carry our past about with us and when I get to the Paradise gates I suddenly seem to feel a ball and chain come out of the past and attach itself to my ankles. Take care of Twice and drive along to Hope as soon as Crop is over.'

On the day after Twice got up for the first time, the siren blew and work re-started at the factory. The strike had fizzled out, bringing no benefit to anyone but a detriment to Paradise by the delay in cropping which entailed a considerable loss of sugar, for cane reaches a peak of sucrose content when ripe and if cut too late this rich sap flows back down the stems into the root of the plant again.

'Well, we've lost a ton or two. I suppose Lindsay is pleased,' Sir Ian said.

'Is he ever pleased?' Twice asked. 'God, how he raved that day!'

'Ravin' is right, me boy. He don't make a damn o' sense half the time but he carries the mob every time. It's sort o' sickenin' to see him doin' it, Missis Janet.'

'It made Twice sick all right.'

136

'Oh, well, he'll leave us alone for a bit now,' Sir Ian went on. 'I see he's down at the port creatin' hell among the dock workers next. Still, the harm's done. All the men have lost a good bit o' pay; these Cambuskenneth men are still lookin' for a grievance an' the sugar producers at the meetin' yesterday passed a resolution abolishin' Crop-over celebrations. We are to pay the workers a small cash bonus on the tonnage instead. Mother's fit to be tied. Says the island's goin' to the devil. Maybe she's right at that. When you comin' round to see her, Missis Janet?'

I looked at Twice. 'Any time now that this one is on his feet again.'

'She's been missin' you. Haven't been many people comin' about either. Sue Beaton ain't been up since that day I gave her the tickin'-off about Miller an' that girl o' yours, Twice, gettin' engaged, an' Mrs Miller ain't been up either, probably because *she*'s frightened about what Mother will say about the engagement an' I don't blame her. By the way, I wonder what Mrs Miller herself thinks about it? You seen her?'

'No,' I said. 'Karen, the little girl, was sick. Freda Miller told me that and of course Twice was sick and I'm afraid I haven't been thinking much about anything outside Guinea Corner here. I suppose Mrs Miller feels a bit three-cornered about the engagement too. After all, it's a pretty queer thing to happen in the life of somebody like her, when you think of it.'

'It's a queer thing to happen in the life o' anybody. Only there's no good goin' on about it the way Sue an' Mother were goin' on that day round at the house.' He gave a sudden shout of laughter. 'By Jove, Twice, did Missis Janet tell you about old Andy that day, standin' up to Sue? You could have knocked me down with a perishin' feather – never known it to happen in me life before.'

# 6

Very soon, Twice was going up to the factory for an hour – and staying for two, of course – and then he was going up for the whole forenoon and then he was back to normal, rushing off to the Bay and further points every day at his usual breakneck speed, and the routine of Guinea Corner settled into its stride again.

One day, I was very pleased to see Mrs Miller from the Manse getting out of her car at the door.

'Hi, there!' I greeted her. 'No children today?'

'I left them down at Ginger Grove. How are you, Janet? And how is Twice?'

'Completely better, thanks. He is away over at the other end of the island today. Come in. Mrs Miller, it seems a lifetime since I saw you! How is little Karen?'

'Och, she's all right. To tell you the truth, there was never much wrong with her but you know what grannies are. It was just a kind of cold and a nasty wee cough and she was kind of fractious with it, you know.'

I left her for a moment to go to the kitchen to ask for tea to be brought in and when I came back she looked at me very directly out of her gentle eyes and said: 'I'd have been up to see you before, Janet, but – well, I wasn't sure what you would think about Tommy and Freda.'

The words and the look on her face were so forthright and honest that I felt I must take care to reply in kind. 'I was taken by surprise at first, Mrs Miller,' I said. 'I've been living here at Paradise for a year or two now and one can't help – at least I can't help – being influenced by where I live and by people around me. Madame and Sir Ian belong to the old island-white tradition and I learned to think a bit as they did. That's why I was surprised and even a little shocked to begin with but that's a lot of nonsense, really, when you come down to hard facts.' Her gentle eyes looked up at me and she listened intently as I spoke. 'Freda is a fine young woman and your Tommy is a fine young man and I honestly and truly hope that they will be very happy.'

'That's very good of you, Janet.'

'When is the wedding to be?' I asked in an attempt to break the intensity of feeling that seemed to lie between us.

'They haven't settled anything yet. It's been hard for them. There has been a lot of trouble, one way and another.'

'I am sorry about that. Trouble about their engagement, you mean? I am very sorry. But you yourself are quite happy about it, aren't you?'

'Well, I've got used to the idea now, Janet. Not that I made any of the trouble. I told Tommy right from the start that it was his own life and he would have to live it his own way, but I don't mind telling you I was real taken aback when he first told me he wanted to marry Freda. It's a funny thing. I liked her and her family and Mama Lou and I never thought a thing about them being black people until Tommy said he wanted to marry Freda. And then it came over me. It was quite a shock, like you said. I don't know why it should be but it was.'

I gave her a cup of tea. I saw that now that she had come to Guinea Corner and had begun to talk to me about this thing, she would not stop until she had talked herself out. She wiped away a tear from the side of one eye as she took her cup from me.

'I wish I had come to see you long ago, Janet,' she said next, 'but Karen was sick and then you had Twice in bed and time went past and I thought maybe you would be like all the rest. I wouldn't blame you if you were but it doesn't do any good, them all going on like that.'

'Who? Going on like what?'

'Miss Beaton and the rest of them – the white people down in the Bay there. White people I hardly know are looking sorry for me, as if they want to offer me their sympathy. I don't want their sympathy for anything my Tommy does!'

'What absolute nonsense! You ought to tell them to mind their own business.'

She smiled a little shakily. 'I couldn't do that. They mean to be kind. And I know it seems funny, Tommy marrying a black girl, but people know their own way best. It's wrong to interfere with them. I know that better than anybody.' She paused, drank some tea and then looked at me out of her pretty blue eyes. 'Being from Achcraggan,' she said then, 'you'll know all the story about me.'

'What story?' I asked. 'I wasn't around Achcraggan much after I was ten years old.'

'I've always thought you knew,' she said. 'When I was young, I left Tommy's father. I didn't know that Tommy was on the way then or I might have thought twice about it. Still, I don't know if I would. It's hard to think at all when things go sore against you. Tommy – my boy's father, that is – and I lived at Dinchory and his mother lived down at Achcraggan. She was a widow and Tommy was her only son and he was always delicate – something in his lungs – that's why he wasn't at the war, the first war, I mean. After we were married, his mother just wouldn't leave us in peace. She was for ever in our house, managing and criticizing and she was saying all kinds of things about me to anybody who would listen. Och, it's all gey silly when you look back on it and no more than an old song now, and the poor old soul was lonely and missing her laddie round his home but I was young and not very patient and in the end it came to it and I left the house one night in a temper. Then there was a German fellow at the prison camp – he used to come out to work with the wood-cutters – Fred Wessler, his name was. It was Friedrich by rights, but I called him Fred. He was nice to me and I wasn't very happy. I went for a walk with him once or twice and then the gossip started. I'm telling you about this for a reason, Janet. You'll see it in a minute. When I knew the baby was coming, I tried to go back to Tommy. It was Tommy I wanted, you know, not Fred Wessler, but old Mrs Miller wouldn't let Tommy take me back. The upshot was that I went away with Fred. Fred was good to me, good to me every day until he died and he was good to my son too. For years, till he was twelve, Tommy thought Fred was his father. In 1918, when the war ended, Fred had to go back to Germany but he left me in London and I took in sewing and I managed until he could get back. Then, later on, he was naturalized and became British. But this is what I am coming to – Fred was a good man and he'd be alive now but it was folk being down on him for being a German that just broke his health and his heart. He'd be in a job and doing well and somebody would find out about it and the trouble would start. We were never left in peace. Oh, well, that's all a long time ago now. But maybe you can see why I would never interfere between my son and the woman he wants and why I would never hate anybody for not being Scotch like myself.'

'Yes, Mrs Miller, I see. And thank you for telling me. I can only say again that I hope Freda and Tommy will be happy. What are your own plans? Will you stay here or go back to Scotland?'

'I don't know yet. I won't stay at the manse with *them* after they're married. That's for certain. I had enough of that myself with my own Tommy's mother.'

'But Mrs Miller, you are a very different person from old Mrs Miller at Achcraggan. She was a terribly sour old woman!'

'Sour or not, no young couple should be cumbered with an old granny round the place.'

'Old granny your foot! Have some more tea. I tell you what, you'll have to take a job of some kind or get married again.'

'Married? Me? Who'd look at *me*? And anyway, maybe I've had enough of that. Not that I was married to Fred. I wasn't. Tommy would never divorce me.'

'That is the wickedest thing in the world!' I said.

'Oh, who's to say what's wicked? Tommy wasn't wicked but he was weak. He couldn't help that. People can't help the way they are born.'

'Is he still alive?'

'No. He lived just a year longer than Fred. When I was up at Achcraggan just before we came out here, I went to see his grave.'

All the strain and reserve that had been in her when she arrived was gone and her face and voice now had a mellow serenity that seemed to glow outwards from her mind, like light coming from a pool of shining hard-won wisdom.

'I think it's likely,' she said, 'that we'll all go back to Scotland in the end. Freda is thinking of the schools and the

141

wonderful chance for the bairns, and Tommy – well, Tommy came out here in a fit of restlessness after Karen died but he says now that the day of the white ministers here is done. There's no need for them, he says. The black people have their own ministers and I think maybe he is right.'

'So do I.'

'I don't know whether you know, but before we came out here, Jack Lindsay, Freda's brother, had put in for Fontabelle Church and it was given to Tommy over his head, as you might say. When I first met him down at Mama Lou's he was quite kind of huffy about it so I just said to him: I don't see how you can blame Tommy for being here, I said. After all, one of you had to get it and he happens to be the one and you'd do far more good for the church if the two of you got together, I said. Maybe Tommy knows a few things you don't, I told him, and I am sure you know an awful lot more about this island than Tommy does. So then I just made him walk up to the manse with me and the two of them got on like a house on fire.'

Everything, to Mrs Miller, was so simple that she made me so that I could only sit amazed while she chatted on about Mama Lou, the astounding success of the Ginger Grove potato crop, the Beatons, and how she had made Mars Andy 'stop wearing that great big old-fashioned helmet thing'.

'You'll just go and get yourself a nice panama hat with a black ribbon round it and go about looking like a gentleman, I said, instead of one of these men that run the messages for the banks down in the Bay.'

'And has he?' I asked, fascinated.

'Has he what?'

'Got a panama hat?'

'Of course! All Andy needs is a little encouragement instead of being bullied uphill and down dale by that Miss Sue all the time. Och, she's not a bad old soul. Just a bit spoilt like so many of the white women out here. They've just never had enough to do, never *any*thing to do except shout at the black people and lay down the law. . . . What's all that I read in the paper about there being a strike at Paradise?'

I told her in outline how the stoppage had come about.

'Is that not terrible!' she said. 'That man Kevin's the proper black sheep of that family – my goodness, I should say white sheep for he's lighter in the skin than any of them.'

'You've met him then?'

'Just the once. He came marching into the manse one night just after we started work on the church and starting getting on to Tommy about the rates he was paying the masons. Jack and Josh were there, in the study, but Tommy was through in the pantry with me at the time and this Kevin comes marching in through the front door and right through to the back of the house as bold as brass. *We* didn't know who he was from Adam but before you could say knife Josh comes in and there was a proper set-to. Josh fairly gave him what-for for sticking his nose in where he wasn't wanted and in the end – you know the size Josh is – more like a gorilla than a man as I always tell him – Josh threatened to throw him through the pantry window.'

'And what happened then?'

'Oh, nothing. He just went away. But I didn't know *he* was the cause of the strike here. I don't read that island paper much – too many murders in it. If I'd known it was Kevin that was making the trouble, I'd have got Josh to take a run up.'

Being Mrs Miller's solution, it would surely have been effective I thought, and it was certainly very simple, so I said with all sincerity: 'I'll suggest to Sir Ian that he sends for Josh next time.'

'Sir Ian! How is he? Now that's a real nice old gentleman if you like. You know he always minds me on old Sir Turk at Poyntdale, the late Sir Torquil's father, you know.'

Mrs Miller chatted contentedly along and by the time she went away I felt that I had spent the afternoon at my home at Reachfar.

CROPOVER, as the end of the sugar-milling season was called in St Jago, had been hitherto one of the peaks of the Paradise year, the other peak being Christmas, but it was part of the disintegration of the mythical quality that Paradise and its people had had for me that this traditional festival was on the wane. A year before, at the 1952 celebration, I had been conscious of a hollow ring behind the gaiety and although there had been the usual lavish supper and dance, the spirit of Cropover – or Harvest Home as I thought of it – was no longer abroad. This was a spirit which I thought I could recognize for, at the age of eight, I had attended a Harvest Home at Poyntdale, and the feeling of pride in work well done to the profit of all coupled with humble gratitude to God for the good harvest was something I had never forgotten. That Harvest Home at Poyntdale was the last in the old tradition that was ever held there, for the Great War had introduced a new economic order and it was strange and haunting to see history repeat itself at Paradise in midsummer of 1953. A new order was here too, a new order that was inevitable but, as Twice had once said, the inevitable can be very hard to accept when it overtakes us.

In this year of 1953, the siren began to blow for the end of Crop at about eleven in the forenoon, a few of the older millhands played a tattoo on the siren as was their tradition for about an hour and then silence fell over the valley while the men read the notices posted on the factory gates to the effect that their 'Crop Bonus' would be paid to them on the following Friday, after which they drifted away to their homes.

Madame had asked us of the European staff to come to the Great House for a drink when the siren began to blow and Twice, who had been up at the factory, drove down to Guinea Corner to pick me up. We drove the little way to the Great House while the siren sent its ululating note across the valley and away up the steep chasms and gullies of the surrounding hills.

'It doesn't sound gay today,' I said. 'It sounds like a sort of Last Post for the death of the old order.'

'Or a reveille for a new order,' Twice said. 'It had to come, Janet. We are lucky here at Paradise that it came so smoothly and we are not the only ones who are sorry that the old order has gone. I've been talking to a lot of the older hands today while we were running the mills down and they said that "New Paradise" as they call the factory now should have had a Cropover to celebrate the increased tonnage, but they voted for the bonus. They can't have it both ways. I pointed out to them that the increase in the tonnage wasn't worth celebrating after the loss of milling time in the strike.'

'How did they take that?'

Twice smiled a little. 'They sort of grinned at me, shrugged their shoulders and looked away. The strike is something that "happened" as they put it — not something they did. All it has got them is a smaller tonnage bonus but they don't think of that either. It happened and there it is. There is nothing to be done about it. They've got a sort of passivity — there's heat, there's rain, there's hurricane and strikes. You accept them all.'

'They weren't passive when it came to striking.'

'That was after Kevin Lindsay gave them a shot in the arm. That strike had no more meaning with most of them than getting drunk on pay-night and creating a bit of mayhem around the village. . . . Well, here we are. Get your pecker up. The old lady will be feeling this more than any of us.'

But if Madame was feeling depressed about the new order at Paradise, she did not show it as she sat on the long broad veranda in her high-backed chair, laying down the law to her staff as firmly and positively as ever.

'There you are, Janet,' she greeted me. 'Come over here and sit down. I was just telling the ladies that everybody has a right to celebrate everything in their own way and it is no use pulling long faces about this Crop Bonus instead of having a proper Cropover. But I am old-fashioned and I should like to have a party as usual, and we can arrange for the young people to dance in the drawing-room here just as well as we can do at the Club. Now, while we are all together, Janet, just go to my desk and get some of that large paper and let us make out a list.' When I came back with the foolscap, she continued: 'Now, Mr Mackie and all you young engineers and chemists, who are your special young ladies for my Cropover party?'

Mackie, a very shy young Scot, at once seemed to grow into nothing but hands and feet under that piercing if poor-sighted eye.

'Well, actually, Madame —'

'Oh, rubbish, Mr Mackie! Don't hum and haw! What about that pretty little red-haired Miss Selby? Janet, put down Miss Selby's name anyhow. Charming girl. Time she was married.'

I wrote down 'Miss Carol Selby' and Madame bullied her way round the rest of the unmarried staff and generally round the island.

'An' Sue an' Andy Beaton, Mother,' said Sir Ian. 'An' the Millers – pretty little woman.'

'Oh yes, Janet, Sue and Andy Beaton – we mustn't forget *them*. And Mrs Miller from the manse and her son —'

Madame stopped in mid-career. My pen stopped at the 'M' of Miller. The glasses of the staff stopped in mid-air on their way up or down. All the insect noises in the garden stopped too. Sir Ian, from his place among the group of men round the table that held the drinks, looked down the long veranda at Madame and she, who had laid her glass aside and was holding the carved arms of her chair in beringed little hands, looked towards him and away beyond him over the wide cane-fields to the far-off hills. After what seemed to be a long time, she spoke into the silence: 'Janet, we had got to the Millers, I think. Please put down Mrs Miller, her son and Mrs Freda Miller, his fiancée. Now, let us go on to the people from the Bay. Mr Sashie, of course, and Mr Don —' My pencil moved over the paper, everybody began to talk at once, ice began to chink in the glasses again and the wind rose, rustling the sun-dried papery petals of the bougainvillaea flowers, but history had been made. A coloured woman had been invited as a guest to the Great House of Paradise.

When Twice and I went home to Guinea Corner, the whole

146

valley was very silent for the siren had stopped blowing now and all the workers had gone home to their villages. This silence would lie over Paradise until Monday of the next week when the maintenance work on the factory plant would begin all over again in preparation for the next Crop. There seemed to be nothing to say for the strange reason that the little event on the Great House veranda had been so terribly big and significant. It was something that we had, literally, never expected to see or hear in our lifetime and we could not get it into perspective straight away.

'Would you like to go out anywhere now that we are off the chain?' Twice asked me after lunch.

'Not specially, darling, thank you. It's terribly hot. I think I'd rather just write home to Reachfar unless *you* want to go somewhere.'

'Not me. I must be getting old. I just want to put my feet up for the afternoon. Will my records disturb you if I play some?'

'Of course not. Play away.'

His record-player had now been restored to its position in a corner of the drawing-room and while I sat down at my writing table he opened the cabinet and began to arrange a pile of discs on the spindle. I began to write my letter.

'Dear George and Tom, Although it is bright hot sun outside, today at Paradise makes me think of that grey day at Reachfar after the last Harvest Home at Poyntdale – the day that you two sent me into the kitchen to steal the black-strippit balls from the jar in the kitchen press. You see, there is to be no Cropover Party here this year —'

I looked out of the window and across the lawn, remembering, and I became conscious of the tenor voice from the record-player that was filling the room: 'Every valley shall be exalted and every mountain and hill made low —'

# PART THREE

## ' – The Crooked Straight and the Rough Places Plain'

### 1

MADAME'S Cropover Party, even in its diminished form, marked the high noon of the cycle of the Paradise year, as if it were a gay luncheon party in the middle of a long day and, as soon as it was over, the disintegration of early afternoon began, as all the guests moved off in different directions to go about their business. There was the customary exodus of part of the staff towards Britain; others were leaving for cottages by the sea or in the hills; the manse Millers, Freda and the four children were going up to a mountain coffee plantation owned by an uncle of Freda's, and Mrs Miller of Hope was leaving for the United States on a round of visits to her son, daughter and other friends there. Twice and I now began to look forward to our month of August at High Hope.

In past years, we had either been on our way to Britain during August or Twice had been very busy with the work on the expansion of the factory, so that never before had we had a prolonged holiday together in the island. We looked forward to lolling about in the cool air of the hills with the plentiful supply of books we had ordered from London and to seeing as few people as we could.

'It sounds selfish,' I said, 'but life in St Jago gets terribly cluttered up with people, somehow. It makes me think of Ginger Grove where you can't turn round without stepping on a baby that's crawling about or bumping into someone enormous like Sister Flo or Josh. I suppose it's part of the general fecundity of this island.'

'It's not that one doesn't like people,' Twice said, joining with me in excusing ourselves for near-misanthropy, 'but one gets a feeling of being rioted over and half-smothered as if one had got lost in a quick-growing jungle of personalities and situations. By the way, Freda and Miller hope to get married about the end of September. She told me yesterday when I was down at the office.'

'I wonder if they will go back home afterwards?'

'I shouldn't be surprised. Anyway, she is leaving the office at the end of the month when I go on leave. It's a nuisance but that's only my point of view. Talking of points of view, isn't it extraordinary how everybody has come round to the mixed marriage? If you go back to this time last year, it would have been unthinkable.'

'You can't go back to this time last year,' I said, 'and once a thing has been thought it can never be unthinkable again. But it is a big step forward in thought for someone like Madame in the course of a single year – to have accepted it, I mean.'

'And having forced other people to accept it.' Twice laughed. 'Madame was absolutely gunning for old Miss Sue at the Cropover party. She hardly let the poor thing open her mouth.'

'If the Millers all go back home at the end of the year, the person I am going to feel sorry for is Mars Andy. He is a new person since Mrs Miller came to the island.'

'Mrs Miller has a tonic effect all round,' Twice said thoughtfully. 'A queer sort of look comes into Sir Ian's eye when he sees her.'

'What do you mean?' I asked.

'He stops blimping and blasting and gets sort of splooshy-looking as if he were hearing Christmas bells across the snow instead of the usual trumpet call to battle that haunts his ears. I suppose a man of Sir Ian's age *could* fall in love still?'

'With Sir Ian, anything could happen,' I said with conviction, 'but can you sort of see Mrs Miller at the Great House? I can't, somehow. For me, her background is a little two-storey stone house in Scotland, not a tropical mansion.'

'That's only an outcrop of Reachfar rock in your mind. If Mrs Miller were called to be châtelaine of a tropical mansion,

149

I'm sure she could do it. She seems to be able to rise to whatever happens to her, whether it's fair or foul, as easily as some trim broad-beamed canal boat going up or down through a series of locks. That's what she always makes me think of. Well, three more days and we'll be off on this leave. By Jove, I'm looking forward to it. And I expect all sorts of things from it, too.'

'What sort of things?'

'You to put on some weight for one thing. It'll be cool up there, you'll be able to get out and walk and I hope your appetite will get better.'

'Stop going on as if I were a delicate invalid! Come to that, I'm not the one that gets bronchitis and malaria and everything. What I am wondering is what Caleb is going to think of it. They were all mad keen to go when I gave them the choice of coming with us or going home or staying here for a month but Caleb is the only one who has stuck to his guns. The three women have dropped out. I suppose it must be a bit of a thing if you have spent your whole life in Paradise Valley with an odd trip to the Bay now and then to be going 'way up in de bush as they call it. I think Cook and Clorinda and Minna think we are mad and that Caleb is mad to come with us.'

It was much easier to get to High Hope than to Craigellachie Heights, although the distance from Guinea Corner to the former was much greater and even the last seven miles of rough track through the bush, after we left the Central Highway, were not so bad as the road to the Heights. And, of course, High Hope was much farther from sea-level than Craigellachie Heights.

When we got out of the car at the side of the little fenced garden, Twice shook his head violently from side to side, then held his nose and tried to blow down it. 'That's better,' he said then. 'That last mile up the Central Highway made my ears pop like fun. How are *your* big ears, Dram?'

Dram and Charlie seemed to have no trouble with their ears and sped off to inspect their new environment without more ado while Caleb, Twice and I unloaded the car and explored the cottage which had been locked up on the day I visited it. It had tremendous picturesque charm but it was, as the picturesque so often is, extremely primitive as Mrs Miller had warned me it was, and Twice was at once fascinated by the water supply. This consisted of three large oil drums set at different levels on a trestle arrangement against the outside of one wall. Into the highest – or was it the lowest? – of these there came a piece of pipe out of the hill immediately above the house and out of the lowest – or was it the highest? – there came another piece of pipe in through the bathroom window and ended in a tap. In the bathroom, hanging from the ceiling, was a four-gallon petrol tin with two bottoms in it, one with holes and one without holes and this last one slid to and fro. The technique of bathing was to put the bottom without the holes into the shut position, fill the can with water from the tap by the medium of a large chipped enamel jug, soap yourself all over with the aid of a handful of water from the tap and then slide the petrol-tin-bottom-without-the-holes to the open position, whereupon you were deluged and rinsed down with ice-cold water from above. This water now ran away through a hole in the floor at the lower side of the house, straight out into a flourishing bed of roses.

The other piece of equipment in this bathroom was what *The Island Sun* advertised as a low-down water-closet, which meant that the cistern was immediately behind the seat and worked by pressing a lever instead of being high-up and operated by pulling a chain. This cistern had a slight variation from the norm, however, in that its lid had been discarded and it had to be filled by hand from the enamel jug which first had to be filled from the tap. After that, you pressed the lever in the usual way. From underneath, a pipe went out through the wall but I never took the trouble to trace its course to its conclusion. On the wall behind the cistern, there was a notice, gaily decorated with painted poinsettia flowers in red and lettered in black which said: 'We call it good manners to leave this cistern full, NOT EMPTY.'

The organization of the cottage was extraordinarily complete, however. It had four bedrooms in all, two on each side of a central living-room, and when we explored them we were a little disconcerted to see bedsteads but no mattresses or bedding. It was Caleb who discovered that all the mattresses, pillows, linen and blankets were lying over trestles out at the back, baking in the sun.

'Blankets!' I said 'Golly!'

'We'll need them up here. We are over four thousand feet up.'

The sheets and pillowcases were very old, much mended and as thin as muslin but they were of linen and all carried a large embroidered monogram. The teapot was of old Coalport but it had a white enamel lid. The lighting was by paraffin lamps, most of them of cheap glass or enamel, but on a table, made of a slab of unpolished mahogany laid across two upright slabs along one side of the living-room, there were candles in two magnificent Sheffield plate candelabra, one with four arms and a bad dent in its base and the other with only three arms and a jagged end where a fourth had been wrenched off. The door to the bedroom which Twice and I decided to use had a very unusual silver-plated handle in the form of a loop made by two beautifully modelled arms ending in clasped hands at the centre. I examined all the other doors but found that they closed with iron hooks that went into staples on the doorposts.

'Twice,' I said, 'look at this door handle.'

Twice came over, bent to the handle, opened the door and looked at the inside. 'Gosh,' he said, 'I haven't seen one of these since I was six and saw the old Duchess in her carriage at the old Duke's funeral. It's the handle of an old carriage door and the door of a very lush and expensive carriage at that!'

The house, furnished with throw-outs from the Great House of Hope, was full of these strange little odds and ends, full of ingenuities and improvisations, but the mattresses were of the best quality and the woodshed at the back was stacked to the roof with logs and, about an hour after we arrived, a Negro man and woman came walking through the bush, up the hill by the little path that first led me to the cottage.

'Good day, sah, good day, missis. We bring de eggs an' milk.'

Caleb, a 'bush boy' himself, whose first job in life had been with us at Guinea Corner, made friends at once with this couple who were so different from the sophisticated industrialized Negroes of Paradise and St Jago Bay as to be one more fascination of this fascinating place.

For me, the fascination did not lie entirely in the non-tropical features of the house, such as the blankets on the beds and the roughly built stone fireplace in the living-room, nor did it lie in the change in climate, although here, when the night clouds came down as a cold wet mist, the log fire was as welcome as on a chilly summer evening at Reachfar. No. For me, the fascination lay in the fact that we seemed to be above what I called 'proper' St Jago. We were above the real bush line. Below us, for miles, the writhing jungle green of trees, undergrowth and trailing vines stretched away, shrouding hill, valley, roads and whole villages, the eternal over-abundant vegetation seeming to swallow them up so that only a high roof showed here and white twist of the Central Highway there as it made its way round the cleared shoulder of a cliff. But behind the house, the bush seemed to be beaten. There were stretches of bare rough grass, outcrops of naked rock, groups of a few trees but it was open, airy, presenting distance to the eye, and about it there was nothing of the secret menace that lay, always, for me in the dense, still yet ever-moving, silent yet ever-whispering bushlands of the lower ground.

'High Hope!' I thought on the Sunday morning as I looked away down over the rolling green hills, over the valleys where the mist lay in long white swathes to the brilliant blue of the sea fifteen miles, as the vulture flew, to the north. 'High Hope indeed! I haven't been able to breathe so deeply since the last time I was at Reachfar.'

I suppose, really, that Twice was right and it was the climate that suited me in a way that the humid heat of the Paradise Valley could never do, but I think, too, that the resemblance between High Hope and Reachfar had much to do with my state of mind. As day followed day, I seemed to recapture something of my childhood. Reachfar had also been rich in outcrops of rock and rich in wild flowers as this place was. At Reachfar, the well had been up in the moor, south of the house, and here at High Hope the spring was a little way above and south of the house too. And from Reachfar, looking west, north and east, you could see the whole sweep of Ross from Ben Wyvis to the west over the Firth and fertile lands and hills to the north and to the east away to the horizon of the North Sea. I had made a song, as I called the rhymes I made in my childhood, about that when I was learning the points of the compass. Here, at High Hope, I had that same urge to make a song and skip and hop from one outcrop of rock to another on the hill behind the house, and although I was too old now to make songs, I was grateful to be able to recapture something of the mood from which childhood's songs are born.

The light heady air made me feel energetic and I spent long hours exploring the rising ground behind the house or sitting in a natural throne I had found that had two boulders for arms, an outcrop of rock for a back and a cushiony pad of short grass for a seat. Sitting in this, one looked due north and when the day was clear one could see the north coast from one end of the island to the other, from St Jago Bay in the west to Hurricane Point in the east. From here, the great valley of Paradise looked, always, like a large saucer filled with beaten white of egg, lying embedded in a carpet of green moss. The white of egg was the cloud of humidity the valley held and the moss was the vegetation of the surrounding hills.

Twice, on the other hand, said that High Hope made him feel relaxed and lazy, so that while I walked about he lay on the veranda or in the garden and read by the hour. For two weeks, we were extremely happy, seeing no one but each other and Caleb, who laughed and sang about his work and, each evening, went down the hill to the little settlement called Hope Town where there was a rumshop and a primitive dance-hall or visited the home of his new friends who brought our milk each day.

# 2

A<small>T</small> the end of a fortnight, I said to Twice over breakfast on the Friday morning: 'This is where there comes an interruption in this idyll of ours, chum. Freda and Mrs Miller have announced that they are coming up for the weekend.'

'Oh damn!' said Twice.

'I know but I simply couldn't help it, darling. I did a lot of hinting about getting away from the madding crowd for a bit and all that but you know what people in this island are – they spend their lives visiting round from one place to another. They're a terribly gregarious lot.'

'Mrs Miller isn't exactly of this island,' Twice carped.

'Oh, yes, she is. Much more than you and I are. But actually it was Freda that put the idea of coming up here into her head. Freda herself has never been as high in the island as this and Mrs Miller took the view that Freda must come up for a weekend and not be beaten by a couple of importees on her own ground.'

'Well, if they want to sleep, they can stay on the veranda with me,' Twice said, 'but if they want to spring about like mountain goats you'll have to look after them.'

'I'll keep them out of your hair, darling. The only nuisance is that I think I'll have to go down to Hope Town. We haven't enough butter and I'd like some bacon and stuff.'

'Send Caleb.'

'I can't, really. I don't know what sort of shop it is or what they've got. It's not far by the bush paths. I'll go down with Caleb. I'd like to see Hope Town anyway.'

'I'll come with you then.'

'Do you want to?'

'Not particularly.'

'Then don't come.'

'You're not going alone.'

'Caleb will be with me.'

Twice merely looked cussed and laid his book aside. 'Stop arguing. Having Caleb with you if anything happened would be worse than having nobody.'

'But what can happen?'

'Nothing probably except that I'd be uneasy till you came back so I am coming.'

'Let's take the car then.'

'A walk will do me good. I'm putting on weight by the hour, lounging around here, and it's cooler walking than in the car when the sun is out. Caleb can come too and carry some of the stuff.'

It took us about an hour, by an intricate system of footpaths through the bush, to get down to Hope Town, which had a church, a post office, an open-air fruit and vegetable market, the dance hall, two rum shops and a grocery run by a Chinese family. The grocery did not carry stocks of many of the things that Europeans use but I did manage to get some tinned butter and bacon and an assortment of other tinned foods.

I had not realized, on the downward journey, how rapidly we had lost height but after the first few hundred yards of the upward climb, I began to find it difficult to keep pace with the long stride of Caleb's bare brown legs and feet on the narrow path in front of me. It seemed, too, to be much hotter than when we came down, shut in as we were, in single file, with the thick green vegetation on either side and the damp brown earth of the path rising like a leaning wall in front of us. I stopped and turned round to look at Twice who was behind me.

'How are you doing?' I panted. 'Golly, it's like a Turkish bath in here.'

'All right.' Twice was panting too. 'Let's have a blow, though.'

'Me keep walkin' Missis?' Caleb asked. 'Me got de buttah, Missis.'

'Carry on, Caleb,' Twice told him. 'The missis and I know the way all right.'

With his deceptively easy-looking stride, the boy went on and disappeared round a bend higher up. It suddenly seemed to be very quiet, there in the bush. There are few birds in St Jago for most of them have been killed off for food, so there was no bird-song and it was windless, so that no vegetation

156

moved. It was very quiet and greenly dim and I became conscious of that furtive, uneasy, moving-yet-still, silent-yet-whispering menace of the bush. Then I became conscious of another noise.

'Twice,' I said and even in my own ears my voice had a queer sharp edge, 'Twice, you are wheezing!'

'I know,' he said, holding his chest and breathing shortly and shallowly. 'I feel sort of odd. Maybe that iced beer we had was too cold after walking or something — Listen! What's that?' There was a drumming noise in the air now and the little green tunnel that was the path seemed suddenly more dark than green. A large splash of water fell on my arm.

'Rain!' I said. 'Oh, damn! Come on, Twice!'

'Darling, it's no good. I can't hurry. I – I can't get enough breath.'

Many times in my life before, I had thought that I had felt fear but now I knew that all these other times had been only a faint mockery of this grim terror that gripped me as, with Twice in front, making his own slow pace, I climbed up and along and up and round all the twists of that foetid, whispering, hot dark tunnel while the icy rain poured through the trees, faster and faster, in bigger and bigger drops on to our steaming skins. I began to think that it had no end, that we had lost our way, that we were condemned to plod like this for ever and ever, until Twice, almost unable to breathe at all, fell to his knees at my feet and I fell on top of him.

We were in sight of the edge of the bush, a little way from the garden fence, and I saw Caleb coming towards us, running, our mackintoshes in his arms.

'Caleb, Mr Twice is sick. Take his arm.'

The boy's big eyes widened and, fearfully, he put his arm round Twice's waist and between us we half-carried him to the house and into the bedroom.

'Caleb, *all* the hot-water bottles. Quick now!'

He ran away, his feet going slap-slap on the bare wood of the floor while I tore off Twice's shirt, shook some raw white rum on to my hand and began to rub his back.

'It's all right, Janet,' he said after what seemed to be a long time. 'I'm all right.' Caleb, his eyes enormous, stood at the end of the bed. 'Caleb, go and make some tea for the missis. Janet, go and change your clothes. You must be chilled to the bone.' Then he lay back on his pillows and began to cough.

I had with me the tablets that had been prescribed for his bronchitis and in a short time his breathing became easier and he grew drowsy, but after I had changed my clothes, had my tea and was sitting by the bright fire that Caleb had built in the living-room, I was haunted by a dreadful uneasiness. I did not know what its origins were and I could not describe its nature, but in my mind, as if symbolic of this uneasiness were the words: 'This place is not Reachfar. It's called High Hope but it's in St Jago. This place is part of St Jago. This place is not Reachfar.' Monotonously, as monotonous as the drum of the heavy rain on the shingles of the roof, the words repeated and repeated themselves in my brain.

By six-thirty in the evening it was pitch-dark, for there is little variation in the length of day between summer and winter in St Jago. The heavy rain persisted and Caleb, hating rain and fearing the chills it brings as all St Jagoans do, was cowering in the kitchen by the wood stove when I went in and said: 'Caleb, do you know if there is a doctor in Hope Town?'

'A dactah, Missis?' The large eyes stared at me, stared round at the walls, stared back at me again and then the head shook from side to side. 'Me say no, Missis. Dactah come to Hope Town only Wedsday.'

'I see. Well, Caleb, we'll have supper when Mr Twice wakes. You will heat the soup? And we'll have eggs and —'

'Me can fix it all, Missis,' the boy said.

I went back to the living-room and sat on by the fire while the rain went on drumming on the roof.

About eight o'clock, Twice woke and we had some soup, poached eggs and some fruit. He was very drowsy and lax but he seemed to be breathing more easily and about half past nine he went off to sleep, so I undressed and got into my own bed on the other side of the room. I lay awake for a long time, listening to the rain, thinking of the car that stood outside but which I could not drive, and then I must have slept for I awoke to the sound of Twice coughing. The rain had stopped,

158

the sky was clear and in the light of a bright half-moon I could see his face, impatient, peevish, as the niggling husky 'cough-cough' wrenched him out of sleep. He turned from his back to his side, his eyes still closed, as I got out of bed and reached for my dressing-gown and slippers. Cough-cough. He rolled over to his other side, a querulous frown between the closed eyes. Cough-cough. Then: 'Ow-ow!' he said on a childish note, sat up, opened his eyes and began to cough violently, his enormous shoulders heaving and straining.

The wood stove in the kitchen was dead but I managed to re-light it to make the hot drink I gave him after he had swallowed the tablets, but when he lay down again the cough came back. I propped him with more pillows to a near-sitting position but every time he drowsed off, the cough would come again, little and niggling at first, then the childish petulant; 'Ow-ow!' and then the violent spasm that left his forehead damp with sweat. From a little after midnight until dawn, this is how it was. For a little time, about four in the morning, I thought the dawn would never come. Outside, the great sweep of the island from east to west was brilliantly clear under the bright moon, land, sky and distant sea all in black, white, grey and silver, nothing moving, but all cold, still and dead as a landscape on the moon. Twice and I, I thought, are the only two people who live and breathe in all this great wide world; Twice is sick; there is nobody to come to help me for this island has got us completely in its grip. The morning will never come. This island has caught us for good and we are frozen here for ever in this moonlit stillness.

'Please God,' I heard myself pray in the words of my child-hood, 'please God, let it be morning soon!'

I had often seen the dawn in St Jago for, in tropical countries, one wakes early if one is a worker, but never had I seen a dawn of the sudden beauty of this one. And this beauty was not born entirely of my gratitude for its coming.

Twice was having a short spell of peace and I had tiptoed out to the veranda for I felt that the pull of my dreadful anxiety might wake him and I looked eastwards, hoping against hope that my prayer would be answered and that day would come at last. The time as marked on the dial of my

watch meant nothing now. There was nothing but this end-
less night that only the dawn could bring to an end when –
and if – it came. It came. Suddenly, as I watched, a wavering,
exploring faint finger of light rose out of the sea beyond
Hurricane Point. It broadened, it lengthened, wavered from
side to side again and seemed to beckon and in another second,
all along the horizon, on either side of it, more fingers came
up, tentative and uncertain at first, then taking courage from
that first slender finger that now, like the hand of a conjurer,
burst into a joyous exuberance of flags and banners of yellow
and gold, pink and scarlet light, which were all reflected,
doubled and redoubled in the silver mirror of the sea. Then,
quickly, from among these trappings of his pageant, came the
golden breastplate of the emperor-conjurer himself, only a
golden rim at first, then a half-circle and then with a blaze –
presto! – the whole shining disc was above the horizon and
the vast sweep of the world was full of his light.

I turned my eyes from the blaze and looked in through the
window of the bedroom. Twice, propped against his pillows,
was still asleep, his face no longer petulant but smooth, still
and at peace. I sat down on the veranda steps and began to
cry with relief and gratitude.

The spirit rises in the morning; hope is reborn; faith is renewed and while, in the bedroom, I slipped quietly into shirt,
shorts and sandals and Twice slept on, it was difficult to believe
in these haunted hours of the night when he tossed, gasped and
periodically emitted his wretched, petulant little 'Ow-ow, dash
it!' of protest against his difficulty in breathing. However, rise
in spirits, hope reborn, faith renewed, I remembered notwith-
standing the terror of the night and as soon as I was dressed I
wrote two letters, one to the local policeman, the other a
message to be read over the telephone to Doctor Gurbat Singh
at Paradise. Then I gave Caleb a pound and sent him off to
Hope Town.

Twice did not wake until after ten and when he did wake
he was cheerful, hungry and wheezing hardly at all.

'You are feeling better, darling?' I asked.

'I feel fine. But *you* look rotten, Flash. I suppose I kept
you awake all night with my coughing and carry-on? Darling,

160

I'm sorry.' He threw the bedclothes back and made to swing his feet out of bed.

'Twice, please don't get up!'

'But I'm all *right*, I tell you! It was only a sudden sort of chill. Flash, don't cackle and fuss like an old hen and look haunted!'

'I'm not cackling and fussing and if I look haunted that's the way I look!' I felt my voice rising and sharpening and took a violent pull at my self-control. 'Only, Twice, please stay in bed and rest for a little while even if it's only to please me.'

'But I've done nothing but sit on my fanny since we came up here. Isn't that resting? I'm not going walking to Hope Town today if that's what's bothering you.' He swung his feet from under the sheets and over the side of the high old-fashioned bedstead. 'Gosh, that's funny!'

'What?'

'My ankles – look how they're swollen. That must have been with walking in those sandals with no heels on them.'

We both stared at his feet. Twice has shapely legs and feet, terribly normal feet that I, finding difficulty in buying shoes to fit my long, too narrow feet, had always envied. The ankles above them were now markedly swollen, the swelling extending down over the insteps and under the soles.

'That settles it,' I said. 'You stay in bed. You've strained your feet in some queer way walking in those sandals and if you don't look out your arches will drop and you'll have big flat kippers of feet like Vickers!'

He looked up at me for a moment, pulled his feet back into bed and under the sheet and said: 'Oh, all right. You win!'

'And while you're mad at me anyway, you might as well know the worst. I've sent Caleb down to the Police Post to get a message phoned through to the Doc at Paradise.'

'Great Heaven! What for? Saying what?' His blue eyes blazed at me.

'Saying to come up for the weekend among other things.'

'Flash, this is ridiculous and I'm bloody annoyed with you! You are going on as if I were an old woman and you an older one!'

'I don't give a damn.'

'But I do! What are people going to think? Dragging the Doc away up here?'

'I don't give a tinker's cuss what anybody thinks!' I snapped and then I noticed that the wheezing noise from Twice's chest was very loud and that his breath was coming in short angry gasps. It was then, too, that I noticed the swelling about his neck, from the bottom of the ears round under the jaws. The jawline, which was usually so clear-cut – a little too clear-cut as a rule when he was as angry with me as he was now – was padded to a flabbiness of outline with swelling. Panic fear, worse even than the fear that had haunted the night, rose in my throat and I began to cry.

'Oh, for pity's sake, Flash, don't,' he said. 'All right. I'm sorry I blew my top. Come here. You got a fright yesterday and I suppose you woke at your usual time this morning instead of snoring on like me and your silly nerves are all shot to hell. All right. Stop crying. I won't say another word and I'll stay here and it's the weekend anyway and Doc will probably quite enjoy coming up.'

'I'm sorry, Twice,' I sniffled. 'It was just such a long time last night that you were coughing and I swore I wouldn't let it happen another night and so I sent Caleb off with the letter at seven o'clock before you could wake up and stop me. I'll go and see about your breakfast.'

I do not remember much about the day, except that I spent a great deal of time looking away north-west down over the green sea of the bush to where the white loop of the highway wound round the shoulder of that hill, but none of the many times I looked did I see the little cloud of dust which would mean that a car was rounding that corner and might be on its way to High Hope. It was Dram, about two in the afternoon, who brought a rush of gladness to my heart by coming to my side on the veranda, pointing his nose at the track that wound away into the bush and quietly saying: 'Uff!' deep in his throat. Twice was asleep.

'A car, Dram?' I whispered.

'Uff!' he said again and moved off towards the gate.

There were two cars, one behind the other. Out of the first

stepped Mrs Miller, Freda and Josh and out of the second came Sir Ian and Doctor Gurbat Singh.

'What's the matter, me dear?' the old man asked quietly.

I stared at them all. Twice and I had come up here to get away from people, to be on our own for a little at High Hope. I had never been so glad to see five people in all the days I had ever lived.

## 3

THE doctor and I went into the bedroom where Twice was now awake and he greeted Gurbat Singh, glanced meaningly at me and said: 'Do I hear Sir Ian's voice outside?' I nodded. 'There you are! A fine to-do. I'm sorry, Doc – the missis here lost her head a bit this morning. She doesn't do it often but when she does it goes off with a bang.'

'No harm done,' the doctor said, opening his bag. He had his back to the bed and I saw the frown on his lean, black-jawed East Indian face as he very slowly took out his stethoscope.

'I'll be right outside if you want me, Doctor,' I said.

He nodded, did not speak and turned to the bed.

I walked out through the living-room, across the veranda past my guests, on down the steps and down to the bottom of the garden to the little gate where the footpath came in through the bush. There, staring into the dense green foliage, I heard again that voice in my brain: 'This is not Reachfar. This is High Hope – it's in St Jago —' but now I knew what the words meant. They meant: 'I am lost. I have lost my bearings. I am in strange, terrifying country – hostile country. I am lost!' I heard quiet footsteps on the garden path, gripped the wood of the gate hard for a moment and turned to face Sir Ian, with the two women beside him and big Josh behind, towering above them all, his big broad black face kind and worried.

'Look here, me dear,' Sir Ian said in a low voice, 'what the devil's the matter?'

'I don't know. I just don't *know*! It was yesterday. We went down to Hope Town —'

In a garbled incoherent flood I poured out the story of the walk back from the settlement, the rain, the coughing, the stark moonlit terror of the long night, the sending of Caleb with the message, Twice's anger, the fact that his ankles were swollen, everything.

'I'm sorry,' I ended. 'I'm sorry to be going on like this but I feel – it's just that I feel —'

Doctor Gurbat Singh, his stethoscope about his neck, came down the path towards us. Mrs Miller, Freda and Josh drew back but Sir Ian stood firm, drew his bushy brows down and snapped: 'Well, Gurbat Singh?'

'I'd like another opinion, sir.'

I felt my legs and spine grow weak and clutched at the wood of the gate which was sun-hot and rough under my fingers.

'Another opinion? Why?'

The young doctor glanced at me for a second, a look of searing pity came into his eyes, a look that I found unbearable, before he said quietly: 'I do not like the condition of the heart, sir.'

'The *heart*?' The word was a whispered shout from deep in Sir Ian's throat.

'Yes, sir. There is also some distension of the liver. This man is *sick*, sir.'

'Dammit we know that! Sorry, Gurbat Singh. Beg your pardon, me boy. Now then, this other opinion, who'll we get?'

'The best man, sir, would be Lindsay, Doctor Mark Lindsay.'

'Lindsay? But dammit, you know what Lindsay is! Lindsay won't —' I turned and looked at Mrs Miller, Freda and Josh standing up near the house, out of earshot. 'Ye know what Lindsay is!' Sir Ian was barking in an undertone. 'Who else? Oh, dammit, never mind just now. Get off down to Paradise an' get up here with the ambulance an' then —'

'I am not going to undertake to move Mr Alexander, sir,' said the doctor in his high-pitched Indian voice.

'You're not goin' to – but dammit, Gurbat Singh — Good God! You mean —?'

'On my own responsibility, I would not move him just now, sir.'

I let go of the wood of the gate for I had discovered that it was not, after all, the wood of the moor gate at Reachfar that I was clinging to and, in any case, I did not need to cling to anything now. I felt vital and strong. I strode up the garden. The doctor ran behind me, laid a hand on my shoulder.

'He is quiet for now, Mrs Alexander,' he said. 'I gave him an injection. Try not to worry. Leave him to rest.'

'I know, Doctor. Thank you. I am not going to Twice.' I went on until I could call softly to the others: 'Please come here.' They came at once, in single file, down the path, Josh coming last. 'Mrs Miller, Freda, Twice is very sick. Doctor Gurbat Singh thinks that something has gone wrong with his heart. He wants Doctor Mark Lindsay to see him but he won't come to sick white people. Freda, please, do you think there is any way we could get him to come?'

Freda's big eyes looked round at us all and then up at her brother. In the hot silence there seemed to be no sound for a long time but in the end it was Josh who spoke.

'Missis Janet,' he said, 'I go to try to make Mark come. Come, Freda,' and he turned away.

'Hold on,' the doctor said. 'I'll give you a letter.'

About ten minutes later, without another word, big Josh and Freda got into the car and drove away down the track through the bush. I felt the strange vital force seep out of me, as if it were being drawn away down the hill beneath the arching trees, along the rough track in the wake of the car that carried Josh and Freda.

'Come, Janet,' Mrs Miller said, 'you've had a bad night of it, lassie. Come up to the veranda and sit down. If anybody can bring Doctor Mark, Josh can. Come now.'

'I must get Caleb to make us some tea,' I said.

'Sit you down. I will see to all that. My, this is a bonnie place. It minds me on Reachfar hill.'

I looked at her. 'It isn't though. This is St Jago,' and I

moved along the veranda and looked in through the bedroom window. 'He is asleep,' I said to the doctor when I came back to the end of the veranda. 'It's queer. He doesn't look sick at all. But he looked terribly sick through the night, when it was dark. Sorry, I'm talking rubbish.'

'Not at all, me dear. Here, drink this,' Sir Ian said and pushed a large glass of whisky and water into my hand.

'I don't think so.'

'You should,' the doctor said, 'and I'd like you to swallow these, please.'

He handed me two little tablets. I did not want to take them. I suspected that they would send me to sleep and I felt that I must not sleep for, if I did, the bush would crawl up and smother Twice, stop him breathing if I was not there to hold it back, but yet the doctor had been kind, coming all this way on a Saturday when he probably had other plans and —'

'Come, me dear, knock 'em back,' Sir Ian said.

I did what they said. I swallowed the tablets and then I sat looking away out to the west where St Jago Bay was, where Doctor Mark Lindsay was and then the white cumulus out on the horizon turned into Ben Wyvis under his winter snow and it was in that direction that I prayed: 'Please God, make Doctor Mark Lindsay come!'

The early dark had come down before I started awake, but Mrs Miller was sitting beside my chair and she laid her plump little hand on my arm and said: 'All right, Janet, all right. And Twice has had milk and bread and butter and he's sleeping again.'

'Did he ask for me?' I inquired childishly.

'Aye did he! And we told him you were sleeping and he said that was fine and not to waken you.'

'Where are the others?'

'Down there in the garden.'

'What time is it?'

'Only seven o'clock.'

'Mrs Miller, I am sorry sleeping like this. I knew those tablets would knock me over.'

'Och, be quiet with you! Would you like a cup of tea?

Or will you just have a drink with the rest of us and then your supper?'

'Oh, lord, the supper —'

'Och, stop worrying, lassie! Caleb and I have the supper all arranged.'

We were a strange little party. It was a beautiful clear evening, quite different from the drumming rain-filled evening before and the moon came up, big and white, but it no longer held the stark cold terror that it had held in the early morning hours. That sort of terror dies in the face of knowledge, no matter how grimly terrifying in its own way that knowledge may be.

'Sir Ian,' I asked quietly, 'has the doctor said anything more to you about – about Twice?'

'Not much, me dear.'

'Will you tell me though? I have to know, you see.'

'Missis Janet, I know that. The trouble is that Gurbat Singh don't know. He's playin' safe an' that's sense, but he don't know. There's one thing. He says the heart action is better than it was when he arrived today.'

'Better? Oh, Sir Ian, has he told Twice anything?'

'He's told him we're waitin' for another doctor, that he – Gurbat Singh, I mean – ain't sure about the swellin' o' the ankles, but he's given Twice some sorta dope, ye see. He ain't takin' in much. He sat up an' had some food but ye could see he wasn't himself, ye know.'

'I see.'

The minutes and the hours ticked past. We had supper. The moon swept in its wide arc across the sky. Twice slept on. We chatted a little of all sorts of minor things. The whole world seemed unreal. I felt unreal. No matter where I looked, I could see only the black outline of that hill shoulder where the road wound round, the road by which a car must come, so I stopped looking anywhere except in its direction, north-west, against a white sky.

'Look!' I said to them suddenly. 'Quick! Over yonder! See the lights? That's a car, probably coming here.'

'Or makin' for Hope Town,' Sir Ian said. 'Saturday night. The market trucks'll be gettin' home from the coast.'

167

'Of course,' I said. 'They couldn't be here yet anyway. They won't come up tonight at all. Nobody would leave to drive up here in the dark.'

I remember very little about the late evening and the night. I suppose that I slept part of the time in the bedroom that I shared with Mrs Miller but the house was a little hive of uneasiness round the still bed where Twice lay, sleeping peacefully with the watchful Gurbat Singh on my bed at his side. Now and again, one would hear movement in the white moonlit stillness, for Sir Ian in the bedroom next to us was watchful and wakeful; Dram, at the foot of my bed, came alert at every small sound and from time to time Mrs Miller's whisper would come: 'Not sleeping, Janet? Try to rest, lassie,' and we would talk to one another in whispers for a little and then the white silence would enthral us and everything about us again.

When the dawn came, I stopped looking towards the shoulder of the hill where the road wound round for, in the night, I had come to believe that I must not try to will a car to appear at that corner. I must wait, patiently, in the belief that the car with Doctor Mark Lindsay in it would come and if I kept on believing that, with patience, the car would certainly come. I had prayed for this man to help us, I had done the most powerful thing I knew to do and I must not go on 'ask-ask-asking' as I had done as a child. If I did, I might exasperate God and the car would not come. The essential thing to do now was to wait, to have patience, to believe that my prayer had been heard and would be fulfilled. This was the most difficult thing of all to do but, for three hours, I tried hard to do it and at the end of the third hour after dawn, at eight o'clock, the car appeared at the gate.

It was difficult to see, through the tears, who was in it, and when two men got out of it, it was still more difficult to believe the obvious – to believe that the miracle had happened – for this tall Negro carrying a brown leather bag and walking beside Josh could be no other than his blood brother.

'Doctor Lindsay,' I held out my hand, 'thank you for coming. You know Doctor Gurbat Singh?'

He merely touched my fingers, nodded and said: 'Where is the patient?'

Gurbat Singh led him away into the room. The patient. That was Twice. To this man, Twice was merely 'the patient'. The world from High Hope on this tropical summer morning looked very stark and harsh and sharply defined and, in spite of the bright hot sun, I felt cold and, in spite of the people around me, I felt terribly alone.

But this, my mind told me, was no time to think of my own loneliness or my coldness. This man was the one man in the island of St Jago who could be of most help to Twice and I must be prepared to be trodden under his feet if that was to be the price of that help. He was calm, I must meet him with calm. He was cold, we must talk of 'the patient'. He hated us but he could help Twice and I could never hate him in return. He had come here, I could only suppose, because he had once taken an oath to help the sick and he was prepared to keep to the letter of that oath, probably under persuasion from his brother and sister.

They stayed in Twice's room for a long, long time and when they came out, Sir Ian, Mrs Miller, Josh and I rose to meet them.

'You'd like us to go, Gurbat Singh?' Sir Ian asked, indicating Josh and Mrs Miller as well as himself.

Gurbat Singh looked at Doctor Lindsay, deferring.

'As Mrs Alexander chooses,' Doctor Lindsay said.

'Then please stay everybody,' I said. 'Will you sit down, Doctor?'

He sat down on a chair beside my own, looked down at his big lean hands for a moment, then looked up at me out of huge brown eyes, in shape very like the eyes of Josh but their light was as cold and brilliant as the light over this place called High Hope.

'I speak after a first examination,' he said. 'I shall know more later but there is no doubt that the heart is seriously affected. I suspect considerable enlargement on one side. I should like, please, the history of the patient.'

I stared straight back into his eyes and it was like

projecting all the essence of oneself against a brown glass screen which turned everything aside.

'Yes, Doctor?' I said. 'Would you please help me by asking what you want to know?'

He nodded. I felt in a curious way that I had found the best response.

'There is a history of bronchitis, I understand. Have there been other illnesses?'

'He once told me that he had pneumonia when he was a child of six but you see, Doctor, I did not know Twice until 1945 and he doesn't talk about himself very much – not about being ill and things, I mean.'

My voice was shaking; I was making a bad job of this; he was despising me even more than he despised most white people – despising me as a fool who could not even help him with the essential things he had to know in order to help Twice – 'the patient'. Full of fear, I stared into his cold dark face.

'I see,' he said. 'He served in the war?'

'Yes.'

'Where?'

'France in 1939. Then Norway for a few months. Then in anti-aircraft in Kent in late 1940. Then in 1941, he went to India and came home – back to Scotland – in 1945.'

'He was a gunner?'

'No, an engineer. He was in REME. I am afraid he has never been anything but an engineer.'

'I see. Never wounded?'

'No. He says he never saw – never saw an angry man.'

Doctor Lindsay's face remained closed but I was conscious of the faint smiles from Sir Ian, Josh and Gurbat Singh. They gave me a queer little injection of strength.

'This condition of the heart is of some standing, Mrs Alexander. This did not happen overnight.' He frowned at me and the strength ebbed away. I felt that he was accusing me of wilful unhelpfulness. 'The sudden change to this altitude, the walk up from Hope Town the other day – these are aggravations, yes, but the condition was there before.' His gaze became terribly concentrated, boring into my face. 'You *must* have observed something unusual between 1945 and now!' His voice was irritable, impatient, as he battered at my stupidity. 'Tell me, did he ever faint?'

'Faint?'

'Yes! Lose consciousness?'

'Don't be stoopid —' I heard Sir Ian begin but I broke in: 'Yes, Doctor! Yes!'

'A-ah!' It was drawn-out, satisfied and it made him seem more human that he could feel satisfaction. 'Now then, what was the earliest occasion that you can recall?'

I wished now that the other people were not there for this was something that was very private and important to me and in that way, precious.

'In the summer of 1947,' I said.

'Yes. And the circumstances?'

This was it. I had to tell him. 'It was on the night that we got engaged to be married,' I said in a low voice. 'Twice – he is very emotional.'

He nodded. 'I understand,' he said and suddenly he did a very unexpected thing. He turned to the others and said: 'I would ask you to leave us, please. Doctor Gurbat Singh, I shall discuss the case fully with you later, of course.'

'Yes, sir,' Gurbat Singh said and they all went walking away down the garden.

I felt very alone but not afraid of him any more.

'These fainting attacks,' he said, 'they were always connected with emotional crisis?'

'In a way, yes, Doctor. That – the one I have told you about – was the only one connected with *us*, as it were, but there were other times. He would lose his temper when any of the workmen did anything very stupid, anything that spoiled a piece of work, you know, and have a sort of black-out for a moment.'

'Yes. Go on.'

'There was a time in Scotland when a labourer went too close to the petrol tank of a truck with a blow-lamp and the tank blew up. Nobody was hurt or anything but it was *stupid*, you see, and Twice gave the man a cursing and then came into the office – I worked in the office – and he blacked out.'

'Yes?'

In a mesmerized way, born of some idea that I was now doing what would help Twice most, I went over several of these incidents, telling him of them while he interpolated little encouraging interjections, and then: 'Just a month or two ago, I noticed that when he became excited or angry he would begin to wheeze as if his bronchitis were coming on. That time Kevin Lindsay came to Paradise and incited the men to strike, Twice came home and I thought he was going to faint— Oh —' I stopped and stared at him, realizing that I was talking to Kevin Lindsay's brother. His face remained unchanged and so did his manner. Instead of 'Kevin Lindsay' I might have said 'John Smith' or 'Tom Brown'.

'I see,' he said. 'Very good, Mrs Alexander. Now, I am not going to tell you that the patient is not very ill. He is quite seriously ill.'

'Yes,' I said.

'His condition can be treated. At this stage I cannot tell you the degree of improvement that can be made, but you must understand that the damage to the heart is of long standing and that to some degree it will be permanent.'

'Permanent?'

'Yes. The heart will never be completely sound again. He will always need great care.'

'I see. Thank you.'

'I would advise that he be moved to a lower altitude right away. Later, do you wish him to be taken to the States or to England for treatment?'

'The States or England? But Doctor Lindsay, now that you have come to us, I thought that *you* would look after Twice!'

Where had my prayer gone wrong? What had I done or said that had led to this?'

'Is that what you wish?' he asked.

'But yes! Please!'

'And what of the patient?'

'Twice?'

'Yes.'

'But Twice will want that too, Doctor Lindsay! Please, I know you are busy – Freda has told me how hard you work

172

but – well, I just thought from the start that if you came up here to us at all, you would look after him!'

'As you wish, Mrs Alexander,' he said coldly, and rose to his feet. 'I should require him to be hospitalized.'

I also rose from my chair. 'We – both of us – are entirely in your hands,' I said. 'Tell me what is to be done and I shall see to it.'

'Be seated, please. I shall discuss the details with Doctor Gurbat Singh.'

From behind, he looked very like his brother Josh as he walked away down the garden to the others. Men are not so very dissimilar in their bodies – it is in their minds that the difference lies, and men's minds are the sum of their race inheritance and their individual experience. Their race inheritance is long, their individual experience is short but it is trenchant. The combination, if it is inimical, is difficult to fight.

In a short time, Sir Ian, the two doctors and Josh came back to where I sat at the end of the veranda.

'We're goin' down, me dear,' Sir Ian said. 'We'll be up tomorrow mornin' with the ambulance.'

'The morning?' I looked at them all and behind them to the long sweep of distance to Paradise and St Jago Bay. The moon would be more full, whiter and harsher than ever tonight. 'In the morning,' I repeated. 'I see.'

Doctor Lindsay went into the living-room, fetched his bag and put it down beside a chair on the veranda.

'I shall stay with the patient,' he said, sat down, took a notebook from the bag and began to write in it.

My relief was so great that I felt light-headed, a little giddy as I walked down to the cars with Sir Ian, Josh and Gurbat Singh. When they had driven away, I leaned against the gate and looked up at the little house, and it and the whole hillside of High Hope seemed to be dominated by the man in the white drill suit whose coal-black head was bent in concentration over his notebook, a man who was as secret, as silent, as potentially menacing, I felt, as the island out of which he had sprung. I went quietly round the edge of the garden and tiptoed in through the back door to join Mrs Miller and Caleb in the kitchen.

## 4

For the rest of that day, I devoted myself to keeping out of Doctor Lindsay's way. I could not leave the house because I had to stay near Twice but I felt that I must keep out of the range of the doctor's notice. There seemed to emanate from him something that warned me and repelled me, just as the whispering bush of the island had always seemed to warn and repel me; something that made me aware that he had been brought into contact with me against his will, by the persuasion of people of his own blood who were my friends, that he resented this and that at a glimmer of excuse, he would go away down the hill, finding his way unerringly through the bush as Negroes do and leave me to face the long stark night alone.

It was very strange to live for most of the time at this deep level and for some of the time, as at meals, on the everyday surface level established by Mrs Miller, for she chatted on about little everyday things, about the arrangements for moving Twice to hospital, of the progress he would make when under treatment by Doctor Lindsay, as if she were quite unaware that this deep level of hostility existed at all. The truth, which came to me during the day only in fitful elusive gleams, was that, for Mrs Miller, this hostility and resentment which I could feel so strongly did not in fact exist. It was smothered and overlaid by the kindly generosity of her own mind which had a childlike belief that all people were like herself, so that if someone was in trouble and you were able to manage a house and arrange meals, as she was, you helped in that way, and if you were a doctor like Mark Lindsay you helped by giving of your special skill.

There were all sorts of questions that I wished to ask the doctor but I did not ask them. There were many things that I wanted to understand about this illness but I pushed them aside. I wanted to know what arrangements, if any, had been made about nurses, for people like us, in the island, had to supply our own nursing staff at the hospital, I knew, but I asked no questions at all and I do not think Doctor Lindsay originated a single remark in the course of the whole afternoon but merely made monosyllabic replies at lunch, tea and supper when Mrs Miller addressed to him some trifling remark about Ginger Grove or the members of his family.

After our evening meal, the doctor told us that Twice could have some milk and biscuits and I carried the tray into the room. Twice was propped up against a heap of pillows, looking amazingly well but unusually limp and lackadaisical in his movements as he reached out towards the food.

'Hello, darling,' he said. 'I seem to be doing an awful lot of sleeping.'

'Yes, but that is what Doctor Lindsay wants you to do.'

The doctor was standing at the foot of the bed, very tall and black.

'Try to eat it all, darling,' I said and turned to go away.

'You may stay for a little,' the doctor said and he himself went away out of the room.

Twice moved his hand towards me in that new, unusually lethargic way and I put my hand into it. 'He says my heart is rocky,' he said. 'He says I am to go to hospital.'

'Yes, darling.'

'Janet, I'm sorry.'

'Oh, Twice, don't be absurd. You couldn't help getting ill, darling. Nobody can. Come, eat your biscuit.'

Lazily and with a flaccid sort of obedience, he raised his other hand and bit into the biscuit.'

'Janet,' he asked, not looking at me, 'how did you get Lindsay to come?'

'Josh brought him.'

'Oh.'

'Josh brought Mrs Miller and Freda up yesterday and then he went back and got Doctor Lindsay.'

'I see. He knows his job, Janet. He knows what he is doing. It's queer. He told me how *I* felt when we were coming up the path from Hope Town. It's queer when somebody tells you something that is your thing and you yourself can't find the words for it. It's a sort of genius, that.'

'Yes, darling. Another biscuit?'

'All right. You mustn't worry, you know.'

'I'm not worrying, darling. Not now, since Doctor Lindsay came.'

'That's right. He's a terribly nice bloke as well, isn't he?'

'Terribly nice, yes.'

The doctor came back into the room, carrying two small white tablets on a saucer and a glass of water.

'More dope?' Twice asked.

'We all intend to sleep tonight,' the doctor said. 'We have a journey to make tomorrow.'

He likes Twice, I thought suddenly, and this was true. It was almost as if there was a tangible and visible bond between them. But he doesn't like me, I thought. I moved to leave the room. 'I should like to talk to you before you retire to bed, Mrs Alexander,' he said with his back to me.

'Very well, Doctor. I shall be in the living-room,' and having said good night to Twice, I left the bedroom.

I threw some more wood on to the fire, sat down and stared into the flames, and when the doctor came out of the bedroom he sat down opposite to me and took out a packet of cigarettes.

'Do you smoke these? They are island cigarettes – not imported.'

'Thank you,' I said. 'I have smoked these ever since we came to St Jago.'

This, I told myself, is one more pathetically small grain of sand added to the bridge across the gulf between this man and me. I smoke cigarettes made from tobacco grown in his island.

'I wished to talk to you about nursing staff,' he said. 'I think you know my sister Florence. I have sent a letter down to her.'

'Sister Flo?' I was unable to keep the delight out of my voice. 'Oh, yes. Yes?'

'I have asked her to take the case.'

'But will she? Sister Flo told me she had completely retired from nursing now. Will she – come to us?'

He nodded. 'She will come,' he said. 'That will be satisfactory to you? Good nursing is essential.'

'I can think of nothing more satisfactory, Doctor. Thank

176

you for arranging this, but she must have help. Do you know of another nurse who is free and would be satisfactory?'

He shook his head. 'My sister likes to work alone when it is possible, and in this case she will manage single-handed. You know the private ward at the hospital?'

'I have been there as a visitor, that's all.'

'It is reasonably well-equipped. I think the patient will be comfortable there.'

I began to feel that we were talking not about Twice, a human being, but about some delicate and intricately balanced machine, and the more he talked the stronger this impression became until he reminded me of Twice himself, working out some problem in engineering of stresses, strains, temperatures and frictions that must be meshed together into harmonious working.

'I am sure he will,' I said, but I could not continue in this way so I took a deep breath and went on: 'I have to tell you, Doctor Lindsay, how deeply grateful I am for your help. I know that, as a rule, you do not take – private patients. I am very grateful.'

He inclined his head in faint acknowledgement of what I had said and then rose to his feet. 'This type of case is a special interest of mine.'

So there it was, I thought. Twice, to him, was not a man but a clinical study, but with his next words he startled me out of this firmness of belief.

'He is an excellent patient. Of course, he has a great deal of character and is unusually intelligent.'

'I believe he is a good engineer,' I said, 'but I have never thought of him as a patient.'

'A man who can do one thing well can usually do more than one thing well,' he said. 'If he does not make progress, it will not be any fault of his in that he has not tried. Good night, Mrs Alexander,' and he walked away into the room where Twice lay, but I felt better than I had felt since he arrived.

The journey to the hospital was accomplished the next day. Twice, asleep, was carried on a stretcher to the Paradise ambulance, then Doctor Lindsay got in beside him and the big white vehicle set off down the hill. Sir Ian's chauffeur drove

Twice's car with Sir Ian and me in the back, and Mrs Miller and Caleb stayed behind to close up the house. Sir Ian was to send for them the next day.

Before I got into the car, I took a last look at High Hope. It was a beautiful place, perched on its hill, with its wide view spread beneath it on all sides, and it reminded me very strongly of Reachfar, but I never, never wanted to see it again. Although I knew it was childish, absurd and near-morbid, I felt that this place had cheated me. It was the last place in St Jago where I would have expected the enmity of the island to manifest itself but it was here that the blow had been struck. I felt that I would never forget High Hope and that terrible night under the merciless white moon when Twice had coughed and gasped and coughed again – I would never forget it and I would never forgive this place. I suppose we must have a symbol on which to hang our consciousness of what we feel to be the injustice of life. My symbol was High Hope.

It seemed to be very hot in St Jago Bay after the climate in the hills, although the hospital was probably the coolest place in this area. It was a community of long, low, white buildings, standing among lawns that stretched down to the beach, and a mile or so behind it the coastal plain rose abruptly into the sugar-loaf hill that was Craigellachie Heights. I remembered noticing the hospital that day I went up there. From the Beatons' front door, it looked like a neat arrangement of little white boxes lying on a green cloth with, here and there, clumps of green-headed dish mops, which were coconut palms.

They carried Twice into a little room at the end of a wide hallway where Sister Flo was waiting. At Ginger Grove, when I had met her, she had been a big, lumpish, untidily-dressed Negress lounging on the veranda and laughing lazily with all the others of that abundant family that lived in that hot green shade, but here she was very different. She was still big but compact and neat in her short-sleeved, plain white dress and the white veil concealed completely the bushy negro hair and made a floating frame about her black face. I suddenly saw her strong resemblance to Josh and her doctor brother.

Twice did not wake even when they lifted him on to the

up-tilted surgical bed, but merely murmured a little in a resentful way, re-settled his shoulders against the single pillow and slept more deeply than ever. He looked very young, strangely innocent and remotely distant and there was nothing for me to do except keep out of the way, I felt, so I went to sit on the wide veranda that ran along the front of the building and stare out at the vast expanse of blue sea that lapped in gentle little waves upon the long stretch of silvery sand. It, too, had a remote, faraway secret life of its own, a life that had its centre away beyond the misty horizon, just as Twice now, had a life that was far away from me, alone, somewhere behind the blue eyes that were covered by his heavy lids in this deep sleep.

I found comfort, however, in looking out over that wide blue distance to the shimmer of heat on the horizon. St Jago here, in these orderly precincts, had been tamed. No vines crept and trailed about the white-painted veranda posts; no quick-growing bush rioted over these green lawns where the water-sprinklers spun continuously to defeat the brassy sun, and compared with this vast sea that lap-lapped for ever at the beach, the island came back into perspective in my mind, into a little volcanic lump on the earth's surface, which is all that it really was.

Physically, I felt very tired and I lay back in the deck-chair and although I did not sleep my mind escaped, at last, from the island into a dream of Reachfar, visiting the Thinking Place above the well, the Picnic Pond where, out of the short rough grass, the juniper bushes grew in grotesque shapes, some like hewn pillars, some round like pincushions and some like parodied forms of animals and men.

When Sister Flo had the room arranged to her liking, she came out to the veranda, placed two chairs just beside the french window that led from Twice's room and then came to me and said: 'Let's sit along there where I can see him.'

I looked into the room before I sat down and he was still sleeping with that faraway look on his face.

'Sister Flo,' I said then, 'I can never thank you and your brother for what you are doing for us.'

'Tchah!' said Sister Flo in the Negro way which has in it a sound from a former century. It is the sort of impatient dismissive sound that I can imagine Doctor Johnson making and I think it must have come into the Negro vocabulary from their white masters of that time, for their dialect is full of survivals of the English of an earlier day, with many words used in the sense which they carry in the authorized version of the Bible.

'It is very good of you to leave your bee farm and come out of retirement like this,' I persisted.

'It's because of Mark,' she said. 'Mark is a demon – all the nurses are terrified of him and the terror makes them stupid, then he grows angry with them and they grow more stupid than ever.' I felt a strong wave of understanding sympathy for the nurses. 'So Freda said to me: Flo, she said, you'd better put on your uniform and go down there to the hospital and so I did.'

'You are not afraid of Doctor Lindsay then?'

'I? Tchah! I am fifteen years older than Mark – one is not afraid of something one pinned into diapers, no matter how clever he may be. For Mark is clever, Miz Janet. Your husband would do no better in New York or London.'

'I am confident of that, Sister Flo.'

While we sat talking in low voices in the doorway, Sister Flo would glance now and again at the bed, but suddenly, at the end of about half an hour, she rose quickly and silently, went inside and took Twice's wrist between her fingers. After a few seconds, I became aware of a curious frightening tension that seemed to emanate from her broad white back and to quiver in the folds of the soft white veil. I got up, went to the foot of the bed, glanced at her concentrated face and then looked at Twice. A strange flicker of movement crossed his face from one side to the other, I saw a pulse begin to throb violently in the side of his throat and a little bubble of spittle began to form at the side of his mouth.

'The bed,' Sister Flo gave the whispered command. 'Wind the handle to your right!'

I grasped the wooden handle, began to turn it, the bed-head behind Twice began to rise and in my mind the words formed:

'Please God, don't let Twice die! Please God, I'll give anything, but don't let him die!'

Twice, his eyes closed, his face still and more remote than ever, was now almost bolt upright in a sitting position and Sister Flo had one hand on his wrist and the other on the bell-push at the head of the bed. There was a frozen eternity into which her wristwatch tick-ticked the seconds and then Doctor Lindsay, big, black and silent was in the room, taking the flaccid wrist out of Sister Flo's hand. He looked away out of the window, out to the far blue horizon and his big brown eyes burned with a terrible concentration. After what seemed to be an aeon of silence, he laid the flaccid hand gently back on the coverlet, nodded at me and said 'All right', then to Sister Flo; 'Put one c.c. in the syringe.'

I felt that I was dismissed but I felt comforted. This man had said it was all right, so Twice was not going to die. I went out of the room on to the veranda and sat down on one of the chairs.

A moment or two later, Doctor Lindsay and Sister Flo came out too and I sat listening while he issued to her a series of short clipped instructions. There might have been no relationship, no bond of any kind between them. Then he turned, looked down at me from his great height and said: 'This reaction was bound to occur, you know. But he has been very quick. I did not expect it so soon. He cheated me a little.'

I tried to smile. 'He is quick – about everything,' I said stupidly. He did not say any more. He went away along the veranda, across the lawn and disappeared into one of the other wards. Sister Flo, with a look of compassion on her broad black face, said to me: 'Come in and see him now, Miz Janet. Come!' and she led me into the room.

An extraordinary change had come over Twice's face. He looked now like a man who was ill, but he had lost that frighteningly remote faraway look that, in its peacefulness that did not belong to this earth, had terrified me beyond any consciousness of my own terror. Looking at him now, with his cheekbones standing out sharply and a faint frown of resentment about his brows, I felt, as he gave a little cough and made a small restless movement, that he was back in the world that I knew, the world that held people like Sister Flo and me, and I began to cry quietly, the tears running down over my cheeks. Sister Flo bent over the bed, a small glass in her hand.

'Thirsty, huh? Come?'

She raised his head a little with her other hand and he opened his eyes as I hastily ran a hand across my face.

'Hello, there,' he said. His blue eyes seemed enormous as he looked next at Sister Flo. 'How d'you do?' he said politely on a questioning note, a little like a well-schooled child and then took a sip from the glass.

'This is Sister Flo who has come to nurse you, darling,' I said.

'Oh.' He looked at her again. 'Thank you.' Then he looked round the room. 'This is the hospital?'

'Yes, Twice.'

'You have been covering quite a piece of country while I've been asleep.'

'Yes, quite a piece of country,' I agreed.

'And you are going to sleep some more now,' Sister Flo told him.

'All right. Whatever you say.'

He closed his eyes and very shortly was asleep again but in a different way this time, as if when he woke he would enter a little more into the world that held Sister Flo and me.

'Four o'clock,' Sister Flo said, looking at her watch. 'You have had no lunch. I did not bother you with it but I am going to arrange for some tea now.'

She went away along the hall to the telephone and it was suddenly as if I came back into the world of time. I seemed to have been here on this veranda, looking out at the sea for ever, and all the other times and places I had known had disappeared from memory, all except the Reachfar of my early childhood which had the character of a timeless dream. Four o'clock. Tea-time. Twice was round the corner. Life was going on.

Sister Flo came back, a maid came with the tea-tray and at that moment the Paradise Rolls-Royce came through the gates, up the avenue between the palms and rolled to a silent stop at the end of the block. I looked at Sister Flo.

'Visitors may come to the veranda,' she said.

I went along to the entrance where Sir Ian stood by the car and, inside it, sat Madame Dulac.

'My dear Janet,' she said, holding out her small gloved hand. 'My poor child!'

I wanted to burst into tears of gratitude to her and Sir Ian for all that had been done for us, but I said: 'Sister Flo says to come to the veranda. Please come and have a cup of tea.'

'Thank you, my dear.'

Sir Ian helped her from the car but when she came to the edge of the veranda she said impatiently: 'Tut, this is no time for an old woman to be vain. Janet, my eyes are not what they were. Is there a step here?'

'Yes, Madame, three. May I take your arm?'

'Thank you, child.'

With an impatient little jerk she held out her elbow and we counted her way up the steps, but at the top she shook Sir Ian and me off.

'Splendid. Where it is level, I can manage beautifully,' and, very much the *grande dame*, she swept along to where Sister Flo waited for her.

'You are Sister Florence Lindsay? How d'you do? I understand that you have come out of retirement to take this case for us. We are deeply grateful. How is Mr Twice?'

Sister Flo indicated the door of the room. 'Resting, Madame Dulac.'

The old lady looked at Twice for a long moment. 'A most unusual sight,' she said then. 'I have never seen that man when he was not moving and much too fast as a rule.' She came to the little wooden table and sat down. 'Now, Sister, I wish you to understand that anything you require you have merely to let me know. I have written in similar terms this morning to your brother, Doctor Lindsay. Thank you. A cup of tea will be very nice and then, Ian, we must go. We can be of no use here and are merely in the way. Janet, how do you intend to arrange your life while Twice is under treatment here?'

I merely stared at her. I had not, during the past few days, thought of myself as having a life to arrange.

'It is going to be very hot and disagreeable for you to drive up and down from Paradise every day. I think the sensible arrangement for the present would be that we take another room in the block here. There are five rooms vacant, I believe, Sister?'

'Yes, Madame. Mr Alexander is the only patient.'

'Quite. People are extremely silly about this private ward. They *will* go to these inefficient amateur nursing homes or to New York or London, of course. Janet, how do you feel about this arrangement? You must sleep somewhere, child.'

I had not thought of things like this. If I had thought at all, I suppose I had visualized spending my nights in a chair on this veranda.

'I can think of nothing I should like better, Madame, if it can be arranged.'

'I don't see why not. I shall see the Senior Medical Officer before I leave.'

'Then that's settled,' Sir Ian said, 'an' we can fetch anythin' you need down from Guinea Corner.'

When the big car had driven away, I went back to Sister Flo at the little table and she said: 'I have heard many times of Madame Dulac and I have seen her too, driving past in her car and on platforms. But today, I have really seen her.'

I had now a feeling of guilt about Madame and Sir Ian as I thought of how, during the past year, I had been condemning them in my mind as people who lived in a dream of the past, taking no regard for present reality. Where, I asked myself now, would Twice and I be at this moment without their help? Was it not the Paradise doctor, the Paradise ambulance, that whole Paradise administration that I had been condemning as a mere myth-inducer that had brought us here where Twice could be treated? In the court of my own mind, I found myself guilty with regard to Madame and her son of Reachfar's two cardinal sins – the sins of disloyalty and ingratitude – and I was bitterly ashamed.

'She is a very wonderful old lady,' I replied to Sister Flo.

'She is that and much more,' said Sister Flo, amazing me.

'She is what this island and our foolish, lazy black people need. But she is old and they don't grow like that any more, no, sir.'

'You amaze me, Sister Flo,' I said candidly. 'Madame can be a terrible old bully. I should have thought you would resent people like her.'

'Tchah! It is good to be a bully for many things. We nurses are bullies, for sick people very often have to be bullied into getting well. And young people need bullying to give them sense. Our black people are young, a young race, and people like Madame Dulac are good for them – discipline, that's what they need and that's what that old lady's got in plenty.'

In the days that followed, I was to come to the knowledge that Sister Flo, in relation to the student nurses and ward maids about the hospital, was simply a black Madame Dulac. She had been trained in the United States, she had spent some years there and some more in a hospital in the Philippine Islands and she would tolerate no St Jagoan slackness of any kind. In her attack upon a junior for slovenly work, too, she showed none of the restraint which Madame showed when dealing with her Negro servants. Sister Flo minced no words but lapsed wholeheartedly into the graphic dialect of the island.

'What you t'ink dis place is? Some trash hut in the Cambuskenneth bush? Git a swab, git down on yo' lazy black knees an' git dat dus' outa here!' she would say, and I would be filled half with pity, half with embarrassment towards the junior member of her own race over whom she stood like a vast, white-clad, black-faced goddess of wrath.

## 5

For the first week, I lived a strange lonely life, mostly in a chair on the veranda in the days, and I looked at the sea a great deal so that, in memory, it is as if I lived at that time cast away on a remote beach at the edge of the world, but this is a case of memory selecting the dominant mood of that time and exaggerating it to the exclusion of all else. In actual fact, the days were quite busy and much more full of variety than my days at Guinea Corner had been, but my whole consciousness was so swamped with the stark despair of that moment in Twice's illness – that moment when I had visualized the wide waste of a world that did not contain him – that this feeling of standing on a beach, a castaway from the only world that I knew, is the dominant memory of the time.

After the first week Twice began to make progress that could be seen from day to day, and he and Sister Flo constructed a close, clinical and rather bawdy little world of their own where they argued about pulse beats, measured urine and indulged twice a day in a protracted toilet for Twice which both of them seemed to enjoy extremely. Twice's many friends brought many gifts and because his diet regimen was so strict their field of choice of gifts was limited to toilet items such a talcum powder, shave lotions, skin lotions and, of course books and magazines. The powders and lotions are an essential part of the comfort of a bed-patient in a tropical country but Twice's room began to look like a well-stocked pharmacy or perfumery, and he and Sister Flo protracted discussions a to whether, today, they would smell in a nautical way of Spic of Seven Seas or in a landward but equally manly way of Heather'n Tweed, as one of their suites of powder and lotio was fancifully named.

Sister Flo, in addition to being a nurse, showed herself t be an able barber, manicurist and pedicurist and never di she allow a chink of dullness, while Twice was awake, where by boredom could get in. In a curious way, by which he di not make a single unnecessary physical movement, she kep him busily occupied all the time. I was grateful to her, grate ful beyond all expression, but at the same time I felt lonel for this world of illness which had, temporarily, claimed Twic was one that I could not enter. I felt clumsy and in the way their little room while they followed their day by day regime of pulse, temperature, baths, meals, medication, rest, measu ings of urine, checkings of blood pressure and enterings of a their findings on their large chart. In theory, I could be in t room any time and all of the time if I pleased but in practice I went in only when I was invited, very much like any of the other visitors.

Every day, Sashie de Marnay and Don Candlesham, friends of ours who owned the Peak Hotel in St Jago Bay, either came for me or sent a car to take me out to their place to lunch and, every evening, when Twice went to sleep at eight o'clock, the car came again to take me to the hotel for the rest of the evening. As Twice himself said, no man was ever ill in greater luxury and I appreciated with all my heart everything that everybody was doing for us, but there it is. I was lonely and the time stands in memory as a period that I spent all alone, stranded on a remote beach at the edge of a world that I did not know.

We had been in hospital for about five weeks when one morning, there was a sort of discreet furore in the silence of the private block and the matron, a sister and three maids arrived and began to prepare a room across the hall. It did not take Sister Flo long to find out what was happening and she came back to tell us that Miss Sue Beaton, who had had an accident, was being brought in that afternoon.

'This place is getting quite fashionable,' said Sister Flo.

'Who is Miss Sue's doctor?' Twice asked.

'Franklin.'

Doctor Franklin was a white physician who practised in St Jago Bay.

Shortly before noon, there was a bustle outside again; the stretcher, obviously very heavy even for the enormous Negro attendants, was brought in from the ambulance followed by Mars Andy, looking in a frightened way into his panama hat while Mrs Miller came behind, directing a man who was carrying two suitcases. Very shortly, Mrs Miller arrived on my little section of the veranda.

'What in the world happened to Miss Sue?' I asked.

'You may well ask.' Mrs Miller sat down wearily in a deck-chair. 'She went up into that awful old pimento loft, the floor was rotten and she fell right through.'

'Mrs Miller! Do they know how badly damaged she is?'

'Not yet. Not till they've done the X-rays.'

'It's a wonder she's alive at all. That place is high.'

'She's alive all right and you never heard the like of her language.'

'She is conscious?'

'Conscious? It's Andy and me and the servants that are nearly unconscious! I've never in all my born days seen a woman like that.'

'I'm going along to the pantry to make you a cup of tea, Mrs Miller,' I said. 'Where is Mars Andy?'

'Down with the doctors. I told him he'd find me here when he came back.'

The 'sympathy department' as Twice called the veranda was now swollen to three permanent members, Mrs Miller, Mars Andy and myself. Mars Andy and Mrs Miller went home to Fontabelle every evening and came down every morning, for Miss Sue seemed to have adopted Mrs Miller as a body servant to herself and could be heard shouting at her nurse, about seven in the morning in a deep wheezy baritone: 'Isn't that Miller woman here yet?' Miss Sue was a thoroughly bad patient in every possible way, so bad that she brought an element of grimly macabre comedy into the clear white gravity of the little hospital block. Her legs encased in plaster, she lay in a half-sitting position in a bed above which there was a maze of handles, levers and pulleys, and she wore a bright pink nightdress with, as a bed-jacket, an erstwhile bridge-coat of brilliant peacock-blue embossed velvet. Above this, her large purple face peered out through the maze of chains and levers, growing larger and more purple by the moment with fury. On either side of the bed she had tables which were laden with a miscellaneous mass of letters, newspapers, pencils, boxes of sweets, bottles of cologne, bottles of rum, a siphon of soda water and entangled among all this was a piece of violent purple crochet work which was an antimacassar in the making that she called 'my needlework'. She refused to eat the food she was required to eat and insisted on eating the food she should not; she would not take the medicines that were brought but would pour them on the floor, fill the glass with rum and toss it off; she ran through the entire island supply of private nurses within three weeks and by the end

188

of the first month was almost entirely dependent on Mrs Miller and Mars Andy except for a few visits from Sister Flo and the nurses on the staff of the hospital.

She was like a little island of lively chaos in the midst of this orderly clinical sea and round her little island hung a cloud of disapproval, exuded by the hospital staff, all the visitors that came to the block and Mrs Miller and Mars Andy, but although I realized that she was behaving badly and being a sore trial to everyone, I could not, somehow, join in the general disapproval. Like her, I was resistant to this non-life for the preservation of life. I discovered this in myself on the morning that Doctor Lindsay was going along the hall after his visit to Twice and Miss Sue's enamel bedpan came hurtling out of her room, missed him by inches and clattered against the wall. I ran from the veranda to the hall, Sister Flo from Twice's room to the hall, and we were in time to see a flustered nurse chasing the bedpan. Doctor Lindsay, very tall and stern of black face, strode into the room.

'Huh, it's you, Mark, me boy?' came the voice of Miss Sue.

Doctor Lindsay said something.

'Even if it had hit you,' came the voice, 'there was nothing in it. That's the whole point! You damn' hospital people got no sense, treating people as if they were hens in a laying battery. *I'll* tell you when I want a bedpan. I can speak, can't I? I'm a woman, not a damn' machine. Now, get out of here, Mark, and go about your business.'

Doctor Lindsay came out and went about his business and I was mean-souled enough to enjoy that moment.

'Janet!' came the voice. 'Janet Alexander, come in here and talk to me!'

I spent a lot of time in her room talking to her or, rather, being talked to by her and Mrs Miller and I could persuade her, even, to take her medicine sometimes, for unbelievable as it may seem, at the root of all Miss Sue's rebellion against the sickroom routine was her innate disability to take any direction of any kind, even for her own good, from a person of colour.

'What are you doing,' she said to me one day, 'having that black boy from Ginger Grove looking after your husband?'

189

'Miss Sue, don't be absurd. Doctor Lindsay is regarded as one of the West Indian authorities on heart ailments.'

'*Doctor* Lindsay, bah! Doctors. I hate the whole breed, white and black. Blackmail, that's what they go in for. If you don't do as I say, you'll die. Lot of poppycock. I'll die when I'm good and ready.'

'But you know, Miss Sue, I think medical science can do a great deal if you cooperate with it —'

'Oh, yes, they can tie you up in plaster and mend a bone here and there.' She slapped the plaster cast about her legs. 'That's all right. Like mending a car or any other machine that goes wrong. But they're not going to go telling me that I must take a lot of pills and muck to make me sleep because my heart is weak. Of *course* my heart is weak – it's been weak for the last thirty years but that's no reason to spend all my time sleeping. I might as well be dead as sleeping all the time. Why, if I took all these damn' pills they have, I'd die anyway because I don't believe in them. Doctor's think it's pills that keep you alive. It ain't. It's your *mind* that keeps you alive more than anything. Where the devil are that Mrs Miller and Andy? They should be here by now!' I made some sort of conciliatory noise. 'She's a decent little woman, Mrs Miller,' Miss Sue went on. 'You knew her in Scotland, didn't you?'

'Not really, Miss Sue. My people knew her when I was a child. I don't remember her in those days at all.'

'She's told me a lot about this place your people have, the place on the hill. What's its name again?'

'Reachfar.'

'Reachfar, that's it. D'you never get homesick? I get home-sick when I'm away from Craigellachie Heights. When I was at school in Edinburgh when I was a girl, I was homesick all the time, crying with it every night. I'm homesick for it right now.'

This deep love for her home was something that I had not suspected in Miss Sue and I felt it make a bond between us in this cold scientific atmosphere which seemed to specialize in disrupting human bonds rather than in creating them.

'They will soon be taking your plaster off, Miss Sue, and then you'll get home,' I said.

190

'Oh, this isn't a serious attack of homesickness. I know it is just up the hill there – not thousands of miles away like your Reachfar.'

'I am never homesick,' I told her. 'I love Reachfar more than any place on earth but I have never felt homesick for it. I've spent most of my life away from it, really, but I am never away from it in my mind if that makes sense. It is sort of built into me, it is part of me and I am part of it somehow. It is the one part of me that has never changed in a changing world and it will never change now, I feel sure.'

'Has it got heather?'

'Lots of it – too much, indeed. Heather is not a good-paying crop, you know.'

She would listen by the hour to talk of Reachfar, its people and its animals and by the hour I talked to her of it, and even when Mrs Miller and Mars Andy and other visitors were there, the talk was often of Reachfar and Scotland and so, for me, this sojourn in this place, with the queer wall of sickroom discipline that it imposed between Twice and me, became less cold and lonely as, gradually, talking to Miss Sue, it became imbued with something of the friendly warmth of Reachfar.

## 6

AT the end of six weeks, Twice was allowed to get out of bed and sit for an hour in a wheelchair on the veranda, which was a great day, but no visitors were allowed and he and I spent the hour alone, side by side, looking out at the sea. Mentally, I was very confused. In one way, I could hardly believe that this was Twice beside me, released at last from the tyranny of the sickbed, and I was swamped with gratitude while, at the same time, I was aware that this was Twice, but a new Twice to whom something had happened that I had not shared and never could share and I resented this wedge of distance that had been driven between us.

We did not talk a great deal. Out of what I felt words did

not come readily, for it had been borne in on me by Doctor Lindsay, through the medium of Sister Flo, that it was essential to meet everything with calm and to avoid all emotion. Twice, still somewhat affected by sedative drugs, seemed content to sit quietly, exploring with his eyes this new freedom of distance to the far horizon and the minutes of the sunlit hour slipped quietly away until, near the end, Twice said: 'This is a hell of a queer thing that has happened to us, Janet.'

'Not so very,' I said, obeying my instructions to meet everything with calm. 'I got ill once and now it's your turn. On the whole, you and I have been luckier about health than many people.'

He stared out to sea. 'This thing of mine is a permanent disability.'

'It's a question of learning to live with it, darling.'

I began to wish that Sister Flo would come to say that time was up.

'There is also the little question of learning to *make* a living in its company. Have you thought of that?'

I had indeed thought of it but I had not reached any conclusion. I wished still harder that Sister Flo would come.

'There is plenty of time to think about that, Twice. We have, after all, got a little money saved. Please, darling, you are not to start worrying. It is the very worst thing you can do.'

He turned to look at me and held out his hand for mine. 'I am not worrying, my pet,' he said, smiling at me. 'I think I am so full of this sedative dope that I can't worry. I feel, sort of, as if I don't know myself any more. I am rediscovering myself as if I were a stranger I have just met. And I am rediscovering you too. You are different, Janet. I used to call you Flash but that seems to have gone. I seem to be seeing you differently. I think of you as Janet now, someone solid and dependable that does not go up in a flash on me any more. It's like making a fresh start – going off in a new direction.' He smiled again. 'It *is* a new direction too – a new way of life. No more booze, no more smoking, no more – he looked down at our joined hands – 'rushes of blood to the head —'

192

'– and throwing things at one another and then jumping into bed,' I finished for him. 'In point of fact, Twice, we are getting a bit old for that sort of thing anyway. Everything has its time and season and when people get into their forties it gets more and more difficult to get away with the ridiculous without looking it.'

He still looked down at our hands on the arm of the wheel-chair. 'I should hate you to be bored, darling. And it looks like a boring prospect, hedged about with limitations.'

'Tchah, as Sister Flo says, I've never been bored in my life and I don't intend to start now and life is always hedged about with limitations of some sort anyhow. The object of the exercise seems to be to accept them and squash them down into unimportance. There is certainly no point in bemoaning them – that only exalts them above their status. All you have to do as this new person you are is to learn to love me and bear with me and everything will be all right.'

'That will be easy. Loving you is the only thing that has come through unchanged from the time – the time before High Hope.'

'Well,' said Sister Flo, 'what are you two doing?'

'Making love,' said Twice.

'So?' She laughed her rich, rather bawdy laugh. 'I didn't notice anything.'

'This is a new mode in making love,' Twice told her. 'Nothing is visible to the naked eye.'

Sister Flo began to wheel the chair into the little white room, laughing as she went, and I was laughing too, for all the loneliness of these past weeks was gone and something in me that had been strangled almost to death by fear had come back to life.

From that day, life which had hung in a state of suspension for me for six weeks seemed to begin again, but six weeks is a long time to spend timelessly on the edge of nowhere and to begin anew with, as my space, the narrow orbit of the hospital and the Peak Hotel and to pick up, in the realm of time, the little day-to-day threads of living had a strangeness, as if I were setting out into an entirely new way of life which, indeed, I was. It was Sir Ian who brought this home to me.

'Been havin' a chat with Lindsay over in his office,' he said to me one afternoon while Twice was having his after-lunch rest. 'He ain't all that bad, that chap, an' he seems to know about doctorin'.'

'I think he is pretty frightening myself,' I said. 'There seems to be such an awful lot of him and I feel that most of him hates the sight of *me* if you see what I mean.'

'Ye know what I think? I don't think it's white people he's got his knife into as everybody says. He ain't the same as that political brother o' his. Ye know, I think it's *women* he don't hold with.'

'What makes you think that?'

'Just odds an' ends he says an' his way o' going on an' that.'

'Well, whatever it is he doesn't like, it makes him pretty frightening. I am grateful for all he has done for Twice, Sir Ian, but I'd be more grateful still if I never had to lay eyes on him again.'

'I see your point, me dear. Well, anyway, I had a long chat with him this mornin' an' I will say for him that he can give a straight answer to a straight question an' he don't go beatin' around the bush an' hummin' an' hawin' an' gettin' nowhere like some o' them.' He drew down his bushy white brows and looked very fierce. 'Point is, me dear, Twice is goin' to have to resign this job o' his with Allied Plant. He ain't fit any longer to go tearin' round the Caribbean in aeroplanes an' that.'

'I know that, Sir Ian.'

Yes, I did know it. I knew it as a bare unconsidered fact but I had not yet started to think forward from it.

'You got any plans, me dear?'

'No. Not yet. It is too early for Twice to start thinking and worrying and making plans. There's Reachfar, of course, so we shall always have a roof over our heads. But I don't know, Sir Ian. I just haven't got round to thinking about it but in the end it will probably work out to going back to Britain where I can take a job of some kind and help out.'

'Hum. I thought you'd be thinkin' that way. I asked Lindsay about that. He says Twice ain't any too fit to stand the British winter.'

'Oh.' This was something I had not foreseen. 'Oh, I see.'

'Gurbat Singh an' the other doctors weren't all wrong, ye know. Twice *has* got bronchitis as they said he had – that's what was hidin' up the other trouble an' makin' it worse as well. Now, what I'm gettin' at is this. Ye'll remember I once said to Twice that if ever he got fed up with Allied Plant, he could come on to the staff o' Paradise?'

'I remember, Sir Ian, but that was when he was a fit man – or when we thought he was fit.'

'He's still fit enough for what Paradise needs. The doctor says what he needs is a regular way o' life – no tearin' about in aeroplanes an' all that – an' a job that don't call for a lot o' hard physical work. All right. I ain't asking him to climb up the cranes at Paradise or swing about from the girders by his toes the way he did before. I want him to sit at a desk, stroll round the factory now and again an' use his brains to get the production up an' cut the costs down. Rob's not gettin' any younger and he can't do everything. Besides, Rob don't seem to see how things are goin' in this island.'

My eyes filled with tears. 'I don't know what to say, Sir Ian —'

'You don't have to say anythin'. When Lindsay gives me the go-ahead, I'll put the thing to Twice. All I want to know is, d'ye think the two o' you will be happy at Paradise?'

'We have been happy at Paradise for quite a time now,' I said shakily. 'If we have to stay in St Jago, I can think of no better place. When Twice is stronger, you will talk to him? I'm sorry I'm crying and making an ass of myself, Sir Ian. I don't seem to be able to help it.'

'That's all right, me dear. You've had a bad time. I'd have the jimjams meself if I was livin' in this place all the time. You go an' put some powder on your face an' we'll go in an' see old Sue for a bit.'

Everybody was very quiet about Miss Sue these days and she herself was a great deal less noisy and rebellious than when she first arrived at the hospital. One day her bed, with her lying in it, was wheeled out of the block and along the covered way to the X-ray room and it was after she was brought back that this new quietness set in.

'The legs aren't mending as they should,' Mrs Miller told me. 'They haven't told her but they told Andy.'

But, I thought, Miss Sue knew without being told that she was making no real progress and that was why she had become more docile. This, however, did not mean that she was in any way an ideal patient. Indeed, the word 'patient' did not apply to Miss Sue at all. She still had more spirit, mental energy and force of character than any dozen other people and her room was more like an untidy magpie's nest than ever, in spite of the best efforts of Mrs Miller and the hospital staff.

I continued to spend a great deal of time with her, more than ever now that Twice was well enough to read and often had Rob Maclean and the other engineers from Paradise to visit him when they talked of nothing but Paradise Factory in any case. Doctor Lindsay encouraged these visits and the engineering talk, I think, by way of helping Twice to make a gradual return to his own world, and one if not more of the engineers was with him every afternoon.

'Miss Sue,' I said one day for I too was coming back into my own world of puzzling about people and relationships, 'Doctor Lindsay is a queer sort of man, isn't he?'

'Mark? Queer? Tchah! He's a fairly ordinary sort of Negro, Mark.'

I felt a little impatient with Miss Sue. Nobody in her senses, I thought, could call Doctor Lindsay 'ordinary' whether he was a Negro or not. 'He is much too clever a doctor to be written off as ordinary!' I said.

'Oh, he's clever enough,' she conceded. 'All the Lindsays are clever – too damn' clever, some of 'em, like that Kevin that makes all the trouble. But they're all Negroes too.'

'When I said he was queer, I didn't mean anything to do with being a Negro, Miss Sue. And queer is a silly word anyway. What I mean is that he has a knack of making me feel that I am in the way, that I am just cumbering the ground and that he could do a lot better job on Twice if I weren't here at all.'

'I suppose he makes you feel that because that is just what he thinks.'

I gasped and stared at her. One can think the things I had

196

thought but when one says them aloud one hopes to have them denied, not confirmed. 'What do you mean – that's what he thinks? How *can* he think it? He knows nothing about me. He has never tried to find out about me.' I was so indignant that any man could think he could ignore me in this way that I spluttered on until I spluttered myself into silence after repeating two or three times: 'What right has he got to think any such thing?'

Miss Sue put her head on one side and admired her progress with her purple crochet antimacassar.

'He thinks it because in spite of his over-the-water education, he is still a bush Negro,' she said. 'He thinks women in general *are* in the way and cumber the ground and all that you said . . . There's a mistake there. I should have put three trebles instead of these three double crochets. Oh, well, a blind man running for his life will never notice it . . . Mark Lindsay's been over the water to Scotland and learned a bit of doctoring but he's still a bush Negro in one way and probably in more than one. He thinks women are for nothing but breeding out of, male children for preference. And if a woman lives to get old, like Mama Lou, and doesn't die in childbirth, he's prepared to stick her in a rocking-chair and make a family fetish out of her. There's nothing very unusual or queer about Mark Lindsay. He is just another Negro . . . I'd better rip this damn' thing back. That mistake'll only annoy me every time I look at it . . . The best one of that Lindsay bunch is Josh. There's no over-the-water education or doctoring or politics about Josh. Josh is a cultivator right through and this is an agricultural island in spite of all their tourist hotels and rubbish. And Josh is a more advanced man than his brothers in spite of their so-called education. I bet Josh don't make you feel you cumber the ground.'

'No. I like Josh.'

'Tchah! Mrs Miller goes on at me for calling them Negroes but facts are facts. They are Negroes and I am white and that's that. *She* may be content with a Negro daughter-in-law but I wouldn't like it.'

'But don't you think the mixture of races is something that has got to come, Miss Sue?'

197

'I'm not bothering my head with what's to come. My own time will be enough for me and I don't like this mixing of colour, and as long as I'm alive I'll say so when I feel like it. Not that it'll do any good. But it does *me* good to get things off my chest and when I don't like a thing, I'll say so. I'm glad you like Josh Lindsay. He's a great admirer of your husband and you too.'

'Oh, rot!'

'Don't be impertinent. I know what I'm talking about. People get the idea I don't like Negroes but that's a lot o' poppycock. Josh has been my neighbour for years and his father and grandfather before him. Josh is a friend of mine. We played together as children, Josh and I, although I'm a good bit older than he is. You know why Josh isn't married?'

'No.'

'Because he could never find a Negro woman to measure up and he wouldn't marry a white woman. What Josh would like is the sort of marriage you and that Twice of yours have – a real sort of partnership. Josh wants more than somebody to go to bed with and breed piccaninnies. That's why I say Josh is 'way out ahead of these brothers of his . . . Aren't they going to give us any tea today? And where are that Mrs Miller and Andy anyway?'

Every Friday since Miss Sue had been in hospital, Josh had come to see her, for he came down to town on Fridays when the lorries brought his produce down from Ginger Grove to the markets and to the hotels. I had always, naturally, left her room if I was in there when he arrived but I remembered now what pleasure his arrival had always given me. When he came in, very large and black, his hat in his hand and a questioning half-shy look in his big eyes, he always reminded me, as he walked awkwardly on tiptoe on his big feet, of George and Tom at home when they were in some strange place and uncertain of their ground. And his first words, spoken in his gentle voice, were always in his own island dialect: 'And how is you this evenin', Miss Sue?' spoken very gently. How dull of wit I had been all these weeks I thought now. Miss Sue and Josh were the deepest and most intimate

198

of friends and that was the main reason for the comfort and pleasure that I had always derived from his arrival.

It was on my eleventh Friday in the hospital that Mrs Miller, Mars Andy and I were all in Miss Sue's room when Josh arrived and, as usual, I got up after the first few moments to take my leave. Mrs Miller and Mars Andy also rose, taking the opportunity to get out for an evening drink at the Peak Hotel while Miss Sue had Josh to entertain her.

'Siddown!' she said to them on this evening, however. 'Plenty of rum here – whisky too – if it's a drink you want. You too, Janet. That husband of yours has a roomful of engineers – he don't need you yet.'

I sat down again on the chair I had just vacated on Miss Sue's left, Josh sat down on her right so that between us hung all the levers and chains and pulleys, and I saw the broad, black primitive face as if in a surrealistic frame of gimcrack modernity, and Mrs Miller and Mars Andy returned to their seats at the bottom of the bed. 'And how is you this evenin' for sure, Miss Sue?' Josh now repeated his question gravely.

'Tchah! Stuck here as usual, Josh. Can't move me legs. These doctors ain't worth a damn. Did you bring down a good load today, Josh?'

'Not bad, Miss Sue, not bad. Twenty dozen head of lettuces for the Peak Hotel all grown on Little Missie's Piece. Now that's a good crop, Miss Sue.'

'So you got your big foot in the Peak, huh? How you get in there, Big Josh?'

'Miz Janet got me in, Miss Sue.'

She looked at me. 'De Marnay's a friend of yours, isn't he?'

'Yes,' I said. I turned to Josh. 'You wait till I can get up to Mount Melody, Josh. The people up there are friends of mine too.'

'The Denholm girl will grow her own lettuces at Mount Melody if she's got any sense,' Miss Sue said.

'But she has got to reclaim her land back from the bush first,' I argued. 'Josh can keep her going for a year or two, can't you, Josh?'

'Yes, *ma'am*,' he said with his big grin and then he smiled at Miss Sue, a gentle smile. 'What Miz Janet says goes, Miss

Sue. This is Mama Lou's orders since Miz Janet's potato crop. That crop is still the best we've had.'

'In Scotland,' Miss Sue told him, 'the station masters at the big railway stations used to wear top hats and potato blossoms in their buttonholes. Josh, by'n'by your goin' to be all out o' land for all dem lettuces,' speaking with the voice and in the dialect of the island as she often did with this friend of hers. 'Gingah Grove not goin' to be nearly nuff for ya.'

'Dis is true, Miss Sue,' Josh replied in kind. 'Gingah Grove gettin' too small for me business.'

Miss Sue took hold of one of the handles that dangled from a chain above her head and hauled herself wheezingly into a more upright position. I attempted to adjust her pillows behind her a little.

'That's fine, dear. Well, Josh, like to buy the Heights?'

I started in my seat and blinked and was aware of myself doing both. Then I looked at the open mouths of Mrs Miller and Mars Andy and then I looked across the bed at the staring face of Josh which seemed to be bigger and broader and blacker than ever, but he was the first to speak.

'De Heights, Miss Sue?'

'That's right. Craigellachie Heights. It's on the market as of now. You've got first refusal, Josh. Twenty-five thousand pounds, that's the price. If you don't want it, it goes to an American hotel syndicate tomorrow . . . What's wrong with you, Andy? Put that damn' hat down an' get everybody a drink. Well, Josh?'

'Me buy it, Miss Sue. Me an' me brudders – we buy.'

'Twenty-five thousand pounds, Josh.'

'Twenty-five thousand pounds, Miss Sue. I agree that price right now,' Josh said in the English of the business world.

'An' no half-breed business, Josh. I got witnesses – I got Miz Miller an' Miz Janet. Hones' business, Josh?'

'Hones' business, Miss Sue,' said Josh in the island dialect once more. 'Twen'y-five t'-ousan' poun' for de Heights. Beg ya give us a week fer raise de money, Miss Sue?'

'A month if ye like, Josh. So that's a bargain?'

She extended her bloated, purplish right hand and Josh took it in his large black one with the pale pink palm and the

200

white round the roots of the nails. For a second, the two hands lay together on the white coverlet of the bed and then: 'For pity's own sweet sake,' said Miss Sue, 'is there nobody in this damn' place can pour out a glass o' rum?'

I was the one who poured the rum while Mrs Miller and Mars Andy still sat in stricken silence, but as soon as she had taken the first sip from her glass Miss Sue bent upon them a cold and scornful eye. 'Well, Andy, I've sold the damn' place over your head – not over me own. I've got this roof here. And you can't go on living at the manse for ever so you'd better get around this town tomorrow an' buy one o' these pink villas they're putting up. Mrs Miller'll help you.' She took another longish swig of rum. 'Come to that, why you don't marry her, I don't know. It'd be a sight more decent than the way you're going on just now. Oh, I know you're both well up in years but you know how people talk.'

'Miss Sue!' said Mrs Miller, scandalized.

'Tchah! If *you* don't arrange it, Andy'll never get round to it. Andy's all right but he has to be thought for.'

'Sue!' said Mars Andy and then seized his hat, put his glass of rum and soda standing in it and peered with anxious intent and acute embarrassment into both.

'Oh, well, please yourselves,' said Miss Sue, 'but there it is. I'm not going to run Craigellachie Heights any more.'

'I have wanted to sell for years, Sue,' said Mars Andy, raising his eyes from his hat with a spark of spirit.

'Oh, be quiet, Andy! You may have wanted to but you never *did* it!'

'I was afraid *you* didn't want to, Sue!'

'Andy, stop arguing and don't be stupid. Josh, these Irish potatoes of yours – you should get a real crop over on the south side on the lands above Mary Vale.'

'Yes, *ma'am*, Miss Sue!'

It was two mornings later that the little nurse who had been on night duty went into Miss Sue's room and then came along to Sister Flo and me where we were drinking early tea on the veranda just after dawn.

'Please to come, Sister Flo,' she said.

'What is it?'

201

'Miss Sue, Sister. She is gone. I saw her at four o'clock. It must have happened since then.'

They went away together. I looked out at the vast expanse of sea. Sometime between four o'clock and dawn, apparently, Miss Sue had got 'good and ready' and had quietly died.

## 7

IT was nearly the end of October when Twice and I went back to Guinea Corner and it was strange to go back to that house which we had left so gaily at the beginning of August to find it quite unchanged, when a change so great had been worked in ourselves and in our lives.

The servants and Mrs Miller from the manse were at the door to greet us, a heap of letters lay on the table in the hall and the house seemed to be full of flowers and fruit, sent by all the friends who wished us well but would not come to visit us until later, when Twice was settled. Sister Flo, out of uniform now and a large, fat, gaudily-dressed Negress again, had come with us and our car was to take her on to her own home. Doctor Lindsay had seen us off from the hospital after issuing many instructions about Twice's diet and way of life.

'Do you think you understand?' he asked me at the end.

'I think so, Doctor,' I said.

He looked at me with what I felt to be cold disbelief and Twice said: 'She understands more than you may think, Lindsay. It may not be my place to say it but she is quite bright.'

He stared hard at Twice for a moment, as if considering these words spoken from a mind that he respected, then looked at me as if I were some new microbe on a slide, a microbe new to medical science, and returned his gaze to Twice. 'It's a short life and a merry one or stick to the rules and live for a while,' he said, 'and if you need me, call me.'

'Won't you come to see us sometimes even if we don't need you?' I plunged boldly. 'It would be nicer that way.'

'Yes, why not?' Twice added.

'Thank you. Perhaps some day when I have a little time,' he said in a grudging way and then he shut us into the car and went away along the covered pathway to his office.

After lunch, Twice went to the bedroom on the ground floor which had formerly been his study to have the afternoon rest which he was still to take for a few more weeks, and Mrs Miller and I sat in the drawing-room, I very happy to be home at last.

'Freda's coming up for me at tea-time,' Mrs Miller said. 'Tommy's away in our car today, seeing about Freda's passport and things.' Freda and Tommy Miller had been married at the end of September. 'Then I'll get away home and leave you and Twice to be nice and quiet on your own.'

'I can never thank you for all you have done for us, Mrs Miller.'

'Och, be quiet with you! We're neighbours, lassie, and there never were better neighbours than Reachfar people.'

I smiled. 'Are you looking forward to going back to Scotland?' I asked her. 'I am going to miss you.'

'Well, I don't think I'm going after all. I think I'll stay for a while with Andy, as his housekeeper down there in the Bay. Yon was an awful thing Miss Sue said yon night about him and me getting married, Janet. It would never do, somebody like me marrying a gentleman like Andy! But the two of us get on well enough and he has to have somebody to look after him and his house, for he is as innocent as a newborn lamb, but I'd never marry him. It wouldn't be right. I think he'll end up by going back to Scotland anyway. He's still got some cousins at home.'

She chatted on in her gentle voice, in her contented way, seeing life very clearly and truly from her smiling blue eyes and I listened to her in relaxed contentment, as she rambled to and fro from Fontabelle to Reachfar, back to Craigellachie Heights and then again to Reachfar until nearly tea-time, when she said: 'I'll go and see about the tea. Talking about Reachfar, there's two letters out there with the Achcraggan postmark. I'll send them in to you.'

It was Caleb who brought in the letters and I chatted to

him for a moment while I turned them over in my lap. One was addressed in the handwriting of George and it was not the usual sixpenny airmail form but a proper letter with high-value stamps on it. George and Tom must be celebrating something, I thought.

'Dear Janet,' it began, 'We hope that by the time you get this you and Twice will be back in your own home with all the sickness and the hospital behind you. You have had a poor time of it and Tom and I are thinking it has been worse than you have said in your letters. Your father is writing to you by this same post but Tom and I wanted to write a bittie too. He is writing to tell you that we have sold Reachfar —'

A thick blackness blotted out for a moment the brilliant light in the room, a cold deathly chill crawled up my spine and I heard Caleb's voice: 'Somet'ing not right for you, Mam?' I tried desperately to gather together my disintegrated mind. 'You mus'n' get sick please, Mam!'

I looked up into his black worried face. 'No, Caleb, I won't get sick. It's all right, thank you,' and he looked down at me uncertainly for a moment before he went away.

Unwillingly, I looked down again at the letter in my hands, reread it from the beginning and then: '– We have had to do it. Since Kate went away, Tom and I have not been able to get a housekeeper to stay. It is too far from buses and things for them. And Tom and I are not as young as we once were to manage the work and we have been losing money this last year or two, even before Kate went to America —'

I read on to Tom's part of the letter. 'George will have told you that we have let Reachfar go to the Dinchory folk. They were mad to get it because of the sheltered outrun – do you mind on the time during the war when Granda sent the three of us up to the moor to mark trees for cutting and we couped the can of paint and never marked the trees to this day? It's just as well the trees are still there for we fairly made the Dinchory folk pay through the nose for that high shelter. So now George and I are going to live like toffs at Castle Jemima with your father. Old Jean is grand pleased for we will pay our way just like lodgers and you know how fond she is of the pennies. We did not bother you with all this when Twice was so sick and George and I are terrible glad that this clever Doctor Lindsay has made him better —'

I went on to read my father's letter and then the one from my brother, trying to absorb this thing that had happened, trying to believe that this loss of part of myself was a reality, struggling to encompass the fact that, for me, Reachfar no longer *was*. My forehead was cold and wet with sweat, my hands were shaking and Twice would soon be awake. I could not go to him in this state. I tried to get up with the idea of shutting myself in the bathroom for a while but my legs would not carry me. Reachfar was gone. The words meant nothing. Written on the paper of the letters, they meant nothing; whispered in my own voice they meant nothing for this was something that, for me, could not be.

With a small lobe of my brain I was conscious that Freda Miller had arrived and was talking to her mother-in-law in the dining-room across the hall but the rest of my brain was struggling in a black maze of non-comprehension when I became aware of someone entering the room where I sat. It was Mrs Miller of Hope, her eyes wide, her face grave. I laid the letters on a table and managed to rise to my feet.

'Janet,' she said, coming to me and pushing me back down into the chair. 'What's the matter? Is Twice worse?'

My mind seemed to come alive; the blood seemed to flow through my veins again.

'No. Oh, no! Twice is marvellously better. He'll be getting up for tea in a moment. You will see him.'

Away at the back of my brain, some knowledge was waiting to emerge but I could not think and help to bring it forth and I could not concentrate on it because Mrs Miller was saying: 'I got back from the States only yesterday. I went to the hospital, they said you had just gone home so I came on here. Janet, what in the world happened at High Hope?'

I told her of the onset of Twice's illness, of the journey to the hospital and all that followed and all the time that thought was deep in my brain waiting to be born.

'My dear Janet, what a dreadful time you've had! I wondered what had happened when I had only one letter from you. It has all been ghastly and I feel hideously responsible. I was the one who sent you up to High Hope.'

'Please, Mrs Miller, you mustn't. In a way, I think now that we should be grateful to High Hope.' This was something that had not occurred to me until this moment for, all the time since we had travelled down that hill, I had shut the place out of my mind. 'The trouble with Twice's heart had been there for a long time. High Hope brought it out into the open. Things weren't so bad, after that first day at the hospital.'

In Twice's room, the record-player which I had had moved in there began to play.

'He is awake,' I said.

'Go to him, my dear. Don't mind about me.'

'Oh, no. He can dress himself and everything now. He gets furious if I fuss and cackle as he calls it. It's odd. Sister Flo, his nurse, even cut his fingernails for him but that wasn't fussing or cackling.'

'You had Sister Flo Lindsay? I thought she had retired.'

'She broke out to nurse Twice.'

'You couldn't have had a better person.'

'I know. She is a marvellous woman.'

I thought again of that first day in the hospital, of the dread moment when tension seemed to quiver in Sister Flo's white veil and I felt again in the palm of my hand the wooden handle that operated the surgical bed.

'And what is the news of Reachfar?' Mrs Miller asked.

Suddenly the thought at the back of my brain came to birth. I remembered the handle turning, the bed rising with Twice inert upon it and I remembered the words I had prayed: 'Please God, don't let Twice die! Please God, I'll give anything, anything, but don't let him die!' Perhaps, I thought, Reachfar is what is required of me. All right. Reachfar is gone. I did not think that this thing could ever happen or that I would ever be able to accept its happening, but I do accept it.

'Actually,' I said to Mrs Miller, 'I have just heard that the family have sold it at last.'

'Sold Reachfar?'

'Yes. It had to come, you know. It was inevitable. My

father, my uncle and Tom are too old to manage it and it is an uneconomic size of property for these days anyway.'

'I find it strange to think of you as detached from Reachfar, Janet.'

I smiled and shook my head. 'I shall never be detached from it. As long as I live, Reachfar will live as part of me. It always has and it always will.'

The other two women came into the room and I had just introduced all my Mrs Millers to one another when Twice appeared in the doorway, dressed in a white shirt and shorts, as I had not seen him dressed since August.

'Hello,' he said. 'Gosh, what a gaggle of Mrs Millers!'

He had turned up the volume of the record-player when he left his bedroom and the voice of a tenor now floated along the air of the hall: 'Every valley shall be exalted and every mountain and hill made low, the crooked straight and the rough places plain —'

'Come and have tea everybody,' I said, and went out to the veranda with my friends the Mrs Millers.

# A SELECTION OF
# POPULAR READING IN PAN